D1515801

THE NAUGHTY LIST

THE NAUGHTY LIST

THOMAS CONWAY

This is a work of fiction. Names, characters, businesses, places, events, locales, and incidents are either the products of the author's imagination or used in a fictitious manner. Any resemblance to actual persons, living or dead, or actual events is purely coincidental or used in a fictitious manner.

Published by Skylands Publishing House

Cover Art and Illustrations by Tara Del Maestro Conway

Snowflake Images in Cover Art by Wilson "Snowflake" Bentley
By adapting a microscope to a bellows camera, and years of trial and error, he became the first person to photograph a single snow crystal in 1885.

DEDICATION

For many years, my two children, Rowan and Hazel, listened to this story around Christmastime and became ardent supporters of this book. Their enthusiasm for the story gave me the motivation to share it with the world.

My wife, Tara, spent countless hours editing the story and putting up with the endless ups and downs of the editing process. Whenever doubt crept into my thoughts, her never-ending support gave me the confidence to continue past all obstacles. Without her, this book would have remained a manuscript that never left our family.

TABLE OF CONTENTS

PART ONE

PART TWO

PART THREE

PART ONE

1

They did not miss Santa Claus.

As surprising as that may sound, the people lining the streets for the Macy's Thanksgiving Day Parade did not even look up from their phones as the parade's final float rolled by without its famous rider. Only the youngest in the crowd cried out when they failed to spot Santa. Their parents, distracted and aloof, ignored the children's plea to look up and find the big guy. No one saw Santa at the parade that year, but his absence barely registered in people's thoughts.

Even for those watching at home, Santa's failure to appear was masked by the excitement of a new Christmas pageant. For years Christmas had slowly been evolving and this year would see the fulfillment of everything people thought they wanted. This promised to be the BEST... CHRISTMAS... EVER!!!

People felt Christmas had gone stale. They no longer appreciated the magic of the season and drifted away from the wonder and excitement that was still reflected in children's eyes. Parents tried to make up for this by outdoing one another with lights, parties, treats, and enormous piles of presents. Everyone held themselves to an impossible standard; to make Christmas better than last year. They were no longer interested in Santa Claus and the old traditions.

They wanted something to help them *win* the yearly Christmas competition.

The ultimate measuring stick of this great contest had become the unwrapping of specifically listed items on Christmas Day. Parents were no longer willing to rely on Santa to fulfill their children's wishes. They had taken control of the holiday in an effort to beat their peers; to show their entire community they were top parents; to win. The whole season was judged a success when their child opened a present on Christmas morning and shouted, "I got it! I got the exact game I asked for!"

On the other hand, every parent dreaded the opposite response. "I wanted *Total Destruction 4*, not *Total Destruction 3*! This stinks — Christmas is ruined!"

Corporations around the world fed into this hysteria. They had forced the Christmas shopping season to intrude upon the revered holiday that had always kicked it off; Thanksgiving. Family gatherings that had customarily centered on a shared meal were replaced with frenetic trips to shopping malls. Parents stood in long lines waiting to get the must-have toy of the season while Grandpa and Grandma were left at home with the children. Shopping malls had become battlefields and "doorbuster" was the Thanksgiving war cry.

You could not blame anyone in particular. The demise had evolved over time as parents began adding their own toys to the ones Santa placed under the tree. Like a snowball rolling down from the top of a steep mountain, Christmas became an avalanche of gifts, wiping out anything that got in the way. No one was especially happy with the way things had worked out, but it seemed like nothing could be done about it.

While people still watched the parade to see the balloons, floats, marching bands and Santa, what they looked forward to the most were the announcements from Eastern Industries. The company lured them in with promises of exclusive, first access to discounts at its stores and the unveiling of its newest worldwide game, *Legend Quest.*

Along the entire parade route, the Eastern Industries' float continuously blared its message, "Check your phone or tablet now! Find your deals! Be the first to enter the new world of *Legend Quest!* Don't delay!"

The excitement spread at the speed of light. Even Einstein would have been surprised how quickly one bit of information could travel across the globe and grab people's attention. The world had never seen such a grand launch of any product, let alone a game that could capture young and old. Just about every person in the world heard that the fantasy world of *Legend Quest* had finally come to life. The gates to this kingdom were flung open and everyone was welcome to join.

As the parade marched toward the finish area, the entire audience was staring down at their phones. The sun on this clear day made the screens tough to see, but no one was going to give up. They were trying to be the first to download and play in the new fantasy realm. By the time Santa's float came by, almost everyone was distracted. The sleigh was empty. Santa was a no-show and no one seemed too bothered by the whole affair.

At the finish area, a thin smattering of concerned sighs rose from the crowd but soon dissipated. A few young children cried out for Santa but their weeping went unnoticed. In the VIP Section, a small, old man looked around in disbelief. This was supposed to have been the moment when Hermey introduced his grandson, Tiberius, to Santa Claus. Like everyone around him, Tiberius was mesmerized by the progress of his interminable download. Hermey tried to grab his attention by reminding Tiberius they had come to the parade to meet Santa; but there was no response. When Tiberius wanted something, he was used to getting it without delay.

Hermey grabbed Tiberius by the arm, stomped from the stands and charged around back to talk to the parade organizers. Tiberius did not seem to notice he was even moving despite his hair occasionally blowing into his eyes. His download was halfway done and nothing could distract him from his prize. Tiberius's father had been responsible for the American launch of this game and Tiberius had been waiting for it longer than anyone. He knew the first people to join *Legend Quest* would enjoy a competitive advantage.

As Hermey approached the back of the stage, he had trouble getting anyone to look up from their phones. He eventually found his friend, Mr. Sarg, the person who was responsible for making arrangements with Santa each year.

At first Mr. Sarg hesitated.

"Santa did not show up this morning. I never thought something like this could happen, but he was simply a no-show today. I guess he's too busy getting ready for Christmas this year," Mr. Sarg said as he glanced at the download progress on his phone.

"A no-show? That's not possible. I know Santa personally and he would never skip out on this parade. He has made it a point to show up every year since the forties, when he turned that debacle at the 34th Street Macy's into a miracle," Hermey shouted. "He doesn't want anyone to find a reason to deny his existence again."

"What can I say?" Mr. Sarg replied robotically. "We don't know why he didn't show up."

"I'll get to the bottom of this, Mr. Sarg," a frustrated Hermey replied. "Come on Tiber. One way or another, we must find out what happened. I promised you a meeting with Santa and I will do everything I can to keep that promise."

Tiberius did not hear a single word. In the middle of the conversation, his download completed and he was working like the mad Dr. Frankenstein to create a new creature for his online world. He was going through the many steps of creation when he was swept along in the wake of Hermey on their way out of the parade area.

Hermey was determined to get to the bottom of this calamity. Santa Claus was his close friend. Although many years had passed since he was at the North Pole, Hermey had never forgotten those days. He looked back at those times fondly and had a special place in his heart for Santa.

A long time ago, Hermey had worked amongst Santa's elves. Although he was never interested in making toys, he did his best to fit in. Teeth are what had taken hold of his imagination. He knew he was born to be a dentist, not a toymaker. Despite this inclination, Hermey figured that was just not possible given his circumstances.

His life changed when he met Rudolph, the red-nosed reindeer. After he helped Rudolph to save the Christmas of the Great Blizzard, Hermey had the opportunity to leave the North Pole to study dentistry. He focused on children's dentistry and became very successful in his own right. He had a fulfilling life. As the years passed, he had a son and then a grandson and reveled in telling each of them about his experiences at the North Pole.

Tiberius always assumed his grandfather was telling tall tales. While he enjoyed the stories about Rudolph, talking snowmen, and the elves; he never believed in anything that could not be seen or touched. Hermey had taken Tiberius to the parade so the young skeptic could meet Santa and look into his wise, old eyes. Then, assured that Santa was real, Tiberius might wonder what other curiosities exist beyond the veil of reason. Hermey hoped with all of his heart that it would teach Tiberius to *believe*.

The pair drove back to Hermey's house. The small man's eyes twinkled every time he looked at his grandson, but Tiberius never looked up from his phone to see this. Hermey could have driven him right off a pier and he would not have known it until he was drenched with water. By the time they parked in front of the tidy house, Tiberius had successfully created his online persona and was exploring the blossoming world of *Legend Quest*. Once inside, Tiberius connected his phone to a power source to ensure hours of uninterrupted play.

Hermey headed straight to his fireplace and began to kindle a small fire. Tiberius looked up for a moment wondering why his grandfather was in a rush to start a fire on such a warm November day. As a matter of fact, he could not recall a time when Hermey was ever cold. Even on the most frigid of days, Hermey never wore a jacket over the customary suit that adorned his slight frame.

"No bother," he thought and his attention went back to his fantasy world.

Hermey opened his roll-top desk, grabbed a sheet of his rare, special paper and began to scribble an urgent note. After a few minutes, his dispatch complete, he threw it in the fire. He had made such a commotion that Tiberius was momentarily distracted from the game.

"Grandpa, why would you waste your time writing a note if you were just going to burn it?"

"Well Tiber, why do you waste your time building a fantasy character when you will abandon it when the next game comes along?" Hermey responded, with a tinge of remorse, as Tiberius fell back under the game's spell.

With his task complete, Hermey urged Tiberius to come along for a drive. There was something of extreme importance that needed to be done. When Tiberius resisted, Hermey once again took the boy by the arm and dragged him into his car.

"Where are we going?" Tiberius insisted, still staring into his fantasy realm.

"You'll see," Hermey responded.

They drove up several long, winding highways; deep into the woods of New Jersey. After about an hour, they turned onto an unpaved section of road. The bumpiness of the ride caused Tiberius to look up from his phone for the first time since they left Hermey's house. They were on a narrow, dusty trail. The trees were bare and it seemed as though they were boring through a tunnel of dead branches and weeds.

By the time Hermey brought his car to a stop, Tiberius's interest had been piqued. In any event, he had lost his phone's data connection and he could no longer play in the fantasy world. He studied the surrounding area trying to figure out where they were. The car was parked in an empty dirt lot that looked out on a small patch of mowed weeds.

"Where the heck are we?" Tiberius was clearly frustrated.

"We are at the Brushwood Pond Radio-Controlled Airfield," Hermey replied distractedly. "We're going to wait to be picked up."

"Picked up?" Tiberius was beginning to tremble with rage. "Get me out of these woods and take me back to a civilized place where I can get some reception."

"I promised you we would meet Santa today and this is where we'll wait for our ride to meet him," Hermey said sternly.

"Do you really expect me to believe we'll get a ride to meet Santa at a remote-control plane field? Are you planning to shrink us first?"

"I expect you to sit here and wait with me," answered Hermey with a commanding tone that caught Tiberius off guard.

Tiberius had not known his grandfather to ever get fired up. In fact, the whole situation was unusual and Tiberius demanded to know more.

"Why did you take me to this... this... place?"

"I told you we're waiting for our ride. I sent a note to the North Pole and in it I said I would be waiting at this very spot to be picked up. I want to know what happened to Santa

Claus. I have a feeling it's something very serious," Hermey replied as he looked toward the northern sky.

"You sent the note?" Tiberius asked with incredulity. "Ha! I saw you burn it in your fireplace. Your note went up in smoke."

"Exactly my dear child," Hermey said. "That's what I intended for my letter. It's the fastest way I know to reach the North Pole."

"Impossible!" snorted the child. "You should really try email or maybe a text message."

"As you may currently notice, not all places have the coverage to receive such messages," answered Hermey with a chuckle.

Tiberius turned red and began to rage. "I need to get back to a place where I can continue my game. You don't understand how important the first moments of a new world are. If I don't get my connection back soon I'll be ruined in *Legend Quest*. RUINED!"

"Your father may spoil you and give you everything you want, but you are with *me* now and *we will* find out what is going on," Hermey said with resolution.

"You silly old fool. I wish you had chosen another day to try and make your fantasies come true." Tiberius's desperate insult hung in the late afternoon air.

The sun soon faded to orange and sunk into the tangled branches of trees. The sky turned into a pallet of colors while the grassy landing field faded into darkness. The changes went unnoticed by the angry child as he continued to hurl various requests, taunts, and even threats. Hermey did not reply. He remained calm as he stared to the north.

Tiberius decided a change of tactics was in order and asked Hermey, "Tell me about the burned up letter — how could it possibly be read by anyone?"

"Well, Tiber, in the days before communications were sent by electrons in a split second, children found that the fastest way to get their wishes to the North Pole was to burn a letter in the fireplace. The smoke from the letter would then rise up out of the chimney and be carried by the wind to the North Pole. Once there, Santa and the elves would decode the smoke and record what the children had asked for," Hermey explained.

"So you wrote a letter to Santa earlier today?" Tiberius asked with feigned interest.

"I certainly did. I want to know why he missed the parade today. I also explained that I promised you would meet him and I would appreciate his help in fulfilling that promise. I asked him to fly his sleigh to this secluded field and introduce himself to you," replied Hermey.

"Ok, great, so what if the supposed sleigh doesn't show up? It's getting dark, we should think about leaving soon," Tiberius muttered as he checked his phone's status.

Before Hermey had a chance to answer, the faint sound of jingling could be heard. Hermey strained to see a wild, jostling craft appearing in the northern sky. The last rays of light illuminated it and Hermey could make out Santa's sleigh. It was coming in fast to the miniature airfield.

Tiberius could not believe his eyes. The flying object was bounding through the sky and heading right for them. In a moment, it was resting gently on the field. It was indeed Santa's sleigh. All nine reindeer were hitched to it! Somehow it had been able to land in a field no bigger than his own rooftop.

"Impossible," muttered Tiberius.

"Get in," shouted a gruff, little driver whom Hermey did not recognize. "We have a lot to tell you, but it's best if we get back to the North Pole right away. We need your help."

Hermey asked, "Where's Santa? What's going on?"

"We need to leave now!" commanded the driver. "You'll find out everything once we get there."

"OK," replied Hermey. "Let's go Tiber, looks like we'll have to go to the North Pole to meet Santa and get to the bottom of all this."

2

Tiberius could not understand what was happening. Here he was, soaring through the sky with nine magnificent reindeer pulling him along. The driver of this flying sleigh was no bigger than he was, but he seemed to have incredible strength. He managed the flying coursers with ease.

"How could Hermey have pulled off this incredible ruse? Was it real?" Tiberius thought to himself. Many questions swirled through the young boy's mind. He wondered how Hermey had known about the radio-controlled airfield. He tried to figure out how Hermey had managed this elaborate trick. How were they able to fly? He looked all around the sleigh for its engine, but found nothing.

After what seemed to be only a few moments, the sleigh began to lose its altitude, descending into a snowy, white abyss. Only the dim light of the late polar afternoon illuminated the snowy landscape. As the descent continued, Tiberius saw they were heading for a faint glow in the middle of nothing. It quickly grew larger and larger until a glittering village came into view.

It was wonderful – like nothing Tiberius had ever seen. Almost every window glowed from the fires within. In the center was a building that towered above the rest. It resembled a wooden fortress in a medieval hamlet. In the front of the building were two large doors that opened spilling a golden light onto the icy street in front. The sleigh gently touched down on the street and slid with ease into the fortress.

Once inside, Tiberius looked around and was astounded by the cavernous dimensions. Giant wooden poles soared to the top. They were taller than any tree Tiberius had ever seen. Each pole was over six feet in diameter and three hundred feet high with beautiful scenes carved into its entire length. At the top, they held aloft a vaulted roof. There were no nails as everything was held together with force and friction. The magnitude of the structure was overwhelming.

Tiberius glanced over at Hermey and saw the same passive look he was accustomed to seeing on his grandfather. As the sleigh came to a stop, Hermey jumped out and was immediately surrounded by a swarm of people no bigger than the sleigh driver. They clamored toward Hermey as they called out his name. A look of acknowledgement swept across Tiberius's face.

"This is marvelous," he exclaimed, "I can't believe how real everything seems!" Tiberius was convinced he must be a part of a pre-launch test run for some new Santa-themed fantasy world his father had created.

"Elves, this is my grandson, Tiberius Kringle," Hermey announced. "I promised him a meeting with Santa Claus."

The elves sighed and looked at each other. No one spoke. A stout lady with tears in her eyes slowly emerged from the corner of the room.

"So good to see you again, Hermey. Santa and I are so proud of what you have done. Especially your work with children."

"A pleasure to see you again, Mrs. Claus," Hermey said while looking around. He couldn't help but notice the sour look on the faces of the usually happy elves. "What's wrong? Please tell me what's going on."

"It's Santa," the sleigh driver whispered. "He left for the parade this morning, but no one has seen him since."

"He was not at the parade," Hermey stated. "I was hoping to introduce Tiberius to him afterward. Tiberius could really use some Christmas spirit and I thought a meeting with Santa would be just the thing. But it seems there's a much greater problem at hand since he never showed up."

"This is terrible!" an elf exclaimed. "Without Santa we can't have Christmas."

Tiberius opened his mouth to speak, but Hermey interrupted. "I see you have bigger issues than a boy who doesn't know the meaning of Christmas. I'm sorry I sent you that letter, perhaps we should head back to New York."

"No!" Mrs. Claus said forcefully. "I sent the sleigh to get both of you. I know you were hoping to introduce Santa to your grandson. We need you *and* Tiberius. Hermey, we need your expertise on the world you've been living in for over fifty years."

"Fifty years?" Tiberius laughed. "My grandfather is over seventy years old. My father is fifty years old."

"Your grandfather has only been a part of the outside world for fifty years," Mrs. Claus explained. "Before that he used to live here with us."

Hermey turned quickly to Tiberius and said, "Tiber, there are many things you're going to learn tonight. You see, this is Santa's workshop. I did in fact live in this village for many years. I used to make toys, although I was never as good as your father at it."

"You mean; this isn't a game? This is real?" Tiberius shrieked in disbelief.

"Please Tiber, just stay calm, observe and try not to interrupt Mrs. Claus."

Mrs. Claus gently took Tiberius by the hand and led him to Santa's office. Hermey, the sleigh driver and another elf followed closely behind. As they entered, Tiberius marveled at the spectacular details of the room. Every element was engraved in the most intricate fashion. The walls, the desk, the ceiling, and the shelves displayed captivating scenes of Santa's handiwork throughout the world. The shelves contained vast amounts of wooden toys placed neatly in rows. The features of each toy were beautiful. They seemed to be perfectly crafted.

Mrs. Claus gestured to her guests to take a seat around a large, oval table. Tiberius sunk into a plush chair while his hands explored the sculpted, wooden head of a lion at the end of each armrest. On the table were carvings of alluring stars, snowmen, and painted Christmas trees. Tiberius appreciated the fine woodwork of his surroundings.

Once all were seated, Mrs. Claus began. "Hermey, let me formally introduce you to Ziggy, your sleigh driver. He is the head of elves now."

"Nice to meet you," Hermey replied.

She gestured to the other elf. "This is Scout and she's in charge of the Elf Information Network, known around here as the E.I.N. She will fill you in on what we know."

Scout was dressed differently than all the elves they had seen so far. Instead of the green tunic and red tights, she wore a dark purple tunic over grey pants. On her head rested a matching purple beret with a gray stripe at the very bottom and five white snowflakes sewn across the front. Her expression was more serious than any other elf.

Scout spoke in a businesslike manner. "Hermey, we have greatly expanded our information gathering since you were last here. The forest elves, scattered around the world, have joined our network and have been able to shed some light on Santa's disappearance.

"I'm sorry to say, but it appears your son, Rudi, is involved in this caper. We overheard some conversations indicating his employer, Eastern Industries, engineered the disappearance. They want it to seem as if Santa has abandoned Christmas and they have started a marketing campaign today with the theme of 'Who needs Santa?' Rudi is featured in the campaign and delivers a message that Eastern Industries will make sure the holidays go on even though Santa is no longer involved."

Hermey could not believe it. Rudi had become quite the cutthroat businessman, but kidnapping Santa was just too much.

"We asked our friends from the North American Aerospace Defense Command, also known as NORAD, if they noticed any unusual air or sea traffic from New York to Baekdu Island in the northern Pacific Ocean. That is the location of the Eastern Industries headquarters. They responded that one express helicopter had made the trip. We assume Santa was on that flight and is a captive in their headquarters."

"Well, why don't you just take your magic sleigh and go get him," Tiberius asked rather rudely.

"Yes, little one that is exactly what we tried to do. However, as soon as the sleigh neared the island, toy drones from Eastern Industries intercepted us. They apparently were just scouts and so we continued on. Soon, hundreds of drones surrounded us and began firing toy pellets at the sleigh. The pellets were not hurting anything, but their sheer number made us turn back."

"Why don't you just get some real warplanes and destroy all the toys?" asked Tiberius.

Mrs. Claus stood up, looked at Tiberius coldly, and lectured, "Young man, we cannot hurt anyone. We are a place of peace and good will. Our mission here is to spread cheer over the earth. Eastern Industries knows that we will not engage in fighting them. That's the reason they only used toys to defend their factory."

"Their toys were effective," Scout sighed.

"Well, sounds like there's nothing you can do. Can I go back home now?" Tiberius asked abruptly. "This was fun and all, but I have an important game to play."

Mrs. Claus, still standing, stared into the boy's eyes. "We need your help Tiberius."

"My help? How could I possibly help a bunch of elves who won't even put up a fight to get Santa back? You don't need me; you need an army… or Special Forces… or something else."

Tiberius stood up and went straight to the door. He was exhausted from the long day and wanted to get home to resume playing *Legend Quest*. He never liked Santa anyway and wanted no part in a plan to rescue him. His father had always complained that Santa's activities interfered with his company's toy operation in America and prevented him from making more substantial profits. Christmas in his house had never been a big event. Watching the excitement of all the kids talk about their family gatherings just made Tiberius angry and deep-down depressed.

Santa never came to his house so he could not imagine why they would want him to help. Before he could turn the knob, Scout put a strong hand on his shoulder and prevented his exit.

"Did you know I am also in charge of keeping the Naughty List?" Scout warned. She tightened her grip and turned Tiberius around.

"The Naughty List?" Tiberius scowled. "I don't believe there is such a thing."

"Oh, I can assure you there is one," Scout responded. "And for the past three years you have been Number One on it."

Hermey slumped down in his chair. The shock rolled like a wave across his suddenly old-looking face. He had assumed Tiberius was most certainly on the Naughty List, but hearing that his grandson was *Number One* devastated Hermey. On top of that, he had never heard of someone holding that position for two years in a row, let alone three.

"Three years?" Hermey asked. "Tiber, what did you do?"

"Nothing all that bad," Tiberius answered. "Just a few pranks here and there."

"Let's start with three years ago," Scout said. "You went through fifty-six caretakers that year. You tormented each one until they left. The worst case was when you tricked Ms. Zelomi by cutting the power and then having your sound system play coordinated howls, screams, and shrieks across the entire house. She really believed your house was haunted. She almost had a heart attack before running out of there screaming."

"Then two years ago, do you remember the Santa your father hired at the flagship store he was running?"

"Ugh, I guess so," Tiberius stammered.

"You should remember, you got him fired," Scout continued.

"I didn't know he got fired," Tiberius said sincerely.

"You sat on his lap and proceeded to pop a balloon of fake blood under your shirt. Then you yelled, 'Santa stabbed me! Run for your lives. Santa is a murderer!' Not only did you get that man fired, thousands of kids developed a phobia about Santa coming down the chimney to stab them."

"It was supposed to be a joke," Tiberius said defensively, staring down at the floor.

"This year, your day-to-day actions have been so bad that I will not go through all the naughty behavior that has piled up, although I fear there will be another climax shortly," Scout said with some trepidation.

Tiberius was overwhelmed to hear these details. None of his actions seemed so bad at the time, but hearing his misdeeds read back to him put them in a whole new perspective.

"How could Scout possibly know all this about me?" He thought, "no one knew about the prank on Ms. Zelomi."

Tiberius returned back to his seat and slumped down next to his grandfather. He could not bring himself to look at Hermey, so he stared blankly at the table. Mrs. Claus walked closer to Tiberius and repeated her plea.

"The elves and I need Santa back. Without him there is no Christmas and we should all fear a world that does not keep Christmas. We need your help Tiberius. We don't know how to deal with this evil company and we think you can help us with that. You know all about games and you are smart and capable. You understand people's strengths and weaknesses. These talents can be put toward a good use."

"I'm just a kid, I can't help you defeat a large corporation's evil plan," Tiberius said. "Anyway, you don't know my father. If he wants something, he's going to get it, no matter the cost."

"You won't be alone. There are many magical things about Christmas we can help you discover and there are many more kids just like you who are good at heart, but sometimes behave badly."

This was the first time in young Tiberius's life someone had said he had a good heart. Up to this point he had been in the care of strangers who seemed to loathe him. He realized right then he was actually eager to be good and knew he may never get a chance like this again.

"Ok, I'll help you," Tiberius said quietly as he finally looked up from the floor. "What do you need?"

Scout handed Tiberius the Naughty List and said, "That's the spirit! Let's start with this. Please look through the names and descriptions of everyone on the list and let us know a couple of kids you think may be able to help. This will be the team you'll work with to save Christmas."

3

The next day the headlines around the world sounded the alarm, "Santa Is Nowhere to Be Seen: Christmas in Peril!"

Fear struck at the very heart of humankind. The idea of not having Christmas was unimaginable. But Eastern Industries was uniquely prepared to take the lead this holiday season. The day after Thanksgiving, they made a world-wide announcement about their fresh, original concept — a holiday savior that would be introduced in all their stores the next day, Saturday. They flooded the airwaves with commercials to announce the unveiling of the man who would save the holiday. In addition, Eastern Industries promised that everyone who came to the unveiling event in their stores would receive twenty-five percent off all purchases and get a free upgrade in the world of *Legend Quest*.

Social media responded quickly and the buzz spread across the globe. People wondered what the supposed holiday savior would be like but they were more interested in the great discounts and upgrades they would receive. Lines began to form Friday night for the opening on Saturday morning.

When Eastern Industries announced that they would broadcast a live message from their headquarters on Baekdu

Island, television and radio stations began to clear their schedules to simulcast the message on their own channels.

Although there had been many Christmas frenzies over the years, this one was shaping up to be the biggest ever. Eastern Industries was primed for it all. They had barricades set up in front of all their stores to keep the lines in good order. Their warehouses were fully stocked and ready to replace all the items that were to be gobbled up in the big sale. Even the number of workers had been tripled over the past couple of months in anticipation of the flood of shoppers.

In Lancaster, Pennsylvania, the line became so long that it extended past the barricades. The well-trained employees began the contingency plan. Numbered tickets were handed out to the people waiting in line and the crowd slowly returned home for the evening. No one was happier about this than August "Gus" Rauch.

Gus's mom had dragged the young boy to the store despite his vigorous objections. Gus had always liked the spiritual aspect of Christmas, but never appreciated the material side. He was certainly not looking to replace it with some overly commercialized imposter. He scoffed at the idea of a holiday savior.

Gus had always been aware of the secrets people kept and was disgusted by how they sometimes acted one way yet felt another. He thought everyone around him was a big phony. Going to the store and waiting for a sale was the last place he wanted to be.

Gus was happy when he finally arrived back home. There he could be with his animals and listen to their stories. To anyone else, the animal sounds just seemed like noise, but Gus was able to understand their language. For some reason, that he did not know, this special ability came to him every year, but only during the Advent season and then disappeared the day after Christmas.

He was not the first child to have been endowed with this rare talent. For two centuries, the Moravians in Pennsylvania had appreciated a unique Christmas miracle that occurred on their farms. On the night before Christmas, if people listened carefully, they had the ability to understand their farm animals. Many families would spend time out in their barns or fields late on Christmas Eve for the treat of hearing what their animals were saying. It was a tradition to give their animals extra feed during this memorable night.

Sadly, over time, industrial farming methods had disconnected people from this amazing gift and they no longer gave any thought to the tradition of listening to their animals. Gus was different. He always paid attention. Only his great-grandfather, Sam, believed him when he claimed he knew what the animals were saying. This time of year, Sam, a retired veterinarian, would have Gus stay with him for a few days to help diagnose the most difficult animal maladies. Understanding what the animals were trying to say usually led to a proper diagnosis. Gus was looking forward to being picked up by Sam the next evening.

Later that night, out in his barn, Gus listened closely as a cow discussed the bad feed she was getting. He listened to the chickens gossiping about what the rooster was up to. His dog simply sat near him and asked to be petted. Gus loved to be with the animals. They never seemed to hide anything. They said exactly what was on their minds at that moment. People were another matter.

Gus would tune in as the animals talked about his neighbors and the activities they were up to when they thought no one was looking. The animals bore witness to countless, daily events. Because of them, Gus knew where presents were hidden in barns or about a preacher sneaking a drink late at night. He knew so many secrets about the people in town that he would often cause problems by leaving clues here or there.

After Christmas, his whole neighborhood would become upset over various rumors Gus had started. The real problem was the rumors were all true. They came straight from the horse's or cow's or another animal's mouth, so to speak.

The next morning, with the numbered ticket in hand, Gus's mom dragged him back to the store. He may have been the only person in the entire place without a mobile phone. Gus was not interested in the sales and he certainly had no interest in *Legend Quest*. He could not believe the level of excitement that was present. Everyone's attention was focused on a large screen that had been placed over the entrance. Just before the doors opened, images of the Eastern Industries logo flashed and the message began.

The crowd murmured as the screen switched to the image of an old man. He was wearing a fur coat that hung down to his ankles. On it were sparkling stars and snowflakes. He wore luxurious boots covered in glistening ornamentation. His hands were kept warm by thick red mittens. On his face grew a beard that was white and fluffy and went down past his belt. His thick, white eyebrows stuck out beneath a tall red cap covered with a beautiful, starry design of white fur. He held in his hand a staff which was taller than he was. The top of the staff was twisted to a point and adorned with silver and diamonds.

Gus wasn't impressed in the least. He thought the new holiday savior was just a fancier version of Santa except he carried a staff. He yawned and wondered when the spectacle would end.

"Greetings patrons. My name is Grandfather Frost and I have come all the way from Baekdu Island in the North Pacific, headquarters of Eastern Industries and I am here to save your Holiday Season! Christmas is dead, but a new Winter Holiday is about to begin. No longer will you have to rely on one man to selectively decide who does and who does not receive presents. If you work hard all year, you'll be granted the savings and deals to ensure you'll always enjoy the best Winter Holiday ever!

"Don't worry about hard-to-find products. Our automated factory at our headquarters can make thousands of each toy as demand warrants. The days of a popular toy being sold-out are over.

"Children, send me your lists. I will make sure they are made available to your hard-working parents and grandparents. You will get every present you desire and only the ones you specifically ask for. Not only will I help you get the toys you crave, but I can also deliver the hardest-to-get upgrades in the world of *Legend Quest*. Visit our website now to begin your very own list.

"Over twenty thousand Grandfather Frosts have been trained and are waiting to meet you. We will be available for visits with each and every child. Not only can you have your picture taken standing next to one of our professionals, but we are also available for your holiday parties and for one-on-one sessions lasting from a minimum of 30 minutes all the way up to an overnight stay at one of our many winter castles around the world. Reserve now to get the best discounts!

"I am also proud to announce that Eastern Industries will support you in your charitable donations as well. When you donate to charities through Eastern Industries, we will handle the entire process from beginning to end, for a nominal fee. We will make sure the money goes to the right place and then record your generosity, for all to see, on our new Charitable Scorecard. Yes, you now have the ability to show your neighbors and the entire world just how selfless and charitable you really are.

"The days of Christmas with its exclusion and mystery are over. The Winter Holiday can now be enjoyed by everyone in the world and we will celebrate it by keeping all the good traditions and removing those that divide and alienate. From this day forward, December 25th will be called Winterval!

"I now declare the Winterval Season underway. Let the snowfall and the shopping begin!"

As the message came to an end, a heavy snow began to fly from the roof of the store. Although it was unseasonably warm, the fake snow fell in droves on the crowd gathered below. There were similar displays all across the world. All Eastern Industries stores, no matter where they were located, had a hefty amount of snow swirling around them thanks to some well-placed snow guns.

The Lancaster crowd walked into the store in an orderly fashion based on their ticket numbers. They found it to be wonderfully decorated. Pleasant holiday music was playing in all sections. Even the smell was fantastic; pine in some areas and peppermint in others. Little did they know the scents included various chemicals that not only increased people's excitement but also their desire to spend. Years of precise research had paid off, resulting in the perfect setting to get people to buy more and more. The uncontrollable impulse to spend seized almost everyone. Those who had taken pleasure in saving and piling up their money the whole year through, suddenly became extravagant.

Eastern Industries could not have made it easier. Upon entering the store, children and parents were given electronic tablets. The children would use the tablet to scan the items they wanted on their list. The parents' tablet would allow them to access various lists and make purchases. For a fee, the shoppers could create a virtual cart and simply scan the items they wanted and have them delivered to their house. On some occasions, the items arrived at the houses before the shoppers got home.

Gus felt as though he had been transported to an alien world. People moved around like robots scanning or filling their carts with various items. Gus's mom kept remarking how wonderful everything was. She felt better than she had in a long time and was really looking forward to the rest of the Holiday Season.

"What will they come up with next?" she wondered.

As Gus's Mom dragged him through the aisles, he noticed Grandfather Frost on a throne in the middle of the store. There were three signs in front of Grandfather Frost, each indicating a different line. The one for people who spent over $200 moved with little delay. The second line also moved swiftly to another Grandfather Frost for a fee of $40. The third line had no requirements, but the unfortunate people in that line seemed to go nowhere. They waited and waited, but Gus never saw them move any closer.

"We have to go, Mom," Gus said pulling at her arm.

"Come on honey, don't you want to meet Grandfather Frost? If I find another item and reach $200, you can get into the fast line for free."

"We need to get home and feed the animals before I leave for Sam's later. I don't want them to be cross. They might yell at me," Gus answered.

"Oh, you and your fantasies. I wish you'd just go online and play *Legend Quest* like everyone else. It's not healthy to sit around and pretend to have conversations with the animals," she sighed.

Gus typed a message in the special request section of his tablet. It popped up instantly on his Mom's tablet. It said, "All I want for Winterval is to leave this store and never come back."

"All right Gus. We'll go home now."

Gus's mom picked up one more item before checking out. She was happy to reach the $200 minimum and carefully tucked the receipt into her purse. She hoped Gus would change his mind at some point and want to meet Grandfather Frost. After all, it was now free.

Grandfather Frost's world-wide announcement shook the North Pole to its core. This was the worst assault against Christmas anyone could remember since the Puritans outlawed it a few centuries ago. At least back then, the anti-Christmas sentiment had been contained to one group, and in that time period, information did not have the capacity to circulate very fast. It seemed the entire world had turned against Christmas within the span of forty-eight hours.

The day after Thanksgiving, Hermey insisted that Ziggy take him back to the airfield where he had left his car. He believed the task of finding Santa was best left to the elves, Tiberius and the other kids they would enlist. He thought the best place for him was fixing children's teeth back in New York, as he always did.

When Ziggy returned, he huddled in Santa's office with Tiberius and Scout. The three ate cookies quietly while each worked on their own tasks. Scout was combing through reports of various activities. Ziggy was writing instructions for some new toys he wanted the elves to work on.

Tiberius had been studying the Naughty List since it was handed to him. The power that was suddenly put on his young shoulders gave him a purpose which had been lacking in his life. He had not even checked the reception on his phone since he had begun his assignment. He was immersed in reviewing the names and notes of the thousands of kids on the list.

Tiberius was always at war with someone. He had battled his caretakers, teachers, tutors, butlers, maids and just about every person his father had hired to guide him through his youth. Even his socialite mother did not escape his crazy machinations. On the rare occasion the two were together, a rather cold barrage of insults would be exchanged. She had no time for him and he resented her for it. When she did make an effort, it was futile, so she had given up a few years ago.

Tiberius liked the idea of being part of a team, especially if he was in charge of picking kids as cunning as he was. At first he looked for boys and girls that were similar to himself, but after reading some of the descriptions, he thought one of him was plenty. He would choose kids who would be able to complement his skills.

As Tiberius carefully inspected the Naughty List, the description of Gus caught his eye. He was fascinated how Gus knew enough about people in his neighborhood to be able to spread effective rumors.

"How does Gus get all the information that roils his neighborhood each year?" Tiberius asked Scout.

"He is descended from Moravian immigrants. His ancestors had the ability to understand the language of animals on Christmas Eve each year. Gus also has this power but he's able to understand them throughout the *whole* Christmas season," Scout said, checking Gus's file.

"Wow. We could really use someone like him. Imagine the possibilities — animals have their eyes and ears on every part of the world. I bet he would be able to communicate with animals that fly or swim near Baekdu Island. That type of inside information could be very helpful in planning out a strategy," Tiberius explained.

"How would we be able to recruit him? He seems like a quiet loner," Tiberius wondered aloud.

"Gus absolutely loves Christmas," Scout answered. "He cherishes his ability to understand the animals and believes his power is due *only* to the magic of Christmas. I don't think we would need to do much convincing."

"How do we get him here? What do we tell his mom?" Tiberius asked, having read that Gus lived alone with his mother.

Suddenly Tiberius wondered if anyone missed him back in New York. He contemplated what his father would say if he knew what his son was up to. The thought made him shiver.

"What about my parents?" Tiberius asked nervously. "My father has many resources at his disposal and he would do anything for me. I bet he's planning a search and rescue operation as we speak."

"Don't worry Tiberius. Hermey has already reached out to your father to let him know you two are getting along great and that you will be spending additional time with him. Your father was surprised to hear it, but happy to know you may have finally found an adult who will put up with you for a while," Scout said with a mischievous smile.

"Oh, I see," Tiberius solemnly replied. "So, how do we go about getting Gus?"

"Gus will be heading over to his great-grandfather's house tonight," Scout replied. "He usually spends a few days there each Christmas season. His great-grandfather, Sam Holder, understands Gus's special talent and believes in the magic of Christmas. I'm sure he would encourage Gus to join us up here."

Ziggy shot out of his seat. He was very excited. "I can put a saddle on Donner and guide him to Sam's farm. Sam knows Donner. Sam helped him over fifty years ago when Donner cut his thigh during Santa's ride. With Gus translating, I'm sure Donner can convince them to have Gus join us here."

"I'll leave tonight and I'll have him here by morning," Ziggy said confidently as he marched toward the door.

"Wait, I found another candidate," Tiberius burst out as he looked up from the Naughty List. "Mithra Bentley from Jericho, Vermont."

While studying the notes on Mithra, Tiberius was impressed with her passion and dedication to studying weather and particularly snowflakes. He thought that her expertise could help them overcome some of the challenges of cold environments and even turn some of those challenges into advantages.

The only concern Tiberius had was Mithra's naughty reason. She had a tendency to sleep through class. That was not the type of cutting-edge naughtiness he was looking for. He was hoping for some sort of destructive behavior that indicated a rebellious attitude. But after further review, he determined she would have to do since no kid in the world had more knowledge about polar weather.

"Oh yes, Mithra and her research are well known up here," Scout said smiling. "I know just how to recruit her... we'll use Jasper."

"Jasper?"

"Yes," Scout answered. "Jasper is a living snowman. His essence is a cosmic dust particle. When the particle is positioned at the center of a snowflake, it becomes Jasper's core snowflake and it gives him the ability to move, just like we do. The more snow you add, the bigger Jasper becomes. Even if Jasper melts, he can form again if his cosmic dust particle is dropped from a cold sky, allowing a snowflake to form around it. If we can get Jasper's core snowflake under Mithra's microscope, her curiosity will take care of the rest."

Out in the stable, Ziggy walked over to Donner's stall and talked about the plans to pick up Gus and to stop by Mithra's farm — a single reindeer operation. Donner perked up when he heard the name Sam. He recalled that Sam had done an excellent job stitching his thigh after it had been cut open during a stormy take off.

Ziggy put a leather saddle on the gallant reindeer and the two of them took off. They shot through the sky as fast as a bolt of lightning and gradually slowed down as they approached Jericho, Vermont. Ziggy looked below and located the Bentley farm.

"Perfect," Ziggy yelled. "The drizzle is turning to snow. Mithra will definitely be out tonight trying to catch snowflakes."

He reached into his pocket and took out the small container that held Jasper's magical, core snowflake. Unfortunately, it had melted and all that was left was a small drop of water and one speck of dust.

"Donner, take us higher," Ziggy commanded. "We need to get enough altitude for a snowflake to form around the dust particle again."

Climbing up to the top of the storm clouds, Ziggy opened the container and emptied the contents into the atmosphere.

"I hope this works," Ziggy said as the speck of dust fell into the cloud. As it descended through the extremely cold temperatures of the upper cloud, frozen water molecules began to bond with it. Millions upon millions of molecules arranged themselves to form a snowflake. It was not exactly the same one Ziggy had brought with him, but rather a new snowflake born from the same speck of cosmic dust at its center.

The new snowflake twirled and fell through the layers of the storm. As it got closer to the ground, it acted more like a glider than an ordinary snowflake. While the other snowflakes gently swirled in the winds, this snowflake moved with a purpose. It had a specific target it was honed in on.

Ziggy was confident it would eventually find its way to land on the black velvet Mithra used to capture snowflakes.

Satisfied with their effort, Ziggy and Donner continued on toward Sam's farm near Kutztown, PA; landing in a barren field just after nightfall. The farm was quiet, but they noticed a glow coming from the farmhouse.

"Land here, Donner," Ziggy instructed. "I'm sure Sam will remember you."

As the two approached the farmhouse, they heard laughing inside. They walked up to the door of the house and Ziggy knocked. The front door cracked open a bit and Sam peered out.

"Who is it?" Sam asked.

"Hello Sam. My name is Ziggy. My pal Donner and I have come from the North Pole," Ziggy answered.

Sam looked right past Ziggy to Donner and asked, "Donner? Is that you?"

The old man flicked the porch light on and stepped out to look at Donner's thigh. Seeing the scar, Sam scratched his head and burst out, "Well I'll be. It *is* Donner. Gus, come out here, I have someone special for you to meet."

Gus went out to the front porch and was shocked to see the reindeer and his companion. Sam was stroking Donner's neck, amazed that the reindeer had barely aged since their encounter over fifty years ago.

"What's going on, Poppy?" Gus asked Sam. "Who is this guy with the reindeer?"

Donner responded in a language Gus understood. "Ziggy is the head of Santa's elves and we have been sent to bring you back with us to help rescue Santa. I am one of his reindeer."

Gus had never known an animal to tell a lie. He did not believe that animals were even capable of lying, but Donner's explanation seemed impossible. He glanced at Ziggy and noticed the pointy ears and then looked back at Donner.

"Please take a ride with us back to the North Pole," Donner continued. "Mrs. Claus can explain how you can help us save Christmas."

"Save Christmas?" Gus asked out loud.

Although he could only understand Gus's replies, Sam knew his great-grandson was talking to Donner. He put his arm around Gus and warmly recalled, "About fifty years ago, Santa's sleigh landed out in my field. Donner had a nasty cut on his thigh and I was able to stitch it up and get them on their way.

"Gus, your special ability is part of the Christmas magic," Sam continued. "Most kids have the ability to see it, but when we get older that magic gets obscured and as adults we are blind to it. Santa's visit to the farm that long ago night lifted the veil from my mind's eye and I was able to see the magic once again."

Sam gave Gus an earnest look and said, "That is why I am the only adult who understands your ability. Everyone else is too blind to understand it."

"Santa Claus is in trouble," Ziggy interrupted. "He left for the parade on Thanksgiving and hasn't been seen since. We want you to help us get Santa back. We believe he's being held at the headquarters of Eastern Industries."

"Eastern Industries?" Gus said raising his voice. "They're trying to ruin Christmas. I hate that company. I'd do anything to try to stop them but how would *I* be able to help *you*?"

"Your ability to communicate with all types of animals could be very useful. We'll give you more details when we get there," Ziggy hurriedly replied and then turned to Sam. "If that's OK with you, Sam?"

"What about the animals?" Gus asked. "I haven't had the chance to help you diagnose them."

Sam stepped back inside the front door and returned with Gus's heavy coat. He helped the bewildered boy into it.

"Gus, you have the opportunity of a lifetime," Sam counseled. "The animals will still be here when you get back. I'll take care of them and make sure your mother doesn't worry. Go with Donner and help bring back the magic of Christmas."

Gus stood speechless as Sam held his shoulders and urged, "Go!"

Ziggy mounted Donner and Gus climbed on behind him. Donner took a few steps and burst into the air. Gus was not quite sure what to make of all this, but he was too excited to think about anything else. He watched Sam and the farm disappear as Donner navigated north through the moonlit sky.

5

Earlier, in a field at the edge of Jericho, Vermont, Mithra stood staring up at the drizzle. It had been a warm day, but as evening approached the temperature dropped and a light rain had begun. She paid particular attention to the clouds. She had not seen this type of formation before. Long silvery bands across the sky reflected the last of the sun's rays and cast a magnificent red glow across the barren landscape.

"This could finally be my chance," she thought. "The perfect conditions to produce a warm snow."

The air was just above freezing, but the humidity was low, despite the drizzle. This circumstance provided an excellent chance to create snowflakes that had partially evaporated on their way down, but still remained snow. Mithra was excited at the prospect of catching and photographing an above-freezing snowflake. It was rare to get this type of snow in Vermont and she was not about to miss her chance.

As the last red of the sky turned to a dark purple, the drizzle began to mix with flurries. She hurried to her barn, opened the freezer and took out the black velvet that was stretched out over a wooden frame. Her plan was to get at least one snowflake to land on the velvet and photograph its unique pattern. For over a hundred years, one Bentley or another had been trying to capture images of snowflakes. But there were very few photographs that had presented a snowflake which was partially evaporated. Unfortunately for Mithra, her initial attempts only collected raindrops as the temperature continued to drop.

Undeterred, she continued her efforts and before long snowflakes began sticking to her velvet frame. She was thrilled to be able to take a closer look under her microscope. Mithra persevered with her work as darkness set in. She hustled to inspect each snowflake, take a photograph and then quickly collect another. The snow was coming down hard and soon the whole landscape had a fresh coating on it. Mithra was attuned to the transformation a snowfall could make to the environment. She noticed the subtle change in light and appreciated the extra quietness it brought.

The calm was suddenly interrupted as her father called out for her from the back door of the house. It was time for her to come to bed.

"Not now, Dad," Mithra yelled back. "Can't you see? The first heavy snow of the season has begun and I simply must get more images. I haven't even finished my meteorological recordings for the day. Please Dad, I promise I'll come in after a little while."

Her father sighed and went back into the house. He knew his daughter well and expected her to continue her chore for the entire night or at least until the snow ended. She always needed one more picture and he knew it was pointless to try and stop her. He and his wife were both meteorologists, so they appreciated and usually encouraged Mithra's passion.

Mithra was the grandniece of Snowflake Bentley, known around the world as the first and best snowflake photographer. Snowflake Bentley had taken over five thousand photographs of snowflakes and put many of them in a book for everyone to enjoy. He considered these delicate gifts from the sky to be miracles of beauty. Each crystal was a masterpiece of design to him and he believed he should capture its beauty before it melted and was lost to the world.

Mithra felt the same way and had decided to follow in the footsteps of her grand uncle.

When it was not snowing, Mithra kept detailed records of the weather. She recorded more information than a meteorological team at a weather station outpost. But when the snow arrived each autumn, she could focus on nothing else. She tracked each variation in weather and carefully analyzed every aspect. She could read the history of a snowflake's journey and knew the difference between the snow at the beginning of a storm and the snow at the end. She was even able to determine the route the storm had travelled based on characteristics of the snowflakes.

Those wonderful and exquisite features of each snowflake revealed a story to her. She could read the history of a snowflake's journey through cloudland by carefully analyzing the details. A snowflake was story writing in what she considered to be the most delicate hieroglyphic ever produced.

Late in the evening, after hours of examination, she eventually looked up from the microscope and rubbed her tired eyes. As she returned her attention down again, she saw what she thought was a snowflake moving, not melting but actually moving. It seemed to be wiggling across the slide almost as if it was waving to her.

"Oh no, it's finally happening," she thought. "My Dad warned me I could start seeing things if I didn't take a break."

Looking back down at the slide, she saw a pattern where the flake had squirmed its way across. To her disbelief, it spelled out two words, BUILD ME.

"OK, I'm now officially nuts," Mithra said out loud. "I guess I really do need to take a break. I might as well give in to my insanity and do what you say — make you into a snowman."

Building a snowman was nothing new to Mithra. But a snowflake asking to be built was definitely a first and absolutely too much to resist, even if she had gone crazy. She shook the snowflake off the slide and placed it in the snow-covered field. She then proceeded to roll the area into three snowballs resulting in a snowman about the height of herself. Not happy with a plain snowman, she went into the barn and found some items to create a nose and eyes. She then ran into the house and grabbed one of her father's old pipes. Her project complete, she stood back and admired her creation.

"Maybe I need to add a hat," she said to no one in particular and headed back to the barn to look for one. As she turned, she heard the sound of someone spitting. Looking back at the snowman, she spotted the pipe on the ground.

"Why does everyone think I smoke a pipe?" the snowman asked.

"Uh, what?" Mithra responded with confusion. Fright spilled across her face.

"I don't smoke," the snowman replied. "Think about it, I would melt half my face away if I smoked. Smoking is about the stupidest thing anyone can do, but more so when you're made of material that easily melts."

"Sorry, I just thought it would make you look like Frosty," Mithra explained in a trance.

"Frosty! I've been here for less than a minute and already you've referenced that crazy story. They got it all wrong… well almost," the frustrated snowman proclaimed.

Mithra was staring blankly at the talking snowman. She was not sure if she had completely lost her mind, but having a conversation with a snowman seemed to be proof enough. She closed her eyes and tried to clear her head.

"How rude of me," the snowman said apologetically. "Thank you so much for building me. My name is Jasper."

"You're welcome… uhm, Jasper… Would you mind trying to explain to me why I am not in the middle of a mental breakdown?"

"My dear girl," Jasper began, "You're one of the sanest humans I have ever come across. Your photos and research are famous where I come from.

"As I'm sure you know; every snowflake has specific material at its core. Usually that material is some type of dust floating around in the atmosphere. Once in a while, a speck of *cosmic* dust enters the atmosphere. Sometimes the cosmic dust is made up of an amorphous organic compound from a frozen world in another solar system.

"The snowflake you saw moving was formed that way. I am the compound the snowflake formed around. I'm able to manipulate snow that attaches to me, up to a certain size."

"Impossible," Mithra responded. "I've never seen a snowflake move on my slide and now I have a talking snowman."

"Not impossible, my dear," the snowman said. "Just as unlikely as finding two identical snowflakes. And I believe you've already accomplished that feat."

"Yes, I have. But how'd you end up on my slide? How do you know me?"

"I don't have time for too many questions right now. I'll let you know that I was dropped from above your house by an elf riding a reindeer and managed to glide my way onto one of your slides. We had complete confidence you would be looking at snowflakes during this storm."

"Elves on reindeer? I guess that's no less likely than a talking snowman."

"Exactly, you're starting to get it."

Jasper proceeded to explain to Mithra about Santa's disappearance. He told her about Eastern Industries and she recalled hearing something about a new holiday. When he got to the part about needing her help she asked, "Why me?"

"It's simple, you're an expert on weather — specifically cold weather and snow. As you know, those are the resources we have in abundance in the North Pole and you're the best person to turn those to our advantage," Jasper concluded. "Would you care to join me on a trip to the North Pole?"

"If you allow me to bring my photography equipment, I would love to go. I can't imagine what it would be like to continue my work there. I'll help as much as I can, but I still don't see how cold and snow can help you," Mithra said with great anticipation.

"I don't understand it all myself, but a team of experts is being assembled and we'd like you to be part of it."

"One problem, what do I tell my parents? I can't just walk out and disappear in the middle of the night."

"Well, I think you should introduce me to them," Jasper suggested.

Jasper waited outside as Mithra went in and cautiously approached her parents, "Uhm, there's somebody outside who would like to meet you."

With some alarm her parents threw coats over their pajamas and stepped outside. Jasper was motionless.

"That's a very nice snowman," Mr. Bentley said. "You forgot the pipe."

Mithra chuckled and said, "This is Jasper. He has come all the way from the North Pole. He has asked me to help get Santa back."

"Nice to meet you," Mrs. Bentley said turning her gaze to the snowman. "Mithra did a great job making you."

"Thank you," Jasper replied.

Mithra's parents froze. They tried to figure out what kind of trick Mithra was playing on them. Before they came up with anything plausible, Jasper went right to the crux of the matter.

"Your daughter is needed at the North Pole to help save Christmas. Eastern Industries has taken Santa Claus and we believe Mithra can help us get him back," Jasper explained. "Her knowledge of snow and weather is indispensable." With a sense of urgency, he added, "We need to leave tonight."

Jasper went on to reveal information about how he had come into being. He talked about the cosmic dust and his ability to manipulate snow and become animated. Mr. Bentley still could not believe what he was hearing. Mrs. Bentley, on the other hand, was fascinated.

Mrs. Bentley had worked on the Alaskan Pipeline before she met her husband and settled on his farm in Jericho. While working on the northern sections of the pipeline, she took a trip to Anaktuvuk Pass, Alaska for a vacation. While not a popular holiday destination, there were many native Inuit people there and she enjoyed listening to their stories and myths.

One particular myth told of a meteorite that had crashed into a snow field deep in the Brooks Range, the northernmost forested area in Alaska. When the local Inuit hunters went out to the site, they observed that the snow seemed to undulate on its own. Therefore, the Inuit considered the place cursed and never returned. Hundreds of years later, they had still refused to take Mrs. Bentley there.

She had tried to adjust a pipeline sensor to detect any cosmic radiation that may be coming from the meteorite's crash site. She was never able to get a reading and was forced to abandon her research when she left to attend to a pipeline emergency. She had never returned.

Jasper's story struck a chord with Mrs. Bentley. "Maybe the 'myth' isn't a myth after all," she pondered out loud. "Is it possible Jasper's core comes from the Anaktuvuk Pass?"

Mrs. Bentley turned to her husband and said, "I must take Mithra and Jasper there, now! I have a theory about Jasper's origin. He may not be the only piece of cosmic dust in existence. There may be more."

"This is all rather sudden, don't you think?" Mr. Bentley exclaimed.

"But honey, what if, at long last, we can get to the bottom of the undulating snow? What if somehow, our discovery can help to save Christmas?" she replied emphatically.

Mr. Bentley had not seen his wife seem so alive in years. And he knew better than to question both his wife and daughter. He could see the determination in their eyes. With a simple shrug, he said, "Pack up your things. If we move fast, we can catch a morning flight that will get you to a connection from Fairbanks, Alaska."

Mithra and her mom got their gear together, making sure to include a cooler to preserve Jasper's precious core for the duration of the flight. Mithra was sure to take her black velvet frame, camera and some other observation equipment as well. She was certain she would have opportunities to discover types of snow she had never had a chance to photograph before.

The Bentleys stepped into their pickup and Jasper jumped into the truck bed. The air temperature was barely below freezing so he was looking forward to heading further north to cooler temperatures. He did not enjoy the whole process of melting and travelling around as a helpless speck of dust. While the idea of being stuffed in a cooler was only slightly better, at least it would keep his core snowflake intact so he could be rebuilt in the cold north.

They arrived at the airport just in time to catch the morning flight to Fairbanks, Alaska. By the time they landed, a local tour company guide was there to meet them at the gate. Mr. Bentley had arranged for a chartered flight to Anaktuvuk Pass. Within twenty-four hours of leaving Jericho, Mrs. Bentley and Mithra reached their destination and settled their brains for a long winter's nap.

6

Gus's arrival at the North Pole temporarily distracted the village from the dark shadow of Santa's absence. The elves were fascinated by his ability to engage the animals and were very interested in what they had to say. Gus recounted the animals' stories to the great amusement of any elf within earshot.

Meanwhile, Tiberius continued to study the Naughty List with Scout and Ziggy. Mrs. Claus would occasionally stop in and check on their progress. There were so many names on the list, but most of them were not a good fit for their mission.

There was John Bull from Great Britain. He was a child that studied magic and put on some spectacular shows. Tiberius thought he might be able to help by using his ability to create illusions and trick people. John was on the Naughty List because he once made his class's grab bag of presents disappear and never gave them back. When Tiberius asked Scout if they could get John, she told him that John did not like Santa Claus because he skipped his house each year. No one could think of a way to recruit John. Besides, he seemed happy with the new changes to the Christmas season.

Then there was Yendi Marley from Jamaica. She was a master of disguise who landed herself on the Naughty List when she impersonated the mayor of her town and cancelled school for the day. Tiberius really liked her description and thought she would be vital to their effort.

"I'm sorry, but I cannot take Yendi away from her town," Scout explained. "She's needed there for the Jonkanoo celebration and there's no way she would miss that. Jonkanoo is a big part of their Christmas and I think she would do more good there than coming to help us."

Tiberius brought up Tomo Gozen, a young climber from Japan. She would lie, cheat and steal to win competitions, despite being good enough to win without resorting to dirty tactics. Tiberius thought her athletic prowess would help the team once they got to Baekdu Island.

"Tomo is currently on a quest to be the youngest person to climb Mount Everest," Scout lamented. "Until she reaches the summit, there's no way to convince her to abandon her attempt. She'd consider that a failure and Tomo does not fail."

Tiberius was getting frustrated. Gus was obsessive about talking to animals, Mithra was nowhere to be seen, and Scout seemed to be rejecting every good candidate on the Naughty List.

"I need someone who can help me plan this whole undertaking," Tiberius burst out, his frustration mounting. "I need some sort of military mind."

Scout considered his remarks and after a while announced, "I think I may know the perfect kid to help you with that, Tiberius."

She took the Naughty List from him and leafed through the pages. She stopped at a boy named Ben David and handed the list back to him.

Ben David was a fourteen-year-old, Jewish kid from Haifa, Israel. His qualifications were excellent. He was the top of his class in both Military Strategy and World History at an elite Israeli military academy. He was on the Naughty List because he had stolen sensitive equipment from his school in order to rescue a friend who was lost during a drill in a dangerous area.

"I think this kid would be perfect. He is smart, capable and he has already led a rescue mission," Tiberius said after reading the description. With some hesitation, he asked, "Why would a Jewish kid want to join a mission to rescue Santa?"

"Santa accepts all religions, Tiberius. He does not exclude anyone. Ben knows this firsthand," Scout explained. "When Ben was younger, he was hurt in an accident and spent many months in the hospital. While he was recovering, Nicola Abdou, the 'Israeli Santa', visited him there.

"Nicola had an unexpected experience when he was a boy that resulted in Santa gifting him an authentic Santa hat from the North Pole. As soon as Nicola donned the hat, he felt the magic of Santa sweep over him.

"From that time forward he made a vow to distribute presents to kids every year. By the time Nicola visited Ben, he was a fat and jolly Santa that had been spreading his message of joy among the people of Israel for more than a quarter century. When Ben asked why Santa would choose to visit him, Nicola responded that he was available to everyone: Muslims, Jews, Christians; in Arabic, in Hebrew, and in English.

"Ben received a collection of history books from this unlikely Santa and his interest in history was born. Ben has always looked back on this moment with the fondest recollection. I think he would jump at the opportunity to come up here and help us."

"Perfect," Tiberius exclaimed. He could barely contain his happiness. "Let's get him up here as soon as possible. I could really use his help to put the rest of the team together and make a solid plan. Oh, I can't wait to meet this kid. He'll be a great fit!"

Everyone in the room agreed that Nicola would be the best person to persuade Ben to help with the rescue, since Nicola was the one that had sparked Ben's love for Santa. They hoped his fame and notoriety would enable him to get Ben out of military school for a few weeks.

Mrs. Claus, silently observing the deliberations, turned to Scout with urgency. "Please have the forest elves send Nicola Abdou a message. It should instruct him to meet me at the abandoned parking lot near the top of Carmel Mountain National Park tonight. I'll be waiting there for him."

In Haifa, Israel; Nicola's doorbell rang. He answered the door, but no one was there. On the welcome mat of his home was an envelope addressed to "Santa Claus." Nicola picked up the envelope and looked it over before carefully opening it. Inside was Mrs. Claus's request to meet at the local park.

At first, Nicola thought the letter was some type of prank. It would not be the first time that someone had teased him about being Santa Claus. He was about to throw away the envelope when a very old piece of paper fell out. He picked up the fragile item and unfolded it slowly. As soon as he recognized his own writing, his hands began to tremble. It was the first letter he had written to the North Pole. Tears welled up as Nicola read the words.

Dear Santa,
I am ten years old. All of my friends say there is no Santa Claus, but I do not believe them. Would you please meet me at the picnic this weekend? It is at the top of Carmel Mountain. I have already told everyone that you will be there.
Yours Truly,
Nicola Abdou

Nicola remembered writing the letter. He also remembered Santa not showing up at the picnic. Everyone had poked fun at him for thinking Santa Claus would actually be there. He could still feel his disappointment, but despite the embarrassment he had never stopped believing.

Even though his family did not celebrate Christmas; to his delight, one present and a letter from Santa were at the foot of Nicola's bed when he woke up that year on Christmas morning. When Nicola unwrapped the present, he was happy to find a Santa hat. The letter that was attached apologized for not being able to meet him at the picnic. It also explained the red and white hat was an original North Pole creation that "whenever you wear it, I'll be in your heart." He treasured the hat and wore it every Christmas season.

Nicola's parents did their best to try and find out who had gotten into their home and placed the present. They refused to believe it could be Santa. Nicola was only encouraged by their failure. The following year, he gave little toys to the younger kids at school, saying that Santa had asked him to help out. Nicola's journey to becoming a Santa himself had begun.

Nicola placed the letter in a safe place, jumped into his Santa suit and drove in his old station wagon up to the meeting spot. As he eagerly entered the abandoned lot, he saw the sleigh and reindeer in the far corner. He stopped the car and got out.

"Nicola!" Mrs. Claus yelled. "So nice to finally meet you. You have done an amazing job spreading Santa's good will to this part of the world."

"Well, I'll be," Nicola said breathlessly as he headed for Mrs. Claus. "I always thought I felt the power of my Santa hat and now here you are, in real life, with Santa's sleigh and team. It's an honor to meet you."

Mrs. Claus gave Nicola a big hug. "Thank you for responding to my message so quickly. I'll get to the point. Santa is in trouble and we need your help."

"Me?" Nicola asked. "What could I possibly do to help Santa? I mean... I would do anything but..."

"Do you remember Ben David?" Mrs. Claus asked in response.

"Yes," Nicola said, thinking back. "He was the little general I visited many years ago. Is he OK?"

"He's fine," Mrs. Claus said assuredly. "But we could really use that little general for a special mission at the North Pole."

Mrs. Claus went on to explain Santa's kidnapping and the team that was being assembled. She finished by asking Nicola to find a way to get Ben out of military school and back to the sleigh.

Nicola did not hesitate. He hopped into his station wagon, started the engine, and began to drive away.

"Be back in an hour," he shouted out the window.

Nicola was a very popular person in Haifa this time of year. All the local people, no matter their religion or politics, loved having the affable Santa in their midst. Nicola used his popularity to gain immediate access to the commandant's office at Ben's school. He made up a reason about why he needed Ben's help until Christmas – something about needing a personal guard who would not intimidate the children. After some consideration the commandant revealed that Ben had been in somewhat of a slump and thought a little time away might actually cheer him up a bit. He agreed to the furlough and called out to his assistant to bring Ben to his office, ready for a four-week civilian assignment.

Ben entered with caution. Being summoned to the office of the commandant usually meant you were in trouble for one reason or another. Ben glanced over at Nicola and let out a slight gasp.

"Hello Ben, remember me?" Nicola asked.

"Yes Santa. I never got a chance to thank you for those wonderful history books you gave me a few years ago. I was pretty miserable in the hospital before your visit, but reading those books took my mind to such wonderful places. I loved learning about the exploits of great people through the ages. It made the rest of my hospital stay fly by. I still study history whenever I get the chance," Ben said with sincere gratitude.

"I'm glad I could make it a little less miserable," Nicola said smiling. He then took a more serious tone. "The commandant has agreed to let you help me this year, assuming you're willing."

"Help with what?" Ben asked.

"Well, with Christmas. I can explain it on the way," Nicola answered hurriedly. "If you don't want to help, I can always bring you right back here."

Ben felt beholden to Nicola and getting away from the school for an adventure was too good to pass up. Within seconds he had jumped into Nicola's station wagon as Nicola launched into an explanation of the situation. Nicola confided that putting on the hat seemed to give him the power of Santa and his life had been a complete joy ever since. Because of Santa's influence, he had helped thousands of kids just like Ben.

Nicola went on to explain that Santa was most likely being held captive on an island in the North Pacific. He related the details Mrs. Claus had told him about Eastern Industries and that Mrs. Claus herself was going to be at the Carmel Mountain National Park, the destination where they were currently heading.

Ben took in this information, but was not sure what was real and what was imagined. He was excited to be out of school and to reunite with Nicola but did not believe what he was hearing was the whole truth. His doubts slipped away as soon as they arrived at the abandoned parking lot near the top of the mountain.

There sat Santa's sleigh with Ziggy in the driver's seat and Mrs. Claus clad in red fur. Mrs. Claus climbed down to give Nicola a big hug. "Thank you for getting Ben to us so quickly.

I wish I could take you with me, but I'm sure you have much to do here this time of year."

Mrs. Claus then turned to Ben. "It's so nice to meet you, young man. Are you willing to help us get Santa back?"

Ben could not talk. He felt a lump in his throat and only managed a nod in response to her question. She took him by the hand and they got into the sleigh behind Ziggy.

"Please keep up your good work Nicola. It is very important and appreciated by all at the North Pole."

"Thank you," Nicola answered. "It's my pleasure to help Santa in any way possible."

Mrs. Claus gestured to Ziggy and he started the team in an instant. The reindeer took a couple of steps across the empty parking lot and bounded up into the air. Nicola watched as the sleigh vanished into the sky.

Mrs. Claus turned to the still silent Ben and said, "Thank you for joining us. Your skills and expertise are sorely needed at the North Pole. Everyone is sleeping right now, so we'll get started in the morning."

A smile started to creep across Ben's face. He thought he had been called out of school to guard Nicola and schlep presents around Israel. Instead, he was overjoyed to find out that he was going to help in a mission to rescue Santa Claus, the real Santa Claus. He felt like he was about to begin the greatest adventure of his life.

7

It was late at night when Ben David arrived at the North Pole. Most of the lights were out and everyone was sleeping. Mrs. Claus retired for the evening and Ziggy showed Ben to his sleeping quarters. The elves had set the kids up in a quaint building next to Santa's workshop.

Despite his great excitement, Ben fell fast asleep. At school, Ben had learned to fall asleep whenever the opportunity presented itself.

Ben awoke the next morning to a village in despair. Although elves are usually known for their cheerfulness, this morning was different. A deep depression was spreading like wildfire across the little village. Everyone found the simple act of getting out of bed to be a tremendous chore. The elves were not used to such feelings and were particularly burdened by the heaviness of their hearts. They had lost their purpose in the world and no longer knew what the future held. Many were on the verge of tears as they went about their daily tasks without their customary singing and excitement.

Tiberius was the most depressed of all. His initial excitement about choosing the naughtiest kids in the world to join him on his raid to redemption had dissipated. Looking through the Naughty List now seemed like an unwanted school assignment. Even Gus was feeling down since the animals were not talking very much.

The sky matched the mood in the village. The morning was gray with a light frozen mist falling. Instead of fluffy snow, the village was being coated with ice. Hopelessness was evident in the face of every elf.

The three boys, Tiberius, Gus and Ben, trudged along the slippery road toward Santa's workshop. Despite the pall hanging over everything, Ben was amazed at what he saw. The quaint little buildings, the decorations hanging from every lamppost, the warm glow coming from the windows; it all was so wonderful in Ben's eyes.

They entered Santa's workshop and headed to the table in Santa's office where Ziggy and Scout were already seated. Tiberius resigned himself to another day of trolling through the Naughty List looking for his next catch. Gus stood behind Tiberius, looking over his shoulder. Scout introduced herself to Ben as he surveyed the room.

On the table were cookies and milk. Ben looked down at this curious meal and asked, "These are nice treats but what's for breakfast?"

"You're looking at it," Ziggy said proudly.

"This won't do," Ben said with the authority of a boy who had spent his life in military training. "We'll need real food if we're going to be able to give you a full day of work."

"Something like a Christmas dinner?" Ziggy asked. "Let me check with our head chef and see what we can fix up."

Ziggy scratched out some orders and passed them to an elf outside of the room.

Ben looked at Tiberius and asked for direction. He was very eager to formulate a strategy to rescue Santa.

"Right now I am looking through the Naughty List to see if I can find more kids for our team and then..." He trailed off without finishing his sentence.

"And then what?" Ben asked.

"I'm not sure," Tiberius said with a shrug. "We really haven't put together a whole plan."

"That's fine," Ben said reassuringly. "Plans are useless anyway, but planning is essential. We may not execute the plans we make, but we must make a plan for every possible contingency."

Fixing his gaze on Scout, Ben continued. "Please brief me on everything we know about Baekdu Island and the location of Santa Claus."

Scout mustered up her most official voice possible.

"We know that Baekdu Island is in the Northern Pacific. It is owned by a hostile country that some people refer to as the 'Hermit Kingdom.' Very little information is known about the country and even less about the island. Until recently, it was thought to be deserted. If any other nation tries to get close to the island, they risk all-out war. Satellites provide only sketchy imagery of a blackened island. Our contacts at NORAD have already confirmed that a helicopter sped away on the morning of the parade and went straight there." She went on to explain the failed attempt to rescue Santa and the toy drones they had encountered.

"I've heard some birds talk about fleeing Baekdu Island," Gus offered. "But they're in shock and unable to answer any of my questions."

Ben shook his head and summed it up by saying, "So we really don't know what we're dealing with."

Everyone in the room looked around at each other but no one had anything to add.

"We'll have to obtain more information somehow," Ben said. "But first we need to shake this village out of its funk! Let's get all the elves together and we'll assign tasks to help us execute our plans."

"As you've noticed, we haven't accomplished much beyond putting a team together," Gus responded coldly.

"Right now we just need to give the elves the impression that everything is under control. I saw the despair that was hanging over the village this morning. They need a sense of purpose," Ben suggested. "Ziggy, can you get the elves together later today for an announcement? I have an idea."

"Sure," Ziggy hesitantly answered. "We can gather on the main floor of Santa's workshop."

"Great. We'll make sure they know how necessary they are to the mission. If everyone agrees, I'd like to ask them to start working on making an army of wooden soldiers and toy planes," Ben announced. "It's crucial they feel they're part of the greater effort."

Ben turned back to Tiberius and suggested, "Let's put the Naughty List down for a little bit and formulate a rough idea of what we're going to do. We need to have an outline before we continue with anything else."

"All good military plans start with a code name," Ben instructed. "Our mission is to get Santa back... Anyone have an idea on what we should call this mission?"

"Operation Get Santa Back," Gus suggested.

"That's too accurate, Gus," Ben replied, holding back a chuckle. "The name has to be more generic."

Tiberius stood up and proclaimed, "Operation Naughty Redemption."

"Perfect," Gus said in agreement.

"Now, what should we call our group?" Ben asked.

The kids were pondering names when Gus offered, "How about we call ourselves the Naughty Team?"

"Works for me," Ben responded. "Let's get to the details."

For the rest of the morning, the three boys and two elves formulated the basic elements of the plan. Gus volunteered to write down the details. The room's energy was rejuvenated by the new planning. They knew little about Baekdu Island except for its dark geography, but they were able to determine that the main factory building was deep inside a mountain that plunged straight into the sea. There was also a wharf for the cargo ships. They dropped off supplies first, and then filled up with toys destined for the warehouses which supplied the stores. Nothing was known about the inside of the factory.

They talked and debated about the best ways to get there, how to access the factory, what type of distractions they could use to cover their operation, and who else they may need to enlist from the Naughty List. It was now December 1st so they had less than four weeks to go until Christmas. The sense of urgency led to quick agreement on a plan outline.

By the time the elves were gathering in the workshop to be addressed by the ragtag team, Gus had boiled their conversations down to the following:

Operation Naughty Redemption
Goal
To rescue Santa Claus from the Eastern Industries Headquarters on Baekdu Island.
Plan
Step 1: Arrange transport to the island.
Step 2: Provide distraction to neutralize Eastern Industries' defenses and surveillance.
Step 3: Locate and retrieve Santa.
Step 4: Get all involved back home safely.

Ben looked down at the words and shrugged. "At least this is a start. We can work on the details later. This should be enough to get the elves to cheer up and get going on their assignment."

With only a very basic plan complete, they stood up and left the room to address the elves. They walked through Santa's workshop to the main area where all the work had stopped and the elves were waiting. Ben climbed up to a spot overlooking the floor packed with elves.

"Elves, as you know, Christmas is in trouble. Eastern Industries is trying to abolish Christmas and replace it with their own profitmaking version of this wonderful holiday. Our only hope to save Christmas is to rescue Santa Claus from Baekdu Island.

"We have developed a plan to rescue Santa and bring him back to the North Pole. We need your help! There is much to get done and little time to do it.

"We'll need thousands of toy soldiers; as many as you can make in the next two weeks. We also need toy planes that can fly and boats to get them there. Can you do it?"

The elves murmured to each other about the tasks being assigned to them. Many were shaking their heads wondering how this could be done in such a short time. Others were discussing ideas on the best way to divide up the elves into teams. The feeling of helplessness lifted from the elves. While the task that lay ahead of them was daunting, they felt empowered by being able to help with the dire situation.

The murmuring soon turned to talking. The voices increased and the elves became very excited. They had a purpose. They finally felt like they could do something to rescue Santa and save Christmas. The talking grew louder with each passing second. A great enthusiasm grew in the room. Before the noise was too loud, Ben yelled one more time, "Can you do it?"

"Yes!" The elves shouted in unison and began to spread out. Bells immediately rang out across the village. Elves ran to and fro with a renewed fervor to begin their important task. In Santa's workshop the buzzing and hammering became louder with each passing second. Within a few minutes, a moving rendition of "Santa Claus Is Coming to Town" could be heard across the village. The elves were back at work. They were happy and the village was alive again.

Ben turned to Ziggy and said, "Well, that worked out better than I expected."

Ziggy put his hand on Ben's shoulder. Tears were flowing down his cheeks. "Thank you Ben. That is exactly what they needed to hear."

Ziggy, Scout and the boys returned to Santa's office with a refreshed spirit. Ben asked Tiberius to find two important components to fill out their team: someone from the Naughty List who had the skills to scale the mountain on Baekdu Island and some type of computer whiz to hack into Eastern Industries computer system with the hope of accessing some of their plans.

Ziggy and Scout gasped when they heard the word "hack".

"Don't worry," Tiberius said to them. "That's why Mrs. Claus wanted help from the Naughty List. We're not recruiting angels for this dirty business."

Tiberius was reenergized. He went back to the Naughty List to find two kids who matched up with Ben's request. He began combing through the pages to find appropriate descriptions that fit the bill.

Although Gus was feeling more optimistic he was not completely cheered up by the improved mood in the village. He was worried about his mom, Sam and the animals on his farm. It had been over two days since he had left and he was only supposed to stay at Sam's for a few more. He shared his concerns with Scout.

"Don't worry," Scout said with a smile. "We have some of the local forest elves keeping an eye on your farm animals and Sam has told your Mom he needs you to stay with him longer this year."

Gus was reassured by this. He knew his mother always worked long hours during the Christmas season and she would not mind Gus spending more time at Sam's farm. He grinned when he thought about forest elves helping out his own animals.

Gus went outside to see what he could learn from the animals. They too were caught up in the excitement and were talking incessantly.

Ben and Ziggy left the room together to arrange plans for the toy army that was being built. Scout and Tiberius stayed behind.

"Where's Mithra?" Tiberius inquired. "It's been a few days and I thought she would be here by now."

"I got a report recently that she's in Anaktuvuk Pass, Alaska. Mithra is with her mother and Jasper," Scout explained. "Apparently she's working with her mother to investigate some old meteor crash that has something to do with Jasper."

"I wish she would hurry up already. We could really use her help here," complained Tiberius. "Can you send the sleigh to pick them up?"

"Jasper said he would send a note once they were ready to come back here," Scout answered. "Whatever they're doing, Jasper thinks it will be worth the delay."

Tiberius turned another page of the Naughty List and grew excited as he read the description of Josef Ruprecht. Josef was a computer genius. When he was eight, his parents tried to fly him to a fitness camp. The morning of the flight, Josef hacked into the airline's computer system and took the whole thing down. The entire airline was grounded that day and Josef never went to the camp. No one ever knew who had been responsible, except for the elves.

"I've heard of this kid," Tiberius said to Scout. "He's the top player on *Empire Battle*. His account is called Big Mauler. Most people have stopped playing *Empire Battle* now that *Legend Quest* has been introduced. But I know Big Mauler is still active on the old game."

"I don't think he'll join us," she replied. "He doesn't like to go anywhere. He sits in his room all day and rarely leaves."

"I think he's the only kid that can get us into the Eastern Industries computer network. We have to find a way. Tell me more about him," Tiberius insisted.

Scout explained that Josef was from Oberndorf, Austria. He was a large child who hated doing anything remotely athletic. He spent all of his time playing computer games or working on his own computer lab. He was very intelligent but seldom used his mind for a good purpose. He was spoiled beyond belief.

"We need this kid. His skills could be the key to our success," Tiberius repeated with determination. He paused a moment before adding, "There has to be a way to bring him here. We just need to learn more about what motivates him."

Tiberius snapped the Naughty List shut and turned to Scout pleading, "We also need Tomo Gozen. She's the perfect fit for our team. Can you find out if she has reached the summit of Mount Everest yet? Maybe she can still join us."

"I'll investigate," Scout responded doubtfully.

8

Nearing the summit of Mount Everest, Tomo Gozen was getting tired. She was feeling lightheaded, but pressed on step by step. She would not turn back. This was to be the pinnacle achievement of her young life, a life she had spent training with monomaniacal discipline; nothing would stop her now.

Tomo's guide checked the time on his wristwatch. He was getting nervous. If they did not summit soon, they would have to turn around or risk descending in a storm. Tomo continued on despite her guide's increasing anxiety.

She was resolute about making it to the top. She had promised her little sister, Kiso, that she would be the youngest person to climb Mount Everest. With just a couple of hundred yards to go, she was not about to give up. Her guide had other plans.

"Too late," he said. "We missed the cutoff. We have to turn back now."

"I won't be turning back until I reach the summit," Tomo yelled back. "I'll go it alone if I have to."

Her guide pleaded with her to retreat but it was futile. Realizing he could not change her mind, he began his retreat and Tomo found herself alone. She knew the dangers of making a late summit but could not face defeat. She had never failed at any activity in her whole life. As a matter of fact, the only thing she feared in life was failure. This fear drove her to try hard at everything she attempted. When she set her mind to a task, she completed it and usually did so in record fashion. This was simply her next feat.

It took another hour to reach the summit. Finding herself alone on top of the tallest mountain on earth, she finally felt the weight of her situation. Her guide had turned back, she could see the afternoon storms approaching, and she had very little oxygen left for the descent. Instead of being scared for her life, Tomo was relieved she had not failed. Despite her success, she took no joy in reaching the mountain's summit.

She did not loiter long at the top. She sent a quick picture from her satellite phone to her sister back in Japan and began the descent. She made it about halfway to her camp when she was overtaken by the storm. It came on suddenly with a fury that surprised her. The winds picked up first and then a blinding snow blew in. She could no longer make much progress. Visibility had dropped to the point where every step became a plunge into the unknown.

As the winds swirled around her, Tomo thought of Kiso at home in their small village at the base of Mount Fuji. The day before, her last call with Kiso had been upsetting. Kiso was in tears about Winterval and the apparent end of Christmas. Kiso looked forward to Christmas each year but not because of the presents or the food. Kiso loved Santa Claus. She loved the Christmas spirit and the wonderful change it brought to life. Hearing that Santa had abandoned the world's children, broke her heart.

Kiso was very different from Tomo. Kiso was a sickly child, but regardless of her various maladies, she always maintained a pleasant disposition. Tomo was the opposite; she was healthy and athletic and wouldn't hesitate to run over an innocent competitor to gain an advantage. The sisters saw in each other their best qualities. Nothing could ever diminish the bond they felt.

Tomo began to feel herself going numb. She thought the end was coming but did not mind. Her busy lifestyle and exhaustive drive to succeed had made her somewhat weary of life. Every morning Tomo would wake up and not want to get out of bed. Every day she faced mountains to climb. Her parents pushed her relentlessly in all activities. She was the best climber in the world but would give it all up to just be a normal kid. Here on the mountainside, it seemed like her climb to the summit might be her last victory. Her only concern was that no one would be able to care for and protect Kiso like she had.

A peaceful feeling began to sweep over Tomo. Her mind was always focused on training for the next activity and now she had resigned herself to this final result. The cold feeling began to give way to a warmth inside her. She felt relaxed for the first time in her life and appreciated the calmness that was settling in her tired body and mind.

Just as she was about to drift off into a long nap, she noticed a red glow piercing the gray of the storm. She could hear the jingling of bells as the glow illuminated the steep cliff on which she was perched. She could not see very well in the storm but she did make out a team of animals pulling a sleigh. A little figure materialized through the snow and approached her. It wrapped a blanket around her and checked her pulse.

"Come on my brave climber," the little figure said. "I'm going to warm you up and take you to a safe place."

Tomo was amazed at how quickly the blanket warmed her to the core. She was led into the sleigh and tucked into the back of it. She laid her head down and fell into a deep slumber.

The next time Tomo opened her eyes, Mrs. Claus was looking down at her. Tomo scanned the room and thought she may have ended up in some sort of heaven. The wood on the walls and ceiling seemed friendly to her. The crackling from the fireplace played a sweet music that filled the room. The shadows cast by the fire danced around the intricate carvings on the walls and furniture. She had woken up in the kid's sleeping quarters in the North Pole and was completely comfortable, both physically and mentally. The gentle Mrs. Claus seemed to be the embodiment of peace and joy. Tomo was happy. She took a deep breath and closed her eyes for a minute.

She was almost surprised when she opened them again and everything was still there. Her mind was at peace. No more thoughts of beating the competition. No more fear of failure. Tomo was caught in the moment and everything else seemed like a distant memory. She spent a long time just lying there letting her eyes wander around the room. For the first time in her life, she had nothing to do.

Just as Tomo was about to speak, Mrs. Claus put her hand on Tomo's head. "Rest here as long as you like. We're in no hurry to move you anywhere. You're safe here."

"Where am I?" Tomo asked sleepily.

"You're at the North Pole. Ziggy, the head of elves, found you at the edge of Mount Everest. He put you in Santa's sleigh and brought you back here," Mrs. Claus explained.

Tomo was not surprised. Everything in her room seemed to be taken from Kiso's dreams of the North Pole. Kiso always talked about the North Pole and Tomo's situation seemed exactly as Kiso described. Happiness continued to grow inside her. She thought about how excited Kiso would be. Then a bit of reality began to invade her thoughts.

"My sister and family must be worried," Tomo wearily said. "Can I call them and let them know where I am?"

"We already sent your sister a message indicating you were safe and would be back home in a few weeks once you recovered fully from the climb."

"I feel better already. I think I could go home right now," Tomo replied.

"Let's not rush anything," Mrs. Claus said with a kind smile. "I'd like you to meet some people first. Sounds like you're up for a little stroll down the street."

Mrs. Claus pointed to a closet. "Please put some warm clothes on. You should be able to find something that fits. The elves made the outfits specifically for you. I'll be waiting outside the door."

Mrs. Claus left the room and closed the door behind her. Tomo put her hand in the closet and felt the soft garments hanging in there. There were no dresses or fancy blouses. The closet contained the athletic clothing Tomo was accustomed to. She dressed and then sat back on the bed to take it all in one more time.

After a few moments, Mrs. Claus called in, "Is everything OK? Do you need anything else?"

Tomo got up, opened the door and Mrs. Claus guided her outside onto the street. Tomo's eyes darted across her surroundings as a light snow fell. Everything seemed so serene and harmonious. She thought to herself, "I wish Kiso could see this."

Mrs. Claus and Tomo entered Santa's workshop and went straight to Santa's office. Tomo walked in to see three boys seated at a table with two elves. There was a large feast spread out that looked undisturbed.

Tomo bowed to the group and introduced herself, "Hello. My name is Tomo Gozen. I am twelve years old. I live in a small village at the base of Mount Fuji in Japan."

"Nice to meet you, Tomo," Tiberius said standing up from his seat. "We're happy you made it up here to join us."

"Join you?" Tomo asked.

Tiberius once again relayed details about Santa's kidnapping, the Naughty List, and the mission at hand. Ben explained some of the challenges they were facing and shared their plan with her.

"Why am I on the Naughty List?" Tomo asked innocently. "I have always tried my best and I listen to my parents. I finish my meals, do my homework, and take good care of my sister. What could I have done that put me on this list?"

Scout looked at her straight in the eye and said, "Tomo, you don't play fairly. We have seen the great lengths you go through to make sure you win."

"I've never been caught," Tomo objected, feeling defensive. "It's not cheating if you don't get caught. My parents taught me that."

"Your parents are mistaken, Tomo," Scout sighed. "Whether you're caught or not, breaking the rules is naughty behavior. It's probably never been necessary for you to break the rules to win, but nonetheless, you've done it at every competition. The organizers may not have known, but we knew."

She reflected on what Scout had said and shuttered. Until this very moment, Tomo had thought she had done nothing wrong. She remembered all the times where she had unfairly hampered her peers in so many competitions. Thoughts of filing down racket strings in tennis, spraying grease on the bottom of basketball shoes, and sabotaging other climbers filled her with remorse. It all seemed so obvious now.

"I think I see your point," Tomo said with regret. She looked back at Tiberius and asked, "What can I do to help? How can I get off the Naughty List?"

"You can teach us how to climb," Tiberius said. "Then you will accompany us when we go to Baekdu Island and rescue Santa."

Tomo bowed again and then took a seat. She had never been asked to join a team before. As athletically gifted as she was, no one would play on her team. She liked the idea of joining this group of naughty kids and trying to save her sister's favorite holiday. She sat back and relaxed in her chair. She was ready to be part of a team, instead of the star.

She felt like a kid for the first time in her life. Sure the task ahead seemed daunting but being part of a group effort really appealed to her.

It suddenly dawned on her; she had been rescued from more than the peril she had faced on Mount Everest; she had been saved from a lifetime of selfish achievements. The warmth she had felt since first arriving, now spread into her heart.

9

Josef Ruprecht woke up on the morning of December 3rd ready to defeat an onslaught of players in *Empire Battle*. Unfortunately, the tides had changed. The pool of players in his favorite game was dwindling and it sometimes took over an hour for a match to be found. Josef had been the top-rated player for a number of years and had a very popular YouTube channel dedicated to strategy. He had earned quite a bit of money from YouTube. But now he was one of the last players hanging on to this dying fantasy world.

Josef was upset over the demise of *Empire Battle*. He had invested most of his profits back into the game. His castle had everything you could imagine in it at max level but without players, it would all be worthless. His YouTube channel no longer generated the hits it used to. The world of *Legend Quest* had ruined his little enterprise.

Josef signed off after an hour of failing to find a battle match. His parents had been yelling at him to get away from his computer and walk with them to town. Since Josef could not find a match in the game, he agreed to join them on a walk to the Silent Night Chapel. This was Josef's favorite place to be. It gave him great pride to know that his ancestor, Joseph Mohr, had composed the poem that later became his favorite Christmas Carol, "Silent Night". The chapel was a beautiful monument to the original site where the song was created.

Josef lumbered down the stairs, threw on his jacket and left the house. While the distance was only about a mile, it took the family over an hour to make it to the chapel. Every now and then Josef would need to sit and catch his breath. Physical activity was something he rarely had to do and he avoided it whenever possible.

Josef was still breathing heavily when he climbed the last couple of stairs and entered the chapel. It was empty. Josef and his parents were the only people in the place. This was very strange. Normally around Christmas, the chapel would be overcrowded with visitors wishing to see the place where their favorite carol had been conceived. It was actually a replica of the original chapel, but no one seemed too bothered by that.

"Where is everyone?" Josef asked his parents.

"They're at the Eastern Industries store," his father replied. "I'm surprised you didn't want to go. Everyone who buys something there today gets a free upgrade in the world of *Legend Quest*."

"I hate *Legend Quest*," Josef said between heavy breaths. "That game has ruined my life."

"Oh honey," his mother sighed. "You should stop playing that old game of yours and join the other kids in the new one. It seems like a lot of fun."

"Fun?" Josef asked indignantly. "*Empire Battle* was fun and I was the best in the world. I have no interest in starting over."

Mrs. Ruprecht turned and left the chapel. It seemed every time she spoke to Josef it made him upset. She could not get through to him. She never really understood it. She gave him everything he ever asked for. When he was hungry, she made him a nice meal. If he wanted to see a movie, she bought it for him. On top of all that, she spent most of their money on his computer obsession.

Josef showed no gratitude toward his parents. No matter how hard they tried, they could not make him happy. His father had given up years ago, but his mother never stopped trying. No matter how rudely he asked her for something, she always did her best to meet his lofty expectations.

Mrs. Ruprecht took them through the center of town on the way back home. She looked up at the local charity scoreboard in front of the Eastern Industries store. It ranked all the families in town that had given money through the Eastern Industries Charitable Network. The Ruprechts were ranked thirty-eighth.

"Looks like the Grubers are ahead of us again," Mr. Ruprecht said solemnly. "I think a charitable donation of another five hundred euros should put us back above them. Maybe we'll even crack the top twenty."

"My God," Josef exclaimed. "A contest for charity? Christmas is officially dead. I can't believe the two of you are participating in this debacle."

"Watch your mouth," Mrs. Ruprecht warned distractedly. She was staring up at the scoreboard, studying the rankings.

"I declare this to be a calamity. Peace and good will turned into the sport of imbeciles. My own parents are unwitting participants in this great tragedy," Josef lectured. "It's a freak of nature that an intelligent being such as myself came from such lowly stock."

Mr. Ruprecht flew into a rage.

"Josef, this is the last straw." Mr. Ruprecht fumed. "When we get home I'm going to find a place to send you away. There has to be somewhere in the world that can straighten you out. If nothing else, at least your mother and I can find some peace for a few weeks."

"I will not be dragged from my home by some false authority figure," Josef angrily replied. "You have tried this diabolical plan before and failed. You will not succeed this time either."

"I'll have you chained if I have to," Mr. Ruprecht thundered. "Your reign of terror over our household cannot be tolerated any longer. It's time for drastic measures."

"I'm not going anywhere," Josef replied defiantly. "As soon as I get back home I'll have the authorities looking to take *you* out of the house for making these horrible threats against your own child."

Josef's mother began to sob. It was bad enough to hear Josef and his father argue but it seemed the whole town was out in front of the store listening to her family fall apart. She hurried away with Mr. Ruprecht.

Josef could not keep up with their fast pace. Before losing sight of his parents, Josef huffed, "I'll turn the tables on you. Just wait and see. You spineless worms!"

By the time Josef got home, his father was on the phone talking to the local schoolmaster about sending Josef away for a while. Josef dragged himself up to his room and logged into his computers, ready to fulfill his evil plans to dispose of his father. Before he connected to the server, everything in his room went dark. His father cleverly had switched off the electrical breaker to the room. Without his computers, Josef knew he could not stop his father.

10

The North Pole was busier than ever. Ziggy and Ben were going from building to building giving the elves advice on the best type of toy soldiers to make. Mrs. Claus was assisting Tomo to see what kind of climbing gear they could find. Gus was running about listening in on various animal conversations. He particularly liked the stories the reindeer would tell him about close calls with airplanes and making difficult landings. Although he was happy to be honing his skills, he was still unsure of how he would be able to help with the mission. He wanted to be more than just a translator.

Back in the office, Scout and Tiberius were stumped on how to get Josef to join their motley team. Scout had talked about Josef's love for "Silent Night" and how deep down he loved Christmas as much as any kid, naughty or nice. No one could figure out a way to turn that into the monumental motivation needed to get Josef to go anywhere.

"Let's just kidnap him and let his parents worry," Tiberius pleaded. "Give me the sleigh and I can take Ben with me. We could tie Josef up and have him back here in a flash."

"Tiberius, we cannot allow you to kidnap anyone," Scout said sternly. "That's taking the whole naughty thing too far. We need to find a way to bring him here willingly."

"Do you have any better ideas?" Tiberius challenged Scout. "What could possibly motivate him to come here?"

"He hates Eastern Industries. He thinks the new *Legend Quest* game is ruining his life," Scout responded. "If we could somehow talk with him for a while, I'm sure he would be willing to join our team."

"I could try to reach out to him through the old *Empire Battle* chat room," Tiberius offered.

Before Scout could respond, an elf burst into the room. She was wearing an outfit similar to Scout's but there were fewer snowflakes on the front of her beret. Scout recognized Berchta from the E.I.N. Berchta was out of breath and straightened up before addressing Scout.

"We have a major problem," Berchta said between heavy breaths. "Josef Ruprecht has enraged his father. Mr. Ruprecht is looking to send his son away for the rest of the Christmas season and into next year. He would like to enroll Josef into a disciplinary school or a fitness camp as soon as possible.

"Our sources indicate that Mr. Ruprecht just got off the phone with the schoolmaster and is calling around to see who will be the first to take Josef off his hands. We estimate you have until tomorrow morning to get him out of there before someone else takes him."

"Well, I guess that's it for Josef Ruprecht," Scout said as she turned to Tiberius.

Just like Josef, Tiberius was accustomed to getting his way and would not give up that easily. He stared down at the Naughty List description of Josef. He reread the section about Josef taking out an entire airline's computer system just to avoid going to a fitness camp.

"I don't think they're going to get Josef to go," Tiberius confidently proclaimed. "He has stopped them once and will do it again. Let's keep thinking this one out."

"Things are different this time," Berchta responded. "Mr. Ruprecht has cut the power to Josef's room. Without computers, Josef is as helpless as any child. I think Mr. Ruprecht is very serious this time. I wouldn't be surprised if

Josef wakes up tomorrow morning and his escort to a disciplinary school is waiting for him."

Tiberius sat back in his chair and looked up at the ceiling. He stared at an image of Santa's sleigh then looked over to carvings of elves cutting down trees. Next to that was another carving of elves building one of the workshops. The walls were not just pictures. They told a story. Tiberius was seeing the story of how the North Pole was first built. The carvings showed the great amount of effort that went into the construction of everything around him. The old images of Santa showed a very fit man, not the fat and jolly image that the world had come to know.

"Santa Claus used to be in good shape," Tiberius said pointing to one of the carvings.

"Yes he was. That was a long time ago when we were first building this village and ramping up our toy production," Scout explained. "He has not had to work that hard for many years. He's still very fit but just carries some extra pounds these days."

It was all coming together for Tiberius now. Mr. Ruprecht had tried to send Josef to a fitness camp once before. Now he was considering a disciplinary school. The North Pole seemed as good a place as any to accomplish the goals Mr. Ruprecht had set out.

"I wish you guys had a computer up here," Tiberius complained to Scout and Berchta.

The two elves looked at each other. Scout whispered something to Berchta but Berchta just shook her head side to side. Tiberius could tell they were debating something they felt passionate about. When Berchta sighed and stared down at the floor, Tiberius knew Scout had won the debate.

"We actually have some computers in the E.I.N. headquarters. I can take you there, if you can give me a good enough reason as to why you need a computer," Scout said.

"I hope it's not so that you can return to one of your online games."

"You don't trust me?" Tiberius said jokingly to hide the actual sting of Scout's comment.

"No," Scout responded with an icy chill in her voice. "Years of being number one on the Naughty List are not going to be erased by a few good gestures on your part. But I'm willing to take a chance to get Santa back here. You're here only because Mrs. Claus has instructed me to work with you. I am bound by oath to follow her wishes. That's the only reason I'm willing to take you inside the E.I.N. But first you have to tell me why you need access to a computer."

"Fair enough," Tiberius murmured. "I think we can impersonate a fitness camp and draw Josef to us. Everyone around here is always busy and working. There great discipline on display with the elves. They work together toward a common goal. We'll try to sell the Ruprechts on the idea that the North Pole is the best fitness camp in the whole world.

"If we can create a quick website to advertise a 'North Pole Fitness Camp', I think I can convince Mr. Ruprecht we are the best place for his son to learn some discipline.

"I picture a site that shows images of the various elves in their daily activities — maybe even some videos of the elves singing while they work as a team. I can help write the text that explains the benefits of the camp.

"We don't have much time. I need this site to be up in three hours. Then I'll place the call to Mr. Ruprecht myself. I'll explain about the health benefits of the North Pole and convince him to allow us to bring Josef here."

Scout contemplated the plan. The website seemed like a good idea and she did not think they would have to mislead or lie to advertise the North Pole as some sort of fitness camp. The elves were good role models for being in shape and having discipline. In short order, she agreed with Tiberius.

"Come with me, Tiberius," Scout said taking hold of his hand. "Berchta, please arrange to get some videos of Tomo climbing. After that, have Ben organize a large group of elves and video them marching in formation. Lastly, see if you can come up with a healthy eating scene."

Scout and Tiberius headed out to the east side of the village. Tiberius observed giant swirls of smoke above a chimney in the distance. He thought it peculiar that the swirls seemed to be flowing into the chimney rather than out. As they got closer, he realized it was their destination.

At the front door, two elves in purple tunics stood guard. Scout looked into a scanner and the front door opened. Still holding Tiberius's hand, she led him into a great room with a large chimney in the middle. Instead of a fireplace at the bottom, the chimney had tubes stretching out of it. Each of the tubes was connected to a bellow that was pumped by an elf. Out of the bellow flowed countless sheets of paper that other elves collected and categorized.

"Is this where you decoded Hermey's letter?" Tiberius asked.

"Hermey's letter and millions of others," Scout replied. "We get letters through smoke, regular mail, email and other methods. This happens to be the smoke collection center."

Tiberius looked around with wonder while Scout led him through the room. He was very impressed by how smoothly everything operated as the elves categorized letters and put them into tubes that shot them down below the floor. Although the elves were very busy at their tasks, more than a few took notice of the new visitor Scout was touring through the facility.

At the end of the room, Scout and Tiberius stepped into an elevator. Scout hit the button labeled "Internet Information Center" and they began to descend. Tiberius looked at the other buttons and noticed that instead of numbers, each button had a label: "Letters to Santa", "Naughty Information

Center", "Santa's Route Planning", "Toy Trend Center", and "Global Weather Forecasts." He was beginning to grasp the enormity and importance of the North Pole enterprise.

They entered a white room with racks of computers blinking and humming in unison. Tiberius was in awe as they passed through rows and rows of equipment and eventually came upon the control center. Facing them was a wall with a giant screen and many smaller screens around it. Each elf sat at a workstation and they all faced the main display. As Tiberius and Scout stepped forward, the elves stopped what they were doing and stared.

"Greetings to all. This is Tiberius Kringle, as I'm sure you all know," Scout announced. "We have given great consideration to forming what we hope will be the perfect team to rescue Santa from Eastern Industries. I don't need to tell you this is a matter of tremendous urgency and your contributions are now necessary for the greater effort. Therefore, I would like you to help Tiberius build a website so that we may recruit Josef Ruprecht."

The elves gasped in unison. Here, more than anywhere else in the North Pole, the elves knew of Josef and his naughty behavior. Josef had hit their network defenses a couple of times looking to hack in but had been unsuccessful.

Before anyone could object, Scout added, "I don't expect you to understand our reasoning but be absolutely clear, Mrs. Claus has instructed us to provide all the assistance that Tiberius needs."

"We have less than three hours to build a website to portray the North Pole as a fitness camp for kids," Tiberius shouted to the room. "Josef's father is about to send his son off to a disciplinary or fitness center and we want to be his top choice. We need to make a convincing website for his father to browse and be assured that this is the best place for Josef to spend time. We'll call it the *North Pole Fitness Camp*."

There was an immediate flurry of activity. The main screen in the room lit up with an image, words were typed over it and within minutes a logo was coming together. Tiberius adapted easily into overseeing the development of the site and directing the elves on its various aspects. The work came along quickly as Tiberius's well formulated ideas were turned into polished webpages within minutes.

The website was almost done by the time Berchta was ready with the pictures and videos they would upload. Tomo's climbing activities looked great. Ben conducting the elves on a long, lively march fit into Tiberius's vision. The only problem was the scene of healthy eating. Berchta had recorded a group of elves sitting around a table eating gingerbread cookies and drinking hot chocolate.

"I'm sorry but that is not healthy eating," Tiberius said turning to Berchta. He tried holding back his desire to laugh but a chuckle slipped out.

"Those are the healthiest cookies we have," Berchta said defensively. "Look at the hot chocolate; we didn't even add marshmallows to it."

"I realize it's what the elves consider healthy but we have to present what Josef's father considers to be healthy. We need the elves to be sitting down to a meal of vegetables, a small portion of protein and they should only be drinking water," Tiberius instructed. "Can you get that back to us in the next hour? We're almost done."

Berchta left the room and, once again, gathered some elves in the eating hall. They were seated in front of plates with a piece of fish and a side of spinach. A clear glass of water sat next to the plates. This was a meal they had never encountered. It seemed like something they would feed to the reindeer.

"When I say action, I want you to take a bite of spinach and then have a drink of water," Berchta instructed the group. "Remember to smile and look like you're enjoying the meal."

The elves looked around at each other with quizzical expressions.

"The spinach is the green stuff on the plate," she added.

At her command, the elves each took a bite. Despite the difficulty, the elves managed to smile as spinach clogged their mouths. When Berchta indicated she was done, they spit it out at once. Every elf turned green as they ran to the back of the room and grabbed peppermint sticks to try and get the taste out of their mouths. Some tried to wash away the taste with mouthfuls of hot chocolate or eggnog.

With the video and pictures complete, Berchta returned to the E.I.N.

"Perfect," Tiberius said after Berchta showed him the new footage. "This website should be enough to reinforce the call I need to make to Mr. Ruprecht."

Tiberius turned to Scout and asked, "Is there a quiet place I can go to make the call?"

Scout smiled a little as she took Tiberius by the hand again and led him to a room behind the control center. She was impressed by the website. While the elves had done all of the coding, Tiberius had given them clear instructions and the final product looked very professional.

Upon entering the room, Scout handed Tiberius a piece of paper with the phone number on it. Tiberius turned to Scout and said, "You better leave the room for this one. I'll have to say some things that aren't completely true."

Scout left the room and waited outside the door. Tiberius picked up the phone, dialed the number, and took a deep breath. It was solely up to him to get this part right.

"Hello?" said a voice on the other end.

"Hello. Mr. Ruprecht?" Tiberius asked. He used his practiced adult voice that was common during his prank calls.

"This is Mr. Ruprecht," the voice responded.

"My name is..." Tiberius cleared his throat. A wave of panic swept the thoughts from his mind. He had been so busy working on the website that he did not fully prepare for the call. He wished he had written some notes.

Tiberius could not think of a name to use. He had made many prank phone calls to his caregivers and had succeeded in fooling them every time, but this was different. So much was riding on the outcome of this call. The pressure was getting to Tiberius.

"I can't hear you," Mr. Ruprecht replied. "Who is this?"

"My name is Tiber Scout," Tiberius said robotically. He was disappointed in the name he just threw out but knew he had to keep the conversation rolling.

"I'm calling you from the North Pole."

"Is this some type of joke?" Mr. Ruprecht angrily replied. "I've had enough trouble for one day. Thank you."

"Wait!" Tiberius said desperately. "Your son's schoolmaster called me today and said you were looking for a place to send Josef for purposes of reform. I run the North Pole Fitness Camp and I think your son would be a perfect candidate for what we do."

The words seemed to come from nowhere, but Tiberius was finally settling in on the call. He continued, "We're a nonprofit organization that can help children learn the proper way to exercise and eat right. We specialize in challenging cases like your son.

"We have a Christmas special this year. For no charge, we'll pick your son up and bring him to our fitness camp. It's a Christmas-themed camp that makes the whole experience fun. Our staff will be dressed as elves and they will encourage the kids to work hard while helping Santa with his tasks. More than just a camp, we offer a fantasy experience that promises to return your son to you on Christmas morning with a whole new attitude."

Tiberius paused to see if Mr. Ruprecht had any reaction. He was laying it on pretty thick; maybe too thick.

"This sounds intriguing," Mr. Ruprecht responded. "Josef is a big fan of Christmas and something like this may persuade him to make some better decisions."

"Please check out our website." Tiberius said quickly. "You'll get an idea of what the camp is about and I can call you back later to confirm a good time for pickup."

He lacked the confidence to try and close the deal.

"Thank you, I will," Mr. Ruprecht said with some hope. "Good bye for now."

"Good bye."

Tiberius hung up the phone and went back to the control room to talk to the elves that were monitoring the site. They were getting hits from a mobile phone in Oberndorf, Austria. For half an hour the site was being clicked on. After they saw no hits for five minutes, Tiberius went back to the room to make a follow up call.

"Mr. Ruprecht, this is Tiber from the North Pole Fitness Camp. Have you had a chance to review our site?"

"As a matter of fact I have," Mr. Ruprecht excitedly replied. "Your camp looks perfect for Josef."

"Great! We can be at your home first thing tomorrow morning to pick him up."

"Is there anything in particular we should pack for him?" Mr. Ruprecht asked.

"Please just have him dress warmly for the sleigh ride to the camp. After that, we'll supply everything he needs for the time he's here with us," Tiberius replied.

"Thank you, Mr. Scout," Mr. Ruprecht said gratefully. "My wife and I will be looking forward to a new Josef coming home."

"See you tomorrow," Tiberius concluded.

"See you then," Mr. Ruprecht said as he hung up the phone.

Tiberius emerged from the phone room with sweat on his brow. Everyone in the control room looked toward him. He gave a thumbs up and the elves let out a hearty cheer.

11

Just before midnight as December 3rd came to a close, Ziggy readied the sleigh and the nine reindeer for their trip to Austria. He fitted them with special shoes as Tiberius had asked him to have the team descend and walk when they were within close proximity of the village. Their trip would only take them a few moments but they had to leave around midnight to arrive in the Austrian morning due to the time difference.

On the side of Santa's sleigh, Ziggy attached a sign Berchta had made for the trip. It was the logo from the website with "North Pole Fitness Camp" printed in bold letters. Everything else about the sleigh remained the same.

Ziggy gave a shout to the team and the sleigh took off in an instant. They bounded through the sky heading southeast. As the sunrise began to shine on the sleigh, it landed a mile from the Ruprecht house in a remote section of woods. Fortunately, the area was covered in a fresh coating of snow. Much to their annoyance, Ziggy had the reindeer walk the sleigh through the snow to Josef's house.

Once in front, Ziggy called a halt to the team and they waited for Josef to emerge. Ziggy was nervous about the whole affair. He could not lie or pretend to be someone else. If Mr. Ruprecht started asking questions, Ziggy would not be able to answer.

Inside the house the phone rang. It was Tiberius calling to let Mr. Ruprecht know Ziggy had arrived.

"Hello?" Mr. Ruprecht said answering the phone.

"Hello, Mr. Ruprecht. This is Tiber Scout from the North Pole Fitness Camp. Is Josef ready?"

Mr. Ruprecht looked out the window and saw the sleigh with the nine reindeer.

"Wow," he said into the phone. "You guys really pull out all the stops. Looks like you sent Santa's sleigh to pick up Josef. I'll get him bundled up and we'll meet your driver in a minute."

"Sounds good," Tiberius replied. "Do you have any further questions? Our driver is in full character, so he'll only behave the way an elf would act if he really did come from the North Pole."

"No questions," Mr. Ruprecht concluded. "I'll bring him right out."

With that he hung up the phone and yelled up to Josef. The boy thundered down the steps. Since the electricity in his room had been shut off for the past day, he was incredibly bored. When he saw the sleigh and reindeer out front, he actually cheered up a little. He was not sure what kind of crazy camp he was going to, but he certainly liked the mode of transportation.

Mrs. Ruprecht sat alone in the kitchen sobbing. Despite his atrocious behavior toward her, she could not help but love her son. Seeing him leave was too much to bear. Josef yelled a goodbye as he went out the front door.

"At least she'll regret this mistake," Josef thought. "When I get back, I'll have her wrapped around my finger even more than before."

Mr. Ruprecht accompanied his son to the sleigh and said to Ziggy, "Hello my good elf, please do your best with my son, he'll be quite the challenge."

"We will be sure to do so," Ziggy said with a shaking voice.

Josef climbed into the sleigh and took a seat behind Ziggy. He put his small bag next to him and leaned back.

"Where are we going?" Josef asked Ziggy.

"To the North Pole," Ziggy said without hesitation.

Mr. Ruprecht laughed out loud and said, "Give my regards to Santa."

"Next time I see him, I'll be sure to," Ziggy replied.

Ziggy gave the reins a slight snap and the sleigh glided over the snow as the reindeer began to trot.

"Where are we really going?" Josef asked again with more authority. "I want to know where you're taking me."

"I'm taking you to the North Pole," Ziggy answered trying to keep the reindeer at a slow pace.

Before they had even made the turn off of the Ruprecht's road, Comet tried to leap into the air. Ziggy pulled the reins back with force and Comet thumped back to the ground. The sleigh came to a stop.

"Not yet Comet," Ziggy lectured. "We need to get out of town first."

"Do you know how to drive this thing?" Josef asked. He was now worried that he was on a sleigh being pulled by a bunch of out-of-control beasts.

Ziggy ignored the question and got the team to begin pulling the sleigh slowly again. He was too scared to look back to see if Mr. Ruprecht had seen Comet's leap to the sky.

"Come on, fellas," Ziggy implored his impatient team. "We just need to get out of sight before we jump up to the clouds."

Josef was now worried. He looked for a way to safely jump out of the sleigh and run home. It was bad enough to be going to some camp but now it appeared his driver was insane.

"Stop this vehicle you crazy imposter," Josef commanded. "I did not sign up for this and I demand to be taken back to my house."

The sleigh rounded a corner and the reindeer were getting anxious. Their feet were not used to this much walking and the special shoes Ziggy had put on them were uncomfortable. Blitzen took a small jump to show his frustration.

"Calm down, fellas," Ziggy said softly. "Almost there."

"Almost where?" Josef screamed. "Pull this sleigh over. Enough with your North Pole Camp gimmicks. I promise I'll go to your camp, let's just take a car or something else the rest of the way."

They turned the corner and were finally out of sight of the homes in Josef's neighborhood. Ziggy gave a sharp whistle and the reindeer soared, lifting the sleigh into the heavens.

Mr. Ruprecht was still standing outside his front door to make sure Josef was not about to come back. He was not sure this odd camp could contain his scheming son. Looking in the direction he had last seen the sleigh, he caught a glimpse of it bounding skyward. He closed his eyes and rubbed them for a moment. When he opened them again, nothing was there.

"Hmmm," he muttered to himself out loud. "Josef has really worn me out. I really need this break from him."

Josef looked down in horror. Below, he saw his town quickly shrink away as the sleigh climbed ever higher. It completely disappeared from view as the sleigh surged through the clouds. Despite the great speed and height, Josef was not cold.

Josef suddenly missed his mother. During his whole life, she had been with him; protecting him from the outside world. Now he was engaged in the most terrifying trial of his life and she was not coming along. He missed her and began to regret the way he treated her. A heavy sadness filled his heart and he began to whimper.

"Don't worry, Josef," Ziggy said trying to comfort the mess in the back of the sleigh. "We'll be landing shortly and Mrs. Claus will explain everything."

"Impossible," Josef moaned. It was the only word he could get out.

12

On the outskirts of Anaktuvuk Pass, the Bentleys had rebuilt Jasper into a proper snowman. Mrs. Bentley was focused on making a device that could pick up the radiation signature of the cosmic dust in Jasper's core. With Jasper as her test subject, she had a sample of the cosmic dust that she was trying to find. This enabled her to investigate various methods to pick up a unique signal. Jasper was excited by the idea of finding more beings just like himself. He figured it would be worth the extra time it took to get back to the North Pole.

Mithra and her mother went into the village of Anaktuvuk Pass to look for a local Inuit guide to take them to the undulating snow field. No Inuit would agree to go. They were fearful of the place and worried about angering the Anirniit; the spirit they believe is in all things.

A light snow had begun and Mithra took the opportunity to photograph some snowflakes while her mother focused on making the sensor work. A young Inuit girl named Pinga took an interest in Mithra's photography. She was fascinated with the magnified view of snowflakes. Mithra spent time with her demonstrating the techniques used to capture the beauty before it melted away. Pinga loved seeing the intricate details of the snowflakes. She could not believe such artistry and design was always present around her, but too small to be seen. She spent the rest of the day observing Mithra at work. Mithra and Pinga discussed many aspects of snow. Mithra mostly talked about snowflakes while Pinga discussed the various types of snow that covered the land. They spoke for hours while Mithra continued to capture new images. Mithra came to trust Pinga and decided to confide in her about her encounter with Jasper.

Pinga loved the story but considered it merely another myth about snow. Pinga had heard many fables from her village elders about different creatures. The harsh conditions that the Inuit lived in gave rise to many superstitions. Pinga dismissed them all. She only believed in what she could experience with her own senses. Mithra liked how pragmatic she was.

When Mithra brought up the undulating snow story, Pinga laughed and said she believed the story was told just to keep people from going to the treacherous section in the Brooks Range. Anaktuvuk Pass was situated at the base of this Arctic mountain range. It was the northern edge of an Arctic forest. She described a deep canyon in the mountains that had a permanent snowfield at the bottom. It was about ten miles up into the range. No one had ventured that way in a long time. It was considered a dangerous place that, besides the superstitions, had many avalanches and grizzly bears.

Mithra was excited to finally be given a clue as to where the snowfield might be located. Later that evening, she met up with her mother at dinner and described the conversations she had with Pinga. Mrs. Bentley was thrilled to hear they now had a possible location to search.

Mrs. Bentley shared her own progress with Mithra. Using a special sensor, she had been able to pick up Jasper's unique radioactive signature from over a hundred yards away. Now that she had a working sensor and Mithra had a general idea where to search, they decided to set out the next day. The two were so excited that they did not realize someone had been listening to their entire conversation.

"Excuse me," a teenage boy said. "I overheard that you are going north into the mountains. I happen to be going in that direction myself. Perhaps we can share a ride."

"Oh..." Mrs. Bentley said with surprise. She wondered how much of the conversation he had overheard and replied, "Why are you heading there?"

"I am on my way to the North Pole," the boy replied. "I am going there to help save Marduk."

"Marduk?" Mithra asked. "Who's that?"

"Most of the world refers to him as Santa Claus. I prefer to use the old Babylonian term of Marduk," the boy answered.

"Fascinating," Mithra said with growing interest. "I'm also on my way to the North Pole to save Santa Claus."

"Looks like we share the same goal. I am Nebo. I come from Hillah, Iraq," the boy replied, extending his hand in friendship. "I have been traveling north on a snowmobile since landing in Fairbanks three days ago. I am only here for the night. I plan to get more fuel and continue north first thing in the morning."

"I'm Mithra Bentley and this is my mother," Mithra said pointing to her mother. "As you may have overheard, we think there's a snowfield with a special type of cosmic dust in it. I believe the cosmic dust may help us in saving Santa Claus... Marduk, as you say."

"How would dust save Marduk?" Nebo asked.

"The dust can make snow come alive. I've seen it myself," Mithra said proudly. "I can take you to someone in the morning that you won't believe exists."

"I believe many things," Nebo said without expression. "I will see you in the morning."

He left the dining area. Mithra and her mother headed back to their room and went to sleep for the night.

The next day, Nebo was dressed warmly as he filled his snowmobile with gas in the dim light of the polar morning. Mithra approached him and said, "Are you ready to meet my friend, Jasper?"

"Meet the unbelievable?" Nebo asked before answering, "I am always ready for that."

Mithra was excited. She could not wait to take Nebo to meet Jasper. She was sure it would get a reaction out of the sedate boy. They walked out to the nearby woods. Jasper stood at the edge waiting for them.

"Jasper, I would like you to meet Nebo." Mithra said with a big smile. She stared at Nebo anticipating his shock when Jasper talked.

"Hello again, Nebo," Jasper greeted the new visitor with a warm familiarity in his voice. "Glad you stayed the night."

"Thanks," Nebo responded without betraying any emotion. "The snowmobile is ready to take you and your friends up to the snowfield."

Mithra was the one with a shocked look on her face. It took her a few moments to get her composure back. Apparently the two had already crossed paths.

"May I ask when you two met?"

"I saw Jasper on my way into town yesterday afternoon," Nebo explained. "I was just going to refuel and continue north but Jasper thought I ought to stay the night and take your party up to the snowfield today. He said he may have some friends buried in there."

Mithra was frustrated that Nebo did not mention the meeting with Jasper to her the night before. She liked to be the one holding all the knowledge. Nebo was a little too mysterious for her taste.

Nebo and Mithra walked back to the snowmobile. They helped Mrs. Bentley pack the equipment into a sled that would drag behind. They picked up Jasper and sped through the valley toward the mountains. By the time the sun peaked over the mountains for its brief noontime appearance, they had arrived at the canyon.

The walls were almost vertical on all sides. The canyon was so deep that the little light the sun offered did not seem to reach the bottom.

Mrs. Bentley unpacked her sensor and immediately got multiple readings.

"This must be the spot," she announced to the group.

Jasper ran over to the edge of the canyon. He peered over the side into the darkness. He was able to make out some movement down below.

"You found it!" he exclaimed. "Let's collect the core snowflakes and get back to the North Pole as soon as possible."

Mrs. Bentley held Mithra back from walking to the edge. Together, the two crawled over and took a look down.

"It's true," Mrs. Bentley said. "Now we just need to figure out how to get down there and back."

Mithra noticed snowflakes falling into the canyon. They were big, wet snowflakes. Her focus shifted to the sky. She saw clouds moving in.

"A storm is coming," she said emphatically. "This type of snowflake is common in the leading edge of an Arctic low coming up from the Bering Sea. We don't have much time until we're stuck in an all-out blizzard."

"We must hurry," Jasper told the group. "Mithra, take a piece of paper and jot down the following."

Mithra reached into her bag and took a piece of paper from her observation notebook. Jasper dictated to her and she wrote:

Dear Scout,
We are at the edge of a canyon 12 miles northwest of Anaktuvuk Pass,
Alaska. We have found more cosmic dust here. We will need some
climbing line and containers to bring them home.
Please hurry. A storm is starting overhead and we don't have much
time.
Your friend,
Jasper

"Now what are we supposed to do with this?" Mithra asked.

"Make a fire and burn it," Jasper replied. "The smoke will carry it to the North Pole."

"The wind is from the north, heading south," Mithra observed while looking up at the clouds.

"I don't have time to explain," Jasper answered back.

Nebo had already gathered some kindling and a little fire sparked to life. Mithra folded up the letter and threw it into the flames. It immediately went up in smoke and drifted away to the north.

"The smoke is going against the wind," Mithra said while rubbing her eyes. "That's impossible."

13

Two hours after midnight on December 4th, Josef arrived at the North Pole. Since it was late morning in Austria he was not tired at all, so Ziggy stayed up into the wee hours explaining why they brought him there and what they expected of him. Josef was relieved he had not been brought to some sort of disciplinary camp. Instead he would have free reign to use his computer skills.

Josef spent the rest of the night in Santa's office complaining to Ziggy about what Eastern Industries was doing to his home town of Oberndorf. It seemed like most people were quick to forget the old customs and were instead racing to be the first to adopt the new ones. Sure there were still decorated trees, but people hissed at someone that referred to them as "Christmas trees". They were to be called "Winterval trees" from now on.

On the streets, people had adopted the meaningless "Season's Greetings" instead of the old "Merry Christmas" salutation. Eastern Industries seemed to be brainwashing the public to think that Christmas was an exclusionary holiday and that Winterval was the more politically-correct, modern solution.

Ziggy was saddened when Josef explained the idea behind the charity scoreboard. Every town in Austria had people competing to be crowned the most generous. He knew many families who were burning through their precious savings to make sure they stayed on top of the list.

Josef revealed that, like himself, most kids were never venturing outside. They were either playing *Legend Quest* or working on their Eastern Industries wish list. Parents seemed to be completely caught up in the high expectations the Winterval celebration was promising. But the stress on parents and other adults seemed to be reaching a breaking point.

Ziggy did not like what he was hearing and was relieved when Scout, Tiberius and the rest of the kids returned to Santa's office to continue planning for Operation Naughty Redemption.

"This is Josef," he said. "He has been telling me all about the damage Eastern Industries is doing to Christmas."

Ziggy let out a big yawn. "I need to get some sleep now. I'll be back in a little while."

"Glad you could join us, Josef," Tiberius said warmly. "I specifically chose you for your superior computer skills."

"I know," Josef replied. "Ziggy explained everything to me during the night. I'm ready to do anything I can to help."

"I'll take Josef to the E.I.N. headquarters and we can set him up with an office there," Scout offered. "I doubt the elves can help in his effort but we'll make sure he has every technological resource available."

Scout led Josef out of the room. Gus followed. The only thing he was interested in doing was communicating with the animals, but unfortunately any animal that had been to Baekdu Island was too shocked to talk about it. Gus wanted to help the team, but it was proving more difficult than anyone had imagined.

"We need to start acting like a team," Ben said to the dwindling group. "I think we should come up with a schedule and stick to it. We should set times to eat, practice maneuvers, work on projects, and sleep."

"Ben, please put together a schedule starting with dinner tonight," Tiberius agreed. "Let's allow Josef the afternoon to get familiar with the systems and starting tomorrow we'll follow your schedule. I guess you'll be in charge of making sure the team works together. That seems to be your strength."

"It's called leadership," Ben said gruffly. "We are lacking that."

Tiberius shrugged his shoulders.

"You're in charge from here on out," Tiberius said. "Once Mithra gets here, my job picking people from the Naughty List is over. I have no idea what to do next."

"You will know what to do," Tomo said, almost at a whisper.

Tiberius and Ben were surprised. Tomo had said few words since she arrived and they had almost forgotten she was in the room.

"I can help Ben with the training. He can make sure we act as a team," Tomo said and then looked Tiberius straight in the eye. "You are our leader, Tiberius. You may not realize it yet but everyone here is looking to you for leadership."

"Ben was born a leader," Tiberius argued. "He has trained his whole life to lead missions. He..."

"Tomo is right," Ben interrupted. "You got us all together, you'll be the one to lead us to our ultimate goal."

"Getting Santa back?" Tiberius asked. "Then what?"

"You are going to save Christmas," Ben said with his usual determination.

Tiberius felt a knot grow in his stomach. He felt helpless. He was only a kid. He had no idea what Christmas was supposed to really be like. For him it always had been about presents and family fights. He did not care much about Christmas. If everyone was counting on him, he feared they would all be disappointed.

Before he could dive any deeper into his growing anxiety, Tomo suggested they get out of the office and go for a walk. Ben and Tiberius agreed.

The three walked around the village until the afternoon. Tomo could sense the uneasiness Tiberius was feeling and made sure they kept their conversation off the topic that hung over all their heads. The walk helped clear everyone's mind. Tiberius realized it had been almost a week since he had arrived at the North Pole and, besides sleeping and eating, he had not taken a break.

Everyone was feeling better when Scout ran up and stopped them in the street.

"Jasper sent us a letter," she gasped. "Read it!"

The three kids huddled around the quick dispatch. It only took a few seconds for them to digest its contents. They stared at each other for a moment before Tiberius's eyes lit with a now familiar twinkle.

"Scout, go wake Ziggy and ready the reindeer," Tiberius ordered. "Tomo, get your climbing gear. Ben, find as many containers as you can. We'll meet by the sleigh in ten minutes."

Everyone ran off in different directions. Tiberius went off to find Mrs. Claus.

"I need Santa's toy sack," Tiberius said bursting into the workshop. "*Please*."

Mrs. Claus was startled at first but regained her composure. "You should put that 'please' at the beginning of your request, Tiberius. No worries, you seem to be making progress."

"I'm sorry," Tiberius responded. "It's a matter of great importance. Please, just trust me."

She walked to the back of the workshop and pulled a velvet red sack from a closet.

"Don't lose this," she warned. "It's very special."

"Thank you!" Tiberius shouted as he ran back toward the stables.

Ziggy already had the reindeer hitched up and ready to go. Ben had a cartload of small containers he began loading into the sack. Tomo threw some lines and climbing gear into the sleigh. Ziggy hopped up and was ready to go.

"Hold it," Tiberius commanded. "Tomo is going with you."

"What?" Tomo and Ziggy asked at the same time.

"You read the letter," Tiberius lectured. "There is a steep canyon and they need climbing gear. Those are two things Tomo will be able to help with."

Tomo jumped in the sleigh and they were out of sight in a flash, leaving behind a swirl of snow.

The storm over Brooks Range had turned into a blinding blizzard. Snow swirled in all directions. The wind was howling over the high ridges. The sleigh circled around the area but Ziggy and Tomo could not see a canyon. Despite Rudolph's nose burning as brightly as ever; it was not enough to find the lost explorers.

"Ziggy, please land the sleigh," Tomo requested. "We need to find the canyon. If we find the edge, we can walk around it until we find Jasper and Mithra."

Ziggy carefully landed the sleigh. Tomo put on her climbing harness and tethered herself to the front of the reindeer team. She told Ziggy and the reindeer to stay far behind her. Without a trace of fear, she blindly marched forward.

Just like her experience on Mount Everest, each step was a step into the unknown. After a few minutes, she took a step forward but her foot kept going down. The reindeer felt a sudden tug on the tether. They stopped.

"Found it," Tomo called, dangling over the canyon wall. Before the reindeer had a chance to pull her up, she had already climbed to them.

Tomo led Rudolph and the rest of the team around the edge of the canyon. Now that they knew where the edge was, they just had to circle it and find the group.

After a few minutes of walking they heard a cry over the howling of the wind.

"Over here," Jasper yelled. "We're over here."

Ziggy and Tomo were surprised to find not two, but three people with Jasper.

"What are you doing here?" Ziggy shouted over the storm.

"We think we may have found where I came from," Jasper replied. "We need to get to the bottom of the canyon and collect any cosmic dust that's down there."

Before anyone could say another word, Tomo, still in her climbing harness, flung Santa's sack on her back and headed straight for the edge.

"Take this," Mrs. Bentley yelled as she handed her instrument to Tomo. "This will point you to each speck of cosmic dust."

Tomo took the sensor and disappeared over the edge of the canyon.

"Who was that?" Jasper asked.

"Tomo," Ziggy answered. "She joined us yesterday. She's a world champion climber. If you need something down there, she'll get it."

Tomo dropped down into the abyss with only a headlamp to guide her. The sides of the canyon were slippery, but she had no problem making a quick descent. When she hit the bottom, it felt like landing on an ocean of snow. Waves of snow moved her up and down.

She looked at the sensor and it pointed to the center of a wave. She scooped the snow into a container and held the sensor up to it. It was still reading the cosmic dust signature.

"Got one," she said aloud.

She continued to scoop snow from the center of each wave until she had collected about fifty containers. The

snowfield was calm, indicating that all the cores had been retrieved. She was surprised to fling the full sack on her shoulders and find it was still as light as a feather. She scrambled up the wall with incredible speed.

She arrived at the top to find everyone and their equipment packed away in the sleigh. She hopped in with the sack and the sleigh launched into the blizzard.

"Did you find anything?" Jasper asked nervously.

"I found about fifty samples."

Jasper's face began to melt with tears of joy. Mithra looked over and smooshed the drops back into his face. Unlike Jasper, her own tears were doing no damage.

After a short time, the sleigh landed on a snow-covered field. The sky was still overcast, but there was no blizzard.

"Where are we?" Jasper asked.

"We're back on my farm," Mithra responded slowly, looking around at her surroundings.

It was night at the farm and the sleigh landed far from the house.

"Mrs. Bentley, this is your stop," Ziggy said.

Mithra and her mother looked at each other.

"I want to go with you," Mrs. Bentley said.

"Santa Claus is about children," Ziggy tried to explain. "We still need Mithra's help but I can't take you with us."

Mithra turned to her mother and said, "Thank you Mom. Thank you for always being there to help me. I need to do this on my own now."

Mrs. Bentley stepped out of the sleigh. Tears streamed down her face. All the emotions from the past forty-eight hours flooded her heart. She had actually found the quivering snow that had captivated her imagination since her youth. Her daughter was now an independent young woman sharing her passion for knowledge. Life was more than what could be observed with instruments. She believed again.

After years of dedicated farming and toil, she now believed there was more to life than material success. She believed in Santa, in Christmas and, most importantly, she believed she was still a kid at heart.

The farm looked fresh and beautiful through her renewed sight. A joy in her heart burst out into song.

"It's the most wonderful time of the year..." she sang as she skipped over the field toward the flickering light coming from her farmhouse.

Ben, none of the kids had ever been a part of a team effort before. They were used to working alone and did not know how a team was supposed to function. Ben knew otherwise.

Ben instructed them on how to prepare. Some joined together to roll a bunch of giant snowballs to use in constructing a defensive fortress. Ben noticed Nebo had incredible strength. He had the power to roll humongous snowballs within a short time. Toward the end of his snowball creation, he resembled a dung beetle pushing a giant, round object.

Josef was not so strong. He sat in the same place and listlessly rolled a number of small snowballs to be used for throwing. Mithra and Gus also focused on forming snowballs to be thrown. Tiberius and Tomo worked on filling in the gaps left between the big snowballs in the structure of the fortress.

The fifty-one snowmen simply watched in amusement. A few would occasionally roll a snowball and throw it randomly, but they were not preparing at all. They were confident superior numbers would be the deciding factor.

"Ben, I think there is a way to stop them quickly," Mithra said. "There's a limit to the size of the snowmen. If we get enough snow to attach to each of them, they'll slow down and eventually stop moving."

"Perfect," Ben responded. "Great plan."

"Ready to go?" Ben shouted from behind the fortress.

The walls were seven feet high and twenty feet long. It was shaped like the letter "C". Inside were hundreds of preformed snowballs.

The snowmen formed into a single long line spread out before the fortress. Jasper took the role of leader and settled behind the others in order to shout instructions.

"Forward march!" he commanded the frozen squad.

"Don't throw snowballs until you're sure you will hit them," Ben yelled.

Josef had been on the losing end of quite a few snowball fights and did not like the odds of this one. Everyone shared his trepidation as the snowmen approached.

"Now!" Ben shouted.

Most of the kids summoned the courage to stand up from behind the wall and launch a barrage of snowballs toward their intended target. The snowmen were taking heavy hits and paused to regroup and scoop up snow. Soon, snowballs were flying in both directions.

"Hit the closest ones," Ben ordered.

The team reacted well to Ben's command. Tomo scored precise hits. Although Tiberius could throw fast, he had poor aim. Josef and Gus cowered behind the wall.

"They're getting closer," Mithra called down to Josef. "We need to launch a bigger offensive. We need your help, Josef."

Josef heard her plea and froze for a moment. He was surprised that *he* was being asked to help win the fight. He mustered as much courage as he could and looked over the parapet of the fortress. Some of the snowmen seemed to be frozen but dozens more were getting close to the snow fortress. His companions were throwing as fast as they could.

Somewhere deep inside Josef a strength rose up. He recalled snowball fights with kids from school. It often ended with the whole school attacking him. But no matter how many came at Josef, he was always able to return a few well-aimed shots. He did not win those snowball fights, but he did enough to deter his assailants and eventually he was left alone. He had thrown snowballs before. He could do it again.

He determinedly climbed over the top of the wall and began his own swift throws. His aim was perfect. He hit the closest snowman flawlessly and rapidly. Soon the target was frozen. He switched to the next snowman and had a similar result. In a short time, it was evident to all that Josef was actually the most effective hurler.

When he saw what Josef was able to accomplish, even Gus finally made an appearance and launched some snowballs of his own. The kids were winning. They were laughing, cheering and having a blast. No one seemed to mind the occasional hit scored by the snowmen.

As the fight wound down, there was just Jasper and one other snowman. No one threw at Jasper as he had never moved from his original spot. He looked around at the carnage and noticed the kids were aiming all their snowballs at Saturn, the last snowman standing.

Saturn took a pounding, but did not freeze. He grew. The more they hit him with snow, the more he grew.

The kids began to move back from the top of the wall as Saturn approached. He was three times his original size and nothing they did seemed to slow him down. He reached the edge of the fort and the team started to retreat.

Nebo picked up a giant snowball at the center of the fort. For a moment, he looked like Atlas holding up the world. He launched the oversized projectile right into the center of Saturn. The behemoth only grew larger.

By this time, the snowman was over twenty feet high. Ben saw their strategy would not work on the last snowman and signaled for surrender. The kids were relieved that Saturn never threw at them. It might have been disastrous considering his size. Saturn himself seemed surprised by this turn of events.

Ben called for his crew to head to Santa's office for their morning debriefing and a review of the battle. Initially, Mithra stayed behind to help knock the extra accumulation of snow off the frozen snowmen. She also wanted to figure out what made Saturn different from the rest.

Once again, the team was gathered in Santa's office with Ziggy, Scout, and Mrs. Claus. Before they got started, Mithra rushed in.

"I'm surprised you're already back here," Tomo said.

"We're a team," Mithra responded. "I think it's important we meet and give our updates together. I can go back outside later and continue to explore the situation with Saturn."

"What about the other snowmen?" Gus asked with obvious concern.

"The elves are helping Jasper wipe off the excess snow," Mithra answered. "Some of them are already back to normal. That was some fight."

"I had a blast," Ben said.

"It was nice to work with such a great team," Josef added.

"I wish we could find a more peaceful way of training," Gus told the group. "I did not like seeing those snowmen become frozen in place."

"Neither did I," Nebo agreed. "But it was pretty amazing to see Saturn grow so large and still be able to maneuver."

The kids continued talking about the snowball fight for a few more minutes. All agreed that Josef had some of the best throws of the day. Nebo's strength had been another nice surprise to them.

As the talk of the snowball fight died down, Tiberius steered the group back to their mission.

"Josef, how did your attempt to get into Eastern Industry's network go yesterday?"

"I did find some weaknesses, but have not been able to infiltrate it yet," Josef answered. "I think I may get inside today."

"Ben, how about transportation?" Tiberius said turning toward his military expert.

"I don't think the elves are capable of building ships that are big enough to transport an army there. We'll look into other ways later today," Ben replied.

"Gus, anything new from the animals?"

"Yes," Gus answered. "The birds that have flown by the island have talked about a large amount of ships coming and going. They haven't seen a human on the island. Apparently, the crews on the ships are not allowed to disembark. All loading and unloading is done by machines without any operators."

"Can you ask the birds if they've noticed anything about the island's defense systems?" Tiberius asked.

"They don't seem to understand me," Gus whispered almost to himself. "I don't know how to better connect with them."

"Thanks, Gus. Keep working on it," Tiberius said. He then turned to Tomo. "Can you work with Ben to see about transportation? We need something to get us to the island and back."

"I can help too after I inspect Saturn," Mithra offered.

"Great," Tiberius said concluding the meeting. "We have a lot to do today, so let's get to our activities and we'll meet up at dinner."

In the Elf Information Network Headquarters, Josef was sitting in the command seat of the control center. The day before, he had setup a network of servers to bounce his attempts around the world to make it tough for anyone to trace them back to the North Pole.

Today, Josef was working with the elves' newest computer, a quantum computer. Quantum computers need to run at super low temperatures and the North Pole was the perfect place for them to operate. Even here, the elves had to make a cooling system to bring the temperature down to the right level. Josef was slowly learning the capabilities of the quantum processor at the core of the machine.

The main advantage of the quantum processor was its ability to perform zillions of different calculations at once. A normal processor can only do calculations one at a time. The encryption algorithm that Eastern Industries was using was the most advanced in the world. Josef had tried to shut down

Legend Quest when he was back home, but he could not attain the computing power to break the algorithm. He hoped the quantum computer would give him the power to crack it.

Learning to work with the quantum computer was tough. Josef was not used to the computer's odd behavior. He started with simple operations. If he asked the computer to divide eight by two, it looked at every possible combination of math equations before coming up with four. When he used numbers with over a thousand digits, the computer got the right answer in the same amount of time.

He then began working with large, prime numbers which are the foundation of encryption. The quantum computer took only a few seconds to answer problems that would take a bank of regular computers millions of years to solve.

He finally advanced to nearly impossible calculations. After a little trial and error, the quantum computer was figuring out problems no one could ever imagine being solved. He was enthralled with the machine. He loved its power and speed.

He was eager to test it against Eastern Industries so he rolled right into his attack on their network. Eastern Industries had a data connection to each of its stores around the world. All of the connections were protected using their advanced encryption algorithm. Josef quickly broke the encryption and could now impersonate a store in the network.

By late afternoon, Josef was working inside the network and trying to get through the final level of encryption. He knew that all the servers on Baekdu Island would be exposed once he got through. With the help of the quantum computer, he was able to break in and access anything he wanted. Within seconds, he was pulling in the plans and activities of the corporate headquarters.

The information was perfect. He found detailed floor plans, operational manuals, robot design specifications, and even the plans for the defense of the island. He was fascinated to find the island had almost no accommodations for humans, it seemed to be fully automated. He began moving the data to a thumb drive attached to the computer he was working on.

Josef was thrilled with the progress. He noticed he was also able to gain entry into the core operation of *Legend Quest*. He stopped working on his original mission and focused his attention on the *Legend Quest* servers. He harbored such a hate for the game that he could not pass up the chance to take it down. With *Legend Quest* offline, people would return to *Empire Battle*. He would, once again, become the leader of online games.

With just a few keystrokes on the quantum computer, Josef went ahead and disrupted the functionality of the game. Across the world, *Legend Quest* crashed. Not content with taking the game offline, Josef looked for the main database. He wanted to erase all the player information so that people would lose their progress in the game.

As soon as Josef found the database, his network was shut down. The elves noticed immediately. Every computer in the E.I.N. started to go offline. The quantum computer was the last to go down, but it was all over in a few minutes. Just before it crashed, Josef managed to remove the thumb drive that contained the plans and schematics.

The E.I.N. network was down hard. Josef assumed Eastern Industries had a reverse hack at the ready to shut down any intruder. He knew he had probably tripped that trap when he targeted *Legend Quest*.

Eastern Industries had not noticed his activity at first. He was inside their network defenses, so his requests to gather information looked like normal activity. When he took down the game, the Eastern Industries security system detected his previously unknown access to the network and sent a crippling virus back toward the North Pole network. It was a quick and effective counter measure.

The elves began to assess the situation. Any device they had connected to the outside was not only down, but completely destroyed. Many of them were sent into calculation loops that burned out their processors. All of the data storage was erased. Even the network equipment fried itself. All that was left were a few old machines that had been powered down prior to the attack.

Josef put his face in his hands and cried. He knew what he had done. He had broken his promise to use his hack only to obtain plans and not to cause harm. Scout also knew. She quickly grabbed him from his seat and escorted him out of the building.

Josef was still crying when Scout returned him to the Naughty Team's quarters for dinner. Mrs. Claus was there waiting for him.

"Tell me what's wrong," Mrs. Claus said with her usual kindness.

"I'll tell you," Scout burst out. "This little troublemaker took down the world of *Legend Quest*. Instead of just gathering the information he was supposed to and closing the connection, he waged war on Eastern Industries and lost. Our entire network is down."

"I'm so sorry," Josef wailed. He could not look at anyone in the room.

"My dear child," Mrs. Claus began.

"I am naughty to the core," Josef moaned pitifully. "I'll never be good. I can't help save Christmas. You should take me to the disciplinary school. My parents were right."

Mrs. Claus stood up and smacked her hand on the table. There was an uncomfortable silence for a few moments. Even Josef had stopped whimpering to look up at her. His self-pity had turned to fear. No one had seen Mrs. Claus exhibit anything but warmth and kindness. Her current state of agitation came as a complete and utter shock to them.

Like a brief summer storm, her emotions left behind an even calmer atmosphere. She put her hand on Josef's shoulder. He felt better. Despite his hatred for himself at the moment, he felt this too would pass.

"I never liked all the gizmos in the Elf Information Network," Mrs. Claus said turning to Scout. "I have put up with all this spying and technology, but maybe this shut down happened for a reason.

"Scout, please get me the Naughty List," Mrs. Claus asked firmly.

Scout immediately left the room. She was happy to get the list, thinking that they were going to look at it to find a replacement for Josef.

"Josef, you are not a naughty boy," Mrs. Claus continued as she looked at his distraught face. "You are a human boy, just like any other kid in the world. Your curiosity and inexperience can sometimes lead you into naughty behavior, but overall, you're a nice kid."

She looked at Josef and took his hand tightly in her own. He looked back at her and into her wise, old eyes. There seemed to be an unlimited depth and understanding in those eyes. He could feel her many years of caring. He could not look away. He fell into a deep, calm trance.

"You are a good child," she continued, while still holding Josef's stare. "You will learn from this mistake and become a better person. That's what mistakes are for. You can't be taught everything in life. It's up to you to fail and try again. It's by making mistakes that we become great. None of you are naughty people. The mistakes and bad behavior can be turned into the great lessons of life.

"Josef, do you know where your family name comes from?"

"Ruprecht?" Josef asked still in a trance. "Not really."

"Knecht Ruprecht was a man that used to follow Santa Claus in your area. It was said he would throw bad kids into a sack or hit them with rods," Mrs. Claus explained. "People used to tell this story to get kids to behave.

"When Santa found out what Knecht Ruprecht was up to, it was Knecht that was thrown into the sack and taken back here. He soon gave up his evil ways and helped us build many of the structures that still stand in this village.

"Knecht never gave up his idea of tracking naughty and nice kids. But instead of putting punishments into place, Knecht introduced the idea of only giving toys to the kids who were not naughty for the year. For a time, it was a useful method as we were not able to make a toy for every child in the world. Even after Knecht left, his Naughty List continued on.

"Recently, we have been able to ramp up production to create a surplus of toys. We certainly have enough gifts for all kids, whether they behaved naughty or nice during the year."

Scout came back into the room. She hesitated a moment before handing the Naughty List to Mrs. Claus.

"You see kids; this list is a relic of the past. Traditions are an important part of Christmas, but so is its evolution. Christmas is not meant to be a monolith carved into stone for people to worship and never change. It is a living, breathing celebration that should evolve with the times.

"Like a fire in the hearth, we need to remove the ash and add fresh fuel to keep it burning brightly. If we do not, it will burn out and leave us forever. Let us celebrate the change in Christmas. Let it be the flames jumping around and giving light to the world we cherish, not just the embers giving heat. While the embers give us the warmth and tradition of the holiday, the flames bring forth the wonder and delight. Both parts are important, but the flames alone give light to the darkness."

She looked down at the Naughty List. She caressed the cover. She glanced around the room. Everyone's eyes were upon her.

"This book has served its purpose. It's time for a change."

Without further ceremony, she tossed the Naughty List into the fire. The fire leaped up and consumed its fresh fuel. The shadows in the room stood out against the new light coming from the fireplace. A weight seemed to lift from everyone's shoulders.

"You are the last flames of the Naughty List," she said to the witnesses of this momentous occasion. "You will show the world why this list has no more connection to Christmas."

17

Winter had finally arrived in New York on the morning of December 7th. Hermey liked to see the snow falling in the city. It hushed the usual noises of the urban island. As he trudged along 48th Street, he dreaded arriving at his destination.

His son, Rudi, had called him the night before. The fifteen-minute outage of *Legend Quest* had the top executives at Eastern Industries in a fury. Rudi was the head of North American operations and shared their anger. To keep all the players happy, free upgrades had to be given out which cost the company millions of dollars in lost revenue.

Rudi got a call from the Chief Executive Officer, Mr. Kim, who explained some of the details of the attack on *Legend Quest*. While Mr. Kim did not know the precise identity of the attacker, he indicated it was a group tied to Christmas since their network location registered as the "North Pole."

As soon as Rudi heard "North Pole," he thought his father may be involved. He remembered the stories his father told him as a youth about the North Pole and the many challenges Santa faced each Christmas. Rudi knew his father did not like his recent business activities, so he was the first person he thought to contact to find out more about his employer's setback.

Hermey came to the main door of the Eastern Industries North American flagship store and entered. He was immediately bombarded with a new type of holiday music. It sounded similar to the tunes he was used to, but all references to Christmas and Santa had been removed. The word "Christmas" was replaced with "Winterval" in all songs and displays.

Hermey was sad when he first walked in, but felt surprisingly better as he walked through the store. After a while, he began to marvel at the wonderful decorations, the orderly behavior of the shoppers, and the majestic throne Grandfather Frost sat upon. Kids and parents walked around with big smiles. Everyone seemed to be in good spirits.

Besides the sights and sounds, pleasant aromas were also wafting through the store to help shoppers get in the Winterval mood. As he passed from one area to another, he noticed each had its own distinctive scent which made Hermey want to stay in the area awhile and purchase something.

"Maybe this isn't so bad after all," Hermey thought to himself.

Hermey resisted the urge to shop a little and headed toward the back of the store. He went through a door marked "Employees Only". On the other side, he was stopped by security.

"I'm here to see Rudi Kringle," Hermey said to the guard. "I have an appointment."

"I need to see your ID," the security guard demanded.

Hermey took out a driver's license and the guard looked it over.

"Oh..." the guard stammered. "Sorry Mr. Kringle, I didn't know it was you. Please step into the elevator and take it to the top floor. A receptionist will be expecting you."

Hermey rode the elevator up; it opened into a typical corporate office. The piped-in smells from the store were not present up here. It seemed very sterile to Hermey.

"Right this way," a young man said as he led Hermey to a conference room.

It was a beautiful room. The large clear windows overlooked a city courtyard with a giant Winterval tree in the center. The happy feeling he had in the store was slowly fading from his consciousness. His mood soon returned to the gloom he had felt before entering the store.

"Is there anything I can get you?" the receptionist asked.

"Just one question," Hermey answered. "When I was walking in the store I felt great. How do you pull that off?"

"You mean the fragrant smells," the receptionist said. "We add a mild, mood-improving vapor to the air to make people feel better. We want everyone in our stores to have the greatest Winterval experience."

"So even the mood-lifting experience in the store is fake," Hermey mused out loud.

"No," the receptionist countered, his face smiling back at Hermey. "The mood improvement is real. Our vapor helps counteract the Seasonal Adjustment Disorder people experience this time of year. When someone buys an item and takes it home, the scent lingers in their house for a few days as well.

"I keep a satchel of pine scent from the store near my bed and wake up happy each morning."

Hermey was disgusted at the thought. It was bad enough his son's company was forcing Winterval onto the world, but now they were manipulating people with specific aromas that altered behavior. In the past, Christmas had always been the answer to the gloom people felt during the shortest days of the year. The charity and kindness, in which the world participated, had brightened the dark days. Now the joy had been reduced to an artificial vapor being pumped into their noses.

Before Hermey's gloom deepened further, an impeccably dressed man entered the conference room and gestured for the receptionist to leave. He wore a perfectly tailored suit. His shoes were freshly polished and his cufflinks sported Winterval trees made from diamonds and emeralds. His black hair was slicked back on his head with some touches of gray on the sides giving him a wise appearance.

"Thank you for coming, Hermey," Rudi addressed his father.

"Good to see you, Rudi," Hermey said. "It's been too long."

"Don't start that stuff with me," Rudi said as his features became tense. "You know how busy work is this time of year."

"I do," Hermey said glancing out the window. "You've done quite a number with Christmas this year."

"It's Winterval now," Rudi said with increasing frustration. "We've buried that old holiday. There's no place in today's world for a holiday that excludes people and creates a belief in a false god."

"Is that how you refer to Santa now?" Hermey asked.

"Please don't get started with your superstitions," Rudi said while waving his hand dismissively. "I'm trying to make the winter celebration into something everyone can enjoy and cherish. I don't want kids to believe in Santa and then get crushed like I did."

"You chose to stop believing," Hermey responded.

"Do you still expect me to believe you're Santa?" Rudi angrily replied. "I was ten years old when I caught you pretending to be Santa."

Hermey's face grimaced when he recalled the Christmas Eve when his own son stopped believing in Santa Claus. Although it had happened almost forty years ago, the pain was still fresh in Hermey's mind.

When Rudi was little, he and Hermey spent all their free time making toys. Hermey could make a few basic ones, but Rudi was a true craftsman with toys. From the time he could walk, Rudi would create the most wonderful wooden toys.

Each year, on Christmas Eve, Hermey and Rudi gave their toys to the local children's hospital for Santa to distribute.

When Rudi was ten, he went up, as usual, to Santa and sat on his lap. On that particular Christmas Eve, Rudi looked into Santa's eyes and realized it was his father in the Santa suit. His life changed at that moment. He ran home crying before Hermey could explain.

Later that night, Hermey told Rudi there are many Santa Clauses in the world. He explained it was the hat that gave regular people the power to act as Santa. Hermey promised he would make sure the one, true Santa from the North Pole would stop by their house that night. He wrote a letter and burned it in the fireplace.

Rudi knew what Hermey was trying to do, but his disappointment was too deep. That night, the sleigh and reindeer landed in front of Hermey's house. Hermey and Rudi went out to meet Santa. Rudolph was at the front of the team with his nose glowing brightly. It was too late for Rudi. He had already shut the door to his heart and nothing could reopen it. He dismissed the whole affair as an elaborate scheme on his father's part. Even when the sleigh flew up to the sky, Rudi would not believe his own eyes.

From that day forward, Rudi hated Christmas. He hated Santa. He hated everything about the holiday except the toys. He still loved making toys and giving them to kids. He continued to do so in future years, but insisted the toys be handed out by him and no one else. He wanted people to realize that gifts do not come from some magical source. His toys came from hard work and dedication. He wanted to be recognized and appreciated for his work.

Santa never returned to Rudi's house. Rudi's conduct had landed him on the Naughty List and he never got off of it.

The father and son grew apart after that. Every year around Christmas, Hermey would try to tell his stories about the North Pole, but Rudi would only get angry. At eighteen years old, Rudi moved off to New York City and started his own successful toy company. With his son gone, Hermey dove deeper into his dentistry practice and lost touch with the North Pole altogether.

Every time Hermey saw his son, he relived the pain of that Christmas Eve. It broke his heart to know his own son hated Christmas. The pain was still present as the two sat down in the conference room.

"Let's talk about the North Pole," Rudi said, shaking off the memories they both were reliving.

Hermey cheered up for a moment.

"I would love to talk about the North Pole."

"Not about Santa Claus and those stories," Rudi clarified. "I want to talk about a North Pole network that hacked into our online game and caused it to crash. I could lose my job over that."

"I haven't heard anything about it," Hermey answered truthfully.

"Look Hermey," Rudi began to lecture his father. "I know that you and Tiberius have been spending time together. The encryption codes that protect *Legend Quest* are unbreakable. It would take the best computer millions of years to crack the codes and someone managed to do it within minutes. I suspect that troublesome child of mine somehow had something to do with the hack. I don't know how he could have pulled it off, but I've learned to never underestimate Tiberius's ability to cause trouble.

"I want to know what the two of you are up to. My job is on the line and my job is my life."

"Tiber is not with me," Hermey began. "Tiber is at the North Pole working with a group of kids to get Santa back from your headquarters."

"Not that again!" Rudi screamed. "I'll have you thrown in jail unless you tell me what's really going on!"

"I am telling you," Hermey sadly replied. "Santa was kidnapped by your company from the parade almost two weeks ago. He is being held on Baekdu Island. He…"

"You are mad!" Rudi interrupted. "You need to get a grip on reality. The Santa that Mr. Sarg hired for the parade never showed up, simple as that. He was probably drunk.

"Look Hermey," Rudi said as he regained control over his emotions. "I know you're harmless and I'm glad Tiberius is spending time with you. As you know, I have no time for him until Winterval is over. Please don't set him up for disappointment like you did with me.

"There's not a caretaker in the world that will watch Tiberius now, so I have no other options. Please keep it together until after Winterval. I've arranged to have Tiberius go to a special school for troubled kids. I just need to get through Winterval and everything can go back to normal."

"I'll do my best to make sure we stay out of your way," Hermey responded. "I'm sorry if Tiber caused any trouble."

"I need you to promise me you'll keep a close eye on him," Rudi said with concern. "If he had something to do with this hack, nothing will save him from going to a juvenile detention facility. Promise me you'll keep him out of trouble until after Winterval."

"I'll go straight to him right now and make sure I know what he's up to at all times," Hermey solemnly promised, choosing his words carefully.

Hermey stood up and left the conference room. He went back through the store and tried to hold his breath. It did not work and he felt better by the time he left. But this time, the mood improvement felt artificial to him and wore off quicker.

As he walked along the streets, his depression quickly returned. He passed a man dressed as Santa Claus ringing a bell for charity. He looked in his bucket and saw it was empty. He threw a dollar in.

"Thanks bud," the Santa said.

"You're welcome," Hermey replied. "Looking a bit light in there."

"You're the first one today," the Santa commented. "No one wants to make anonymous contributions anymore. I've barely collected anything this whole season."

"Where's all the charity going?" Hermey asked.

"Over there," the Santa said pointing to an electronic deposit machine.

The machine was an Eastern Industries collection point. People were lined up to insert money and simultaneously watch their ranking move up on the screen. When they reached certain levels of charitable giving, they received vouchers for free services and products at any Eastern Industries store.

Hermey walked by the machine. He noticed the people in line did not look happy. They were tired. Although they willingly gave to the machine, it seemed more like the machine was taking the money from them. Charity had been reduced to a competition and they were all obsessed with beating their friends and neighbors.

Hermey continued his trek through the city. On a sidewalk, he tried to wish people a "Merry Christmas."

One woman replied, "It's 'Happy Winterval', you old fool."

Another passerby commented, "Don't spew your hate speech near me. 'Merry Christmas' is offensive. Christmas is dead. Good riddance."

Hermey looked up at billboards showing Grandfather Frost inviting people to his magical castle. A gym he passed by had posted a sign of Santa Claus in a red circle with a slash through it. The words underneath read, "Don't be a fat, old man this Winterval; try our two-week workout special and feel as good as Grandfather Frost."

Everywhere Hermey looked, there were signs of Winterval. Eastern Industries was succeeding in erasing Christmas altogether. Even the headline of the day's paper announced, "President's Council on Fitness says Santa is a bad role model. Obesity should be eliminated, not encouraged."

Winterval was at its height and Hermey waded through the mess it was creating. People were consumed with the new holiday, but they were not happy. People were working harder than ever, but they could not get ahead in the great competition.

The poor and needy were the worst off. Normally, this time of year brought in extra help for the people who needed it most. Instead, Eastern Industries was sucking up the charitable resources and funneling it to their own bottom line: profit.

Eastern Industries had won over the minds of the people. It was evident in everything. Almost everyone in the world was swept up in the hysteria. They were running so fast that they did not have time to look back at what they were leaving behind.

18

The Naughty Team was settling into the routine Ben had created. Everyone was participating in the workouts and meetings. No one had benefitted from the routine more than Josef.

He was still a large child, but he was quickly building strength and endurance. His morning routine now included pushups and sit-ups along with the usual stretching. During specialized training, he was able to keep up with the other kids on tasks that had seemed impossible only a few days before.

Josef also got back to work on the information he had managed to save before the North Pole network went down. He used one of the old machines to read his USB stick and to decipher some of the plans he had downloaded. He had detailed maps of the island and floor plans of the factory itself. He studied the schematics of the robot machines to identify any weaknesses.

By the afternoon of December 8th, Ben and Tomo were still unable to come up with a solution for providing transportation to the island. They needed a ship and had no idea how to get one. In addition to the Naughty Team, they had to bring the toy soldiers the elves had been working on. What they needed was an aircraft carrier, but they did not have the raw materials to build anything larger than a dinghy.

Mithra was still trying to figure out what distinguished Saturn from the rest of the snowmen. With the help of many elves, she continued to add snow to him until eventually he was thirty feet high. That seemed to be the limit. When she added any additional snow, he began to have trouble moving.

Mithra did not take out his core snowflake. She feared it may prevent her from building him to the great size again. Instead, she worked with a few volunteer snowmen to see if there were changes she could make to allow them to reach his size.

At first, she experimented with the type of snow used. She rebuilt some snowmen with heavy snow, while others were rebuilt with light, fluffy snow. She tried ice, sleet, and even different materials mixed in with the snow. Nothing worked like it did for Saturn.

After a while, Mithra and some elves decided to try a reverse approach and melt Saturn back to a smaller size. They used hair dryers and carefully began to melt his outer layers. Soon, Saturn was back to the height of the other snowmen, but he looked dirty.

"There is something in that snow," Mithra observed to the elves. "He should be as white as when he was created, but he looks almost rusty."

She stared at the smaller Saturn and pondered the rusty appearance. She ran through some possibilities in her head.

"Of course!" she exclaimed snapping out of her deep thinking. "Rust comes from iron. Iron is a conductor, but not a very good one.

"Do you have any copper or silver dust around here?" Mithra asked the elves.

"Not much," an elf answered. "But we have plenty of gold dust."

"Even better," Mithra said. "Gold is a very good conductor and it will not tarnish or oxidize. Let's mix some gold dust into the snow and create a gigantic snowman. Make it... hmmm... make it fifty feet high."

It was almost noon. Mithra wanted to continue unraveling Saturn's mystery, but she thought it important to head in for lunch with the rest of the team.

As the team was finishing lunch, Tiberius addressed them.

"It's really important we figure out our transportation to the island today. There are only sixteen days to go until Christmas Eve. If we include the duration of the voyage to Baekdu Island, we have very little time to figure out this problem."

"If we can determine the route and distance, I think we can get a good estimate of the travel time," Mithra said. "I've been studying the weather patterns of this area for years. Fortunately, the wind blows from North to South and we'll have the wind at our backs the whole way down.

"In fact, it may be too much wind. This time of year there are constant storms and the winds can reach fifty miles per hour or more. Whatever vessel we build; it will need to be able to handle a winter hurricane.

"We'll also be dealing with sea ice. Recent years have seen a decrease in the amount of sea ice, but we'll encounter it at various points along the trip."

Ziggy spread out a large nautical chart on the table. Tiberius located Baekdu Island and started measuring the distance from the North Pole.

"The island is over two thousand nautical miles away," Tiberius groaned. "Even at twenty knots, average speed, it will take us over four days to reach the island."

"We are not quite at the North Pole," Ziggy responded to Tiberius. He pointed to a spot below the North Pole and added, "This is our approximate position."

"That is closer," Tiberius observed. "But it's still going to be a long trip."

Everyone in the room was surprised by Tiberius's expertise with the nautical chart. He was using parallel rulers and fixed-point dividers like an old salt.

"How do you know all this?" Ben asked.

"I spend summers sailing on my father's yacht with his professional crew," Tiberius explained. "I've sailed to many places with them. My father rarely is able to go with us, so I get to decide where the yacht travels.

"We've been in some pretty serious storms, but nothing like what we should expect sailing through the Arctic Ocean in the middle of winter.

"In order to get a boat to sustain twenty knots and carry a heavy load, it will need to be over two hundred feet long."

"We don't have the resources here to build something that big," Ziggy stated.

"It's true," Ben added. "Nebo and I have been working with the elves to design a boat that will carry a large load but we just don't have enough wood. We could build a frame of that length, but not an entire ship."

"Are there other resources we can use?" Tiberius asked.

"How about constructing a giant iceberg boat?" Gus asked.

"It would melt once we entered the open sea and continued south," Tiberius answered.

"Maybe not," Mithra said pensively.

"It would be impossible to get an iceberg to move at over twenty knots, break through ice and then move through open water," Tiberius countered abruptly. "We need to consider ideas that actually have a chance."

"It's not impossible," Mithra said raising her voice. "A ship has been made out of ice before."

Everyone in the room turned their attention to Mithra. They had come to respect her deep knowledge of the polar environment. The attention made her uncomfortable.

"Back in World War II…" she began, "…the allied forces worked with a substance they called pykrete. It was a combination of fourteen percent sawdust and eighty-six percent ice. They conducted many tests with the substance. They fired bullets at it, put incredible loads on it, and subjected it to heat. Pykrete passed every test. It seemed to be the perfect ratio for their purposes.

"They found the material to be as strong as concrete and better in many respects. They planned to build an aircraft carrier with it.

"At one point, they built a scaled-down model for evaluation. By the time the model was completed, the war and technology had progressed to a point where the monster ship was no longer needed. It took the small model over three years to melt away, so we know it is durable.

"We have plenty of water here. If we can get our hands on tons of sawdust, I think we can build a giant ship in short order."

"We *have* tons of sawdust!" Ziggy said excitedly. "We've kept the sawdust from all the toys we've made over the years. There are piles of it just outside the village."

"All we need to do is build a watertight frame for the boat and then fill it with water and sawdust," Mithra continued. "If we let it freeze overnight, we'll have a ship that can withstand the journey to Baekdu Island."

"Genius!" Ben exclaimed. "I can get started on the frame this afternoon. How long should we make it?"

"The original design called for a ship over two thousand feet long," Mithra recalled. "They planned to use it to launch planes that could not land on a conventional aircraft carrier. I think we could go about three hundred feet long."

"We'll need to make it very wide," Tiberius interjected. "I think we should build it five hundred feet long. Given the conditions in the Arctic Ocean, we want something that will not get rolled by the large waves."

"How would we control such a boat?" Gus worried aloud.

"I'm not sure," Tiberius answered. "But right now, I think this is our only solution to getting a ship to Baekdu Island. So let's start working on it and hope we can solve the rest of the problems on the fly."

After lunch, most of the team stayed together to work on the ship. Josef headed off to the old computer he was working on and Mithra went to see if the elves had made any headway with the new snowman.

To her delight, the large snowman was nearly complete. He was almost fifty feet high. It seemed like every elf in the village had come out to work on him. He had a slight golden hue from all the gold dust the elves had sprinkled in.

Mithra, scientific as always, quizzed the elves on the exact amount of gold dust used in the snowman. She took precise measurements of the snowman's dimensions. Finally, she isolated a speck of cosmic dust from Polaris, one of the star group of snowmen, and put it in her vapor diffusion chamber.

A new snowflake was born. The elves helped her mold it into a large head and they hoisted it to the top of the giant snowman. It began to move.

"We did it!" the elves shouted.

The snowman was just as active as the little ones. He could walk, talk, and wave his arms. All the other snowmen wanted to have gold dust in their bodies. They clamored around and asked to be rebuilt.

"Slow down," Mithra scolded them. "I'd like to see if I can blend some sawdust in there with the gold dust. It may make you less likely to melt or get damaged."

Mithra realized the snowmen were eager to be remade, but she knew that the team needed her help to build the ship. She left the snowmen and headed over to the ship building area.

148

She shared her success with the group. They were amazed that a snowman even bigger than Saturn had been created.

Tiberius showed Mithra the plans he had developed for the construction of the ship. She looked them over and thought they looked great. Tiberius called everyone together.

He assigned Mithra and Nebo to the task of piping water to a mixing tank that would be located above the boat building area. This is where the sawdust and water would be mixed. From there, a tube would direct the pulpy water into a frame.

Ben, Tomo, and Gus would work with the elves to assemble the frame. Tiberius provided them with the necessary specifications and blueprints. He had designed a ship he hoped would withstand storms and also have the ability to break through ice. Those were his two biggest concerns for traveling through the ocean this time of year. For the rest of the afternoon, the teams worked diligently at their tasks.

Ben directed the elves on various activities concerning the frame. Tomo spent most of the afternoon suspended over the growing structure helping to move materials to the high points. Gus oversaw the waterproofing of the seams.

On the tank project, Mithra made sure they had an accurate mix to achieve a perfect fourteen percent sawdust ratio. Nebo used his incredible strength to carry the heavy tank walls up the hill.

The speed with which they completed the frame was unparalleled in any building project the world has ever known. Within a few hours, a five-hundred-foot boat frame had been created. A holding tank for over a million gallons of water was ready on the hill above the build site. The elves even fabricated a conveyer belt to bring the sawdust from its storage area to the mixing tank.

By the time the team broke for dinner, they had the pieces in place to begin pouring the pykrete mixture the next day.

At dinner, they talked about ways to power the ship. Mithra reminded everyone they would have the help of the wind at their backs. Tiberius wanted to build masts and sails for the massive craft, but could not figure out how they would be able to handle the size needed to propel the giant ship.

As they were eating, an Arctic spider crawled across the table. Ben raised his hand to smash the little critter, but Gus grabbed his wrist and held on hard. Ben was surprised the wispy, little fellow was able to stop him.

"Don't hurt him," Gus sternly rebuked Ben.

"I don't want to get bitten by a spider," Ben replied.

"He won't bite you," Gus assured his overbearing companion. "He is going to spin a web for us on that little tree decoration in the middle of the table.

"If a spider puts a web on your Christmas tree, it is said to be a sign of good luck," Gus explained.

The spider worked its way around the tree. It moved up and down the branches and when it was done the tree was covered in its silky web. No tinsel had ever looked so beautiful. The flames from the fire made the web flicker in brilliant colors. All the kids were fascinated by the transformation of this little tree.

"How did you know the spider was going to do that?" Tomo asked.

"She told me," Gus said flatly. He was still listening to the spider.

"Go ahead and touch the web," he said to the kids. "The spider says she spins the strongest silk in the world."

They all took a turn touching the web. It was amazingly sturdy. Tiberius took one piece of the spider silk with both hands and could not break it.

"That's incredible," he observed. "I've never seen a fiber this strong. I love the way it catches the light. This place never ceases to amaze me. Gus, can you talk to animals as well as understand them?"

"Sometimes I think they understand me, but I'm not sure."

"Try it."

Gus held out his hand near the spider. He stared down at it and thought, "Please crawl on my finger. Tell me where you would like to go."

The spider crawled on his finger and somehow Gus knew to put her down in the far corner of the room.

"I think she understood me!" Gus gasped.

He had never been able to communicate with such a tiny creature. Sure the dogs and cows would react to his talking, but a spider understanding his thoughts was something completely new. His ability to understand animals was morphing into a capacity to have a two-way conversation with them.

"How many spiders are around here?" Tiberius asked Gus. He was surprised to see any insect existing in such a cold environment.

Gus looked at the spider and pondered Tiberius's question. Gus seemed lost in thought when he simply uttered, "millions."

19

Ben summoned the team together the next morning. Josef was nowhere to be found when they started their exercise routine. After a couple of stretches, Josef burst into the room. He was already sweating.

"Is everything OK?" Tomo asked.

"Yes," Josef replied. "Everything is great. I woke up a little early and decided to go for a walk. After a while, it turned into a jog. When I realized how late it was getting, I ran as fast as I could to get back here."

Ben smiled and said, "Wow! You're really starting to get into physical exercise."

"I've never felt better," Josef said with a smile. "I always thought exercise was just hard work. Now I really enjoy moving around. Thanks for teaching me how to do it."

"My pleasure," Ben responded. "Please join us for the rest of the routine."

Josef fell in with the others and the morning workout continued. Gus was unusually active this morning as well. Everyone felt pretty good about the way things were going. They did not know how, but they all believed they would succeed in getting Santa back by Christmas.

After a very active morning, the kids headed to the debriefing at ten o'clock. As they entered the room, Hermey was seated with Scout, Ziggy, and Mrs. Claus.

Tiberius ran up to his grandfather and gave him a big hug. "I'm so glad you're back here," Tiberius cried out.

"It's good to be here," Hermey responded, a little surprised by Tiberius's emotional greeting. "I certainly don't want to be down south anymore. Things are not good. Anyway, Tiber, I promised your father I would keep a close eye on you. He was pretty upset over the whole *Legend Quest* outage."

Josef blushed and said, "Sorry about that. I made a mistake attacking their servers and I'll never do that again. I've learned a lot since then."

Mrs. Claus interrupted the conversation by politely saying, "Naughty Team, this is Tiberius's grandfather and our old friend Hermey. He used to live and work with us."

Hermey shook each kid's hand before they all sat down for the debriefing. Tiberius asked Hermey to get them up to date on what was happening down south.

"It's terrible," Hermey began. "People are all caught up in a giant competition to make their own Winterval better than their neighbor's. Greed is rampant and Eastern Industries is cashing in on the whole spectacle."

Hermey went on to describe his experience walking around in New York. He made sure to mention that people did not seem happy unless they were being influenced by one of Eastern Industry's mood altering scents. He talked about how the concept of Christmas was now repulsive to people, describing his encounter with the woman that had been offended by "Merry Christmas."

"Eastern Industries is trying to destroy Christmas by redefining it," Hermey explained. "They have recast it as a holiday that excludes non-Christians. It's now considered politically incorrect to reference Christmas in any way as it may alienate people."

"It's worse than I thought," Mrs. Claus observed.

Tiberius rose to his feet and said, "I guess it's more important than ever to get Santa back. The world needs him to bring the joy and wonder back to the Christmas season.

"Today we will pour the pykrete for the ship. I don't think we'll need the whole team for that, so Josef, please continue to work on interpreting the plans for the Baekdu Island factory. Tomo, you can practice your ice climbing. Gus, I want you to go with her and continue to get as much information as possible from the animals. Everyone's abilities seem to be increasing here at the North Pole and yours could very well be the key to our success."

Gus rose in his seat and smiled. He liked the positive attention he was receiving. Talking to animals used to get him in trouble and now his talent might be able to help save Christmas. He slipped into a daydream about being the hero.

"Ben, Nebo, Mithra and I will pour the hull of the ship today and then set out to make the other parts that will turn it into a sailing vessel," Tiberius said with determination.

As everyone headed for the door, Hermey reached out for Tiberius and asked him to stay behind for a moment. When the two were alone in the room, Hermey looked into Tiberius's eyes. "You have changed, Tiber."

"Actually... I haven't," Tiberius responded matter-of-factly.

"You hugged me... You're leading a team... You seem like a different person."

"I am no different," Tiberius explained. "Mrs. Claus and the others have me concentrating on my best qualities. For too long, it was only my worst qualities that got me any attention. I came to believe my naughty behavior *was me*. I believed *I was* a naughty person.

"After I arrived here, I began to focus on my strengths. Mrs. Claus and the elves had faith in my ability to lead this team and eventually I began to believe it too. Ben has helped me find my physical strength. We all build each other up and bring out the best in ourselves.

"I'm still the same person, Grandpa. I've just learned to see the good in myself. By focusing on my best traits, I feel them growing stronger inside of me. The urge to cause trouble is receding. I want to be good. I want to succeed. Most of all, I want to save Christmas."

"You mean save Santa?" Hermey asked.

"No, I mean save Christmas. Santa is just the living personification of the greater force within us. He is the one who gives without reward. He shows compassion without recognition. He is what we all should aspire to be. I don't just want to save him; I want to save the Santa in everyone. To me, that *is* Christmas."

Hermey hugged Tiberius with all his might.

"Thank you, Tiber," Hermey said holding back tears. "That's exactly what I needed to hear after what I've been through the last couple of days."

"Come look at what we're building," Tiberius said excitedly. "I think you'll be pleasantly surprised."

When Hermey and Tiberius arrived at the ship's construction area, Mithra was already pumping water and sawdust into the mixing chamber above the frame. She was making sure the conveyer belt's timing matched the water's flow to achieve the desired ratio.

Nebo controlled the outlet of the pykrete solution tube and was soon guiding the mixture across the bottom of the frame. The keel of the vessel filled first and Nebo continued working up the frame from there.

Ben was not sure what to do, so he stood by the mixing tank with Hermey and Tiberius and watched the ship as it slowly filled.

"That's some vessel. How many people are sailing on it?" Hermey asked in disbelief. He was awestruck by the immensity of the project.

"It's not just people," Ben explained. "Ziggy and the elves are making toy soldiers to help neutralize the island's defenses."

"Mithra found a way to develop a battalion of snowmen too," Tiberius added. "She figured out where Jasper's core came from and uncovered fifty more."

Ziggy walked up to the group as they continued to observe the ship's creation.

"Want to see what the ship is going to carry?" Ziggy asked. "We have, uhm, quite a few toy soldiers completed."

"Sure," Ben answered. He was already feeling like a fifth wheel as he stood around watching the others at work.

They walked back into the village and down the main street. In the near distance, there was a line of twenty toy soldiers spread across the width of the street.

The soldiers were three feet high. They had red jackets with gold buttons painted on their chests. Their legs were painted bright white, with a red stripe down each side. Their tall black hats stood four inches above their heads and matched the color of their boots. Their faces had two black dots for eyes, a black mustache, and a red dot on each cheek. They each carried a wooden rifle with a gold-plated bayonet on the end.

Behind the first line was another line, and another, and another. Ben's eyes widened.

"There must be over a thousand of them," Ben gasped.

"Actually, there are over ten thousand," Ziggy said with pride. "Watch this..."

Ziggy gave out a call to march. A thunderous sound filled the streets as ten thousand soldiers began to march in perfect unison. Ben and Ziggy had to scurry out of the way.

"How do they move?" Ben asked, unable to hide his shock.

"We fitted each soldier with servomechanisms to give them some limited movement. Over the years, we have been making more and more robots for Santa to deliver. So we thought we would use the robot technology to create moving soldiers to enhance the specifications you had requested.

"They have a microprocessor in their bodies that allows us to control them with some commands or a remote-controlled transmitter. I was hoping you would approve of them."

"Approve?" Ben stammered. "Ziggy, these are amazing!"

Tiberius watched in disbelief as the army continued to parade by. Hermey just smiled.

"How many more do you plan to make?" Tiberius asked Ziggy.

"I think we can get another ten or fifteen thousand before you depart for the island."

Ben turned to Tiberius. "I think we're going to need more ships."

After the impressive demonstration by the toy soldiers, the group left the review and headed back to the ship building area. Mithra was waiting for them.

"Once this freezes overnight, we'll have a giant block of pykrete shaped like a ship's hull," Mithra said. She turned toward Tiberius. "I'll need you to design the mast, rigging, and rudder for the vessel. We'll need to be creative since the original World War II project was never successful at developing a rudder that could withstand a long voyage."

Mithra turned to Ben and added, "Please work with the elves to create a plan for cabins down below. Once the pykrete is solid, they'll be able to use their wood carving tools to shape the interior. Be sure to leave at least fifteen feet of pykrete around the outer hull. At that thickness, our ship will not sink, even if it hits a rocky reef."

Ben nodded. He was happy to have a task again. He hesitated a moment and asked, "Do we have the capability to build more than one ship?"

Mithra drifted off into thought. It was her usual reaction to a tough question. She stared blankly ahead for a while.

"Today is the ninth of December. This hull will be done on the tenth," she began to calculate out loud. "If we get this hull out of the way, we can put the frame back together and pour again on the eleventh. So the second ship would be ready on the twelfth. Assuming we can keep that pace, we can have a fifth hull out of the frame by the eighteenth.

"I think everything here is under control," Mithra concluded. "Tiberius, Hermey, why don't you join me by the snowmen and we can try out some new things. I would love to see if we can add strength to the snowmen by using pykrete."

Mithra filled a sack with sawdust and the three hurried over to the group of snowmen. Polaris was still enjoying normal movement and the other snowmen were anxious to expand to his size.

"Can I be next?" Orion asked. He was from the constellation group of snowmen.

"Sure," Mithra responded. "We're going to use a mix of sawdust and gold dust for you. We'll start by making you regular size."

Hermey and Tiberius rolled up the snow Mithra had sprinkled with the two dusts. They made a snowman in the usual pykrete proportions but in this case, instead of ice, they used snow. When Mithra reformed Orion's core snowflake and put it in the snowman, he did not move. She checked the snowman with her detector and confirmed the cosmic dust was inside.

"This isn't going to work," she concluded. "Wood is a good insulator, so the sawdust we placed in Orion must be blocking the electrical pathways."

"What do you mean insulator?" Tiberius asked.

"An insulator is a material that will not allow an electrical current through it. It is the opposite of a conductor," Mithra explained. "It seems that pykrete and snowmen are not a good combination. I guess I'll have to stick to gold dust."

Tiberius looked at the static snowman. He was disappointed they could not enhance his strength with the pykrete. Then he realized he did not know how strong the snowman was in the first place.

"Jasper," Tiberius called out. "How much weight can you lift? How strong are you?"

"I don't know," Jasper said. "I don't think I have ever tested my limits."

"Let's find out," Mithra said. She loved conducting experiments and wanted to know everything she could about the snowmen.

For the rest of the afternoon, Mithra, Tiberius, and Hermey ran the snowmen through different routines. They tested speed, strength, and endurance. Speed and strength were easily measured, but endurance was a mystery. No matter how much activity they did, the snowmen never tired.

20

The next morning, Tiberius had trouble focusing on anything except the construction of his burgeoning fleet. While everyone else was engaged in their morning exertions, Tiberius only went through the motions. He still had some big problems to tackle if they were to reach Baekdu Island before Christmas.

He had a long list of items that seemed impossible to obtain at the North Pole. He needed tall masts, strong sails, and a way to steer the giant vessels.

He was encouraged by the results of the tests they had performed on the snowmen the day before. As it turned out, Jasper and the others could lift thousands of pounds. Their snow bodies were incredibly tough. Melting or getting too big were the only things that could possibly hurt them. They were faster than any human being; they could also climb as well as Tomo, if not better.

Tiberius knew their strength would be very helpful in regard to handling a vessel in a storm. Unfortunately, since masts, sails and rigging were still non-existent, he did not know what exactly they would be handling. His burden was heavy and it showed.

"Tiberius," Ben called out toward the end of the exercises. "What's weighing you down today?"

"It's the ships," Tiberius confided to Ben. "I just don't know how we're going to build masts, sails and a rudder. I don't think we can do it by the nineteenth. If we don't leave by that morning, we won't make it to Baekdu Island by Christmas Eve. This whole operation will have been a waste of time."

"You made us a team," Ben said trying to reassure Tiberius. "That alone has been worth the time. Let us help you as a team.

"We'll all head back to Santa's office and we won't leave until we have a working plan that will get us to Baekdu Island by Christmas," Ben promised Tiberius.

Mrs. Claus, Hermey and the elves were already in Santa's office when the kids arrived.

"We will not leave this room until we have a means to get the ships safely to Baekdu Island by the morning of the twenty-fourth," Ben began.

"We need to figure out the details of moving the ships we are to build," Tiberius interjected. His voice was shaky and betrayed the confidence he was trying to project.

"Mithra, can we use pykrete to build the masts?" Ben asked.

"No," Mithra said with her usual directness. "Pykrete is like cement and cannot handle the stress of a mast since they need to be flexible. Even if it could, the masts would be so massive that the ship wouldn't be stable."

"Any other ideas?" Ben asked the group.

"Most masts these days are made out of aluminum," Tiberius responded. "Ziggy, is there a source of aluminum somewhere up here?"

"We don't have excesses of any metal, except gold," Ziggy said.

"Too soft," Mithra responded.

"How about wood?" Tiberius continued. "Old ships used wooden masts. With the right wood and strong supports, it might work for us."

"We don't have anything long enough," Ziggy responded with regret. "If we had the right lumber, I am sure the elves could make a mast out of it."

Tiberius looked around the room. It was completely made out of solid wood. Tiberius recalled when he first arrived. The giant room he first entered had tremendous pillars of wood.

"This building is composed completely of wood — where did it come from?" Tiberius asked.

"The elves brought it north with them," Mrs. Claus said to everyone's surprise.

"Brought it with them?" Tiberius asked. He was puzzled by this. He had just assumed the elves had always been at the North Pole. "Where did the elves come from?"

Mrs. Claus turned to Ziggy and Scout. They both shrugged their shoulders, indicating they did not know the answer.

"Let's go out to the main workshop," Mrs. Claus suggested. "I would like to show you some more carvings."

They filed out of the office and into the great room. Mrs. Claus pointed to the wood panels near the door. There were carved images of elves frolicking around giant trees. Even though Ziggy and Scout had been in this room many times before, they had never studied the images until now.

Mrs. Claus pointed up. The carvings changed from only elves in the forest to elves and people living together in the forest. Continuing up the wall, the carvings showed more and more people in the forest with the elves. Way up the wall, was a disturbing image of men cutting down a giant tree. Above that, no one could really make out the details.

Down at the bottom again, Mrs. Claus gestured to an image of an elf being mischievous. He was running into a log house and appeared to be stealing some food. Above that, another image showed an elf running with a key and a pair of glasses.

"What's this all mean?" Mithra asked, unable to decipher the message.

"I think it's the story of the elves," Gus guessed out loud.

"That's exactly what it is," Mrs. Claus said. "Santa carved the elves' story into the walls after they helped him build this room. He wanted to make sure their history was preserved. There are very few elves who know the full story, but it's always here, right above their heads."

"Hundreds of years ago, the elves lived throughout the forests of the world," Mrs. Claus said with the tone of a teacher. "They lived in hollowed-out tree trunks, burrows in the ground, and some lived high up in the trees. The elves used the natural resources near their dwellings and rarely travelled more than a few miles from their homes.

"Europe is where humans first began to live in the same forests as the elves. While the number of humans was small, the two intelligent species coexisted but rarely came into contact with each other. If they did, it was usually an elf observing a human from a distance. It was rare for a human to spot an elf in the forest.

"The elves moved silently through their habitat. They traveled through the underbrush and left little trace of activity. Even as the human presence in the forest grew, an elf sighting continued to be rare. The few people who did spot an elf and told about it, were dismissed as mere story tellers.

"About seven hundred years ago, humans began to abandon the forest lifestyle and started to farm in order to provide food and sustenance for their growing population. For the next four centuries, forests were cut down and the remains were plowed under to create fields for the purpose of growing crops. Large animals were brought in to feed in the new pastures and serve as a source of meat for the humans.

"After a while, most of the old forests were cut down. Europe became one big pasture and there were few areas left for the elves to thrive in. Silently, the elves were forced into the smaller and smaller forests that had managed to survive.

"But not all the elves moved on. Some stayed behind and began to come into conflict with the humans. In retaliation, the elves started with light mischievous activities. They would steal an important key or run off with a person's glasses. Other elves might steal an axe from a woodsman as a means to protect their homes.

"People began to connect the stories of the elves with the objects that had mysteriously vanished. Once the connection was made, the stories became exaggerated; way beyond anything the elves actually did undertake. Things got quite out of hand. For example, when someone became sick or disabled, it was attributed to an elf casting a spell. Fabricated stories of such things as elves stealing babies, terrorized the people.

"Their extreme anxiety elicited a perception that the elves were evil spirits. They soon adopted superstitions to keep the elves away. In the heart of the forest, people hung symbols over the door to ward away the so-called evil elves. Elves had gone from performing mythical, amusing antics to actually establishing fear in people's hearts. Beyond explanation, elves were blamed whenever something bad happened.

"Almost 300 years ago, the situation became unbearable for the elves. This compelled them to either become more mischievous or to hide in the few large forests that still remained in Europe. That's when Santa Claus and the elves first met — in a special forest in northern Finland. Santa and I had setup a workshop at the edge of the forest because the wood from the forest was the best in the world. Trees stood over 300 feet tall. Santa would use newly fallen timber to make toys that were unequalled in quality.

"Santa and a band of old craftsmen liked the isolation of the forest as it allowed them to make toys year-round. On Christmas Eve, Santa would ride out of the village with a team of donkeys and deliver the toys all across Europe. He always wished he had the capacity to distribute more toys, but he only had enough to give presents to the kids who were the neediest.

"As more elves moved up to the same forest, they took an interest in Santa's activities. He was different than the humans who had crowded them out of their forest homes. They liked what he was doing. They especially liked the idea of a midnight delivery of the presents. After all, it was their own style to stay out of sight.

"Some of the elves began showing up to help Santa and the craftsmen. At first, the elves were not very skilled at crafting toys. But over time, Santa taught them to be world-class toy makers. Santa and I really enjoyed the elves' company as they were always happy when working.

"Eventually, the human expansion reached the quiet forest Santa had settled down in. The amazing trees provided badly needed wood for the world's growing lumber demand. In a very short time, the forest was being cut down and the elves faced another catastrophe.

"A powerful elf called Lucia, began a quest to find a new forest to live in. Lucia was known among the elves as, *The Carrier of Light*. She always brought glowing candles with her as she navigated through the dark, northern winter's night. Unlike other elves, she travelled far and wide. Despite her great strength, Lucia was still as nimble as any elf. For years, she journeyed through the frozen north looking for a place as special as their beloved Finnish forest.

"Ultimately, over two hundred years ago, she found this precious site." Mrs. Claus gestured with her arms to indicate the great room where they were gathered. "When she got here, her compass spun around wildly. She thought she was at the North Pole, but it was the magic of this spot that spun the compass. We are actually quite a bit south of the geographic North Pole."

"I knew that," Mithra said proudly. "By my calculations, we are..."

"Mithra," Mrs. Claus interrupted. "Your calculations will not work here."

Mrs. Claus pointed to a wood panel that resembled a snow globe. It showed a young, female elf with a candle inside. The reflections of the candle stopped at the edge of the globe and there was no light outside it.

Mrs. Claus whispered into Ziggy's ear and he quickly left.

"What Lucia discovered was a type of natural phenomena surrounding this area. The center of which is under this very building. We refer to it as 'the bubble'. Everything inside the bubble is invisible to the outside world. Lucia burned a candle made from the wax of the mistletoe berry. That's the only type of light that will illuminate the bubble. Lucia knew she had stumbled upon a very unique place.

"When she returned to the forest in Finland and told us about her wonderful discovery, it piqued our interest. By that point, the reindeer had joined our small group and a decision was made to move to our enchanting location. We were joyously overwhelmed with the beauty and resources available to us. The elves had a great love for the surroundings since it possessed the untouched charm of their old forests. We all knew at once this was the perfect spot for us.

"At first, the elves lived in the small forest around the edge of the bubble. Santa and I built a modest house and workshop and continued to make toys. As time went on and more forests were destroyed, a greater number of elves moved here. Santa's workshop grew crowded and we needed more space to accommodate the influx in our population.

"At one point, Lucia returned to the old forest in Finland and cried at the sight. Lumberjacks had chopped down all but the biggest of the trees. She summoned the elves who were still living there and together they cut down the remaining trees. It was her desire to save some part of the forest and bring it back to the elves' new home.

"Since the trees were over three hundred feet tall, it took a long time to drag them up to the North Pole. The trees were revered by the elves and they really wanted to commemorate them and their journey. So they milled them into the large posts and beams of this exquisite building. The leftover sections were carved into the beautiful story panels you see all around us."

"What about the animals?" Gus asked. He was fixated on a carving of a tree falling down. He noticed the birds flying out of it and the animals running on the ground.

"The animals were left behind," a voice behind them replied. It was an old voice.

"Children," Mrs. Claus said gesturing to the elf who had just spoken. "This is Lucia."

Lucia was standing next to Ziggy, who had escorted her into the room. Lucia was holding a candle. She was shorter than Ziggy and her face, reflecting her years of hard work, was the only feature that indicated her old age.

"You must be hundreds of years old," Mithra gasped, a little embarrassed by her own outburst.

"It's not polite to discuss age," Lucia said turning a wry smile toward Mrs. Claus. "Age is not very relevant here."

Mrs. Claus glanced at Lucia with a deep understanding. It was a look resulting from centuries of friendship. They perused the great walls of the tall building. They moved their focus to the soaring beams above the storytelling panels, then down along the massive posts supporting the structure.

Mrs. Claus turned to Lucia with some remorse. "We need our posts and beams for another purpose now."

Lucia silently nodded in agreement.

Tiberius was overwhelmed by confusion and worn down by his concerns in regard to ship-building. "What in the world are you two talking about?" he burst out.

"This sacred wood is going to provide the best material possible for us to build our masts and rigging," Nebo said. He shifted his gaze from the story panels to the massive, wooden supports.

"You can't do that," Tiberius said, shaking with anger. "If you tear down Santa's workshop, what's the point of saving Santa? He'll have nothing to come back to."

"We have a whole village now," Mrs. Claus said, trying to calm the irritated boy. "This building is important to us, but saving Christmas is more so. We must make every sacrifice to bring Santa back."

Tiberius began to cry. The pressure had finally overwhelmed him. He felt it was his fault that the building might be destroyed. He was desperate to find another way, but nothing came to him.

Nebo reached over and held Tiberius's hand in his own. Tiberius looked up with tears streaming down his face. Nebo looked him in the eye and said, "Everything ends up as dust, Tiberius. You, me, everything in the world will return to dust. We are all just temporary sparks of life in this vast, dark universe."

"That's supposed to make me feel better?" Tiberius wailed, sinking further into his despair.

"Yes," Lucia replied. She held her candle up and sprinkled some powder on the flame. For a moment, the whole room sparkled with its light before it receded back to its original glow.

"Was that not beautiful?" Lucia asked.

"It was amazing," Tomo chimed in with a smile.

"Too often, you humans are caught in the trap of time. You measure everything by time. If you can let go of time, you will find more happiness," Lucia tried to explain to Tiberius.

"The sparkle of that powder only lasted a few seconds, but some of you will never forget the bright light it cast on this room. You may even tell stories of this moment to your own children. That one brief interval of time may live on for eons in the stories and imaginations of future generations.

"It does not matter though. Everything begins and ends. If you learn to let go of time, you can live with the cycle of nature rather than regretting its unchangeable course. Once you realize nothing will last forever, you will learn to love the world around you rather than fear its inevitable change and demise.

"Appreciate this moment Tiberius and do not mourn the loss of the building. For when it is physically gone, it will be reborn for its new purpose.

"I am happy to see the building reach its end in this way. Too often things fall into disrepair and waste away. These precious timbers are the last vestige of the forest that once filled us with great joy. I can think of no better outcome than to be reborn as the deliverer of your courageous team on its valiant journey."

21

Feeling inspired, Ziggy moved quickly to begin the deconstruction of Santa's main workshop. He asked Mrs. Claus and Lucia to give the elves the order with clear direction to save the panels and store all other precious carvings.

The team moved on to their new meeting space located in the building where they slept. Tiberius was starting to feel a bit better. His emotional morning had produced some good results, but he hoped there were more to come.

"The posts and beams from the main building will work for our masts and rudders," Tiberius recapped to the group. "We still need to figure out the rigging and sails."

"What's rigging?" Tomo asked.

"Rigging refers to the lines needed to secure the masts in place," Tiberius responded. "It also includes lines that control the sails we need to make."

"We have plenty of ribbon," Ziggy said. He was thinking of the ribbons the elves used to decorate the presents.

"That will not be strong enough," Ben answered before Tiberius could reply.

"Not necessarily," Tiberius countered. "What are the ribbons made out of?"

"Some are satin, others are cotton," Ziggy replied.

"Cotton may work," Tiberius said, pondering his own answer. "If we take thin cotton ribbons and then weave them into larger ribbons, we'll create a stronger ribbon. Repeat this process a few more times and we may end up with a line that can handle the loads we intend to put on the rigging.

"Cotton ribbon could also be spun up into sail cloth," Tiberius said with a smile. "I think this will work."

"Then that's it," Ben concluded. "We now have a plan to complete the remaining parts of the vessels."

Tiberius turned to Ziggy and asked, "Can the elves do all this work before the nineteenth? They're building hulls, tearing down a building, sewing sails and rigging; on top of the toy soldiers they're already making."

"Yes," Ziggy responded. "We'll just have to supply less toys this year."

"Ha," snorted Josef without meaning to. "I think Eastern Industries is producing more toys for the world than kids could ever handle. What we need to do is make sure the less fortunate have something under each of their trees this year. That's the one area that Eastern Industries will not cover."

Since Tiberius's main issues had been addressed, he turned his full attention to his team.

"Josef, how's the data you saved from the Eastern Industries hack working out?"

"I have complete plans of the factory. I'll be printing those out for Ben to analyze and find weak points," Josef said confidently. "I also have design schematics for a number of toys and robots in the factory. Some of the plans are disturbing."

"What do you mean?" Mithra asked.

"They have drones that are capable of firing objects and they possibly have other weapons as well. They have robots that carry swords. They have designs for underwater mines. It seems like they have the capability to engage with much tougher military equipment than what Ziggy saw on his first flight there."

"Ziggy, how many toy planes have you made?" Tiberius asked, turning toward the head elf.

"We have about five hundred," Ziggy answered. "They can be programed to fly a pattern or remotely controlled, similar to the soldiers, but they can only fire soft, toy darts."

"Can you create more?" Ben asked anxiously.

"We should be able to double that number."

Tiberius was now concerned about the defenses they would encounter. It seemed every time he overcame one hurdle, the next one loomed larger. He took solace knowing he had a reliable, hard-working group by his side. He had full confidence in Ben as his expert in regard to countering any obstacles they might face.

"Ben, please go with Josef and review the information he has found," Tiberius said, rising to his feet. "Mithra and Nebo, I want you to check on the ship and double and triple check that it's solid. We need to get the frame back together by the end of the day in order to pour again tomorrow.

"Tomo, please escort Gus to a hill high above the bubble. I would like him to see if he can get any more information from any birds that may be passing by.

"I'll go teach the elves how to weave the cotton ribbon together to form a stronger braid. Knowing them, we should have some sails to test no later than tomorrow.

"Dinner is at 6 o'clock tonight. Please make it back by then."

Tiberius hurried around that afternoon with Hermey by his side. Hermey watched as Tiberius met with the elves responsible for ribbons and decorations. Tiberius gave them expert instruction on how to braid the ribbon to make line. They already knew how to form a strong cloth from the cotton fabric.

Satisfied with the elves' progress, Tiberius went to check on Mithra and Nebo. As he got to the hull's building site, he saw Nebo trying to push the giant vessel out of the frame. Nebo budged it a little, but could not move it out. The elves had done a careful job removing parts of the frame, while keeping most of it intact for the next day's pykrete pour. Before Tiberius could head over to Nebo, he turned to see Mithra approaching with fifty snowmen. They were various sizes now. Some were as big as Polaris. Others were the size of Jasper. There were about five snowmen that were only a few inches tall.

They all gathered around Nebo and together they pushed the giant hull from the frame and moved it toward the water. They stopped short of the water's edge.

"Is it ready to go in?" Nebo called up to Tiberius.

"Hold on," Tiberius yelled down. He walked down to the vessel and attached the first four lines the elves had made. "Go ahead."

Nebo and the snowmen gave the vessel one last shove and it quickly slid into the water. A huge wave spread out from the front of it. Two snowmen held each line and then tied them to large boulders at the water's edge.

Tiberius leaped onto the floating mass and, after a thorough inspection, was very impressed. Mithra had done it. The giant iceberg boat was sitting nicely in the water.

Behind Tiberius, a large group of elves boarded the vessel with their woodworking tools and some rough plans that Ben had worked on the previous day. Tiberius reviewed the plans and made some adjustments for the masts and rudder. The elves went right to work.

Next, Tiberius headed over to the E.I.N. to check on Ben and Josef. Hermey stayed behind to work with Nebo and Mithra. Hermey did not like the E.I.N. He had never gotten over the fact that Rudi had been placed on their Naughty List.

An E.I.N. elf met Tiberius when he entered the building and escorted him down the elevator to the server room. It was very quiet. There were only a few elves present who were trying in vain to repair the damaged equipment. He headed to the office where he had made the staged phone calls to Josef's father.

Ben and Josef were looking at the same screen. Tiberius hunched over to get a view. It displayed the plans for Baekdu Island.

"Have you found a way in?" Tiberius asked.

"Yes," Josef responded. "There are a couple of options. The least complicated seems to be the loading dock. I think our ships could sail right up to them and unload cargo just like any other ship. We can assign a squad of toy soldiers to guard our route and we'll march right onto the factory floor."

"Sounds too simple," Tiberius responded. Every time he thought something would be easy, it turned out to be much more difficult.

"It is," Ben replied. "The problem is we still don't know where Santa is being held and the factory is huge. There are over 30 levels to it. It goes deep inside of the mountain on Baekdu Island. We have some guesses as to where he might be, but we haven't identified those locations on the plan."

"What are the other ways in?" Tiberius asked. He assumed the main entrance would be the most heavily guarded.

"The other side of the island is rocky and shallow," Ben answered. "They have some smaller gates further inland, but our ships would need to beach on the rocky shore to get us up there.

"There is also a gate high up on the mountain. We're not sure what it's for but we assume only a flying machine would be able to access it. The walls on the side of the mountain are too steep for any vehicle or person to climb."

"What about Tomo?" Tiberius asked Ben, thinking about her ability to scale pretty much anything.

"I'll have to ask her. From what I see, that mountain goes practically straight up and is covered with ice. It's almost like Eastern Industries melted the whole island on a cold night and then let it freeze into a solid chunk of ice. "Their defenses are unknown as well. Josef has found plans for some pretty serious robots and drones, but we don't know if they've been built yet. If they have assembled all the items in their plans, it will be very difficult to get close to the island, let alone enter the factory."

"If I can get inside their factory, I think I may be able to interfere with some of their computer systems," Josef said looking up from his computer for the first time. "When I was in their network, attacking the *Legend Quest* servers, I came across their island defense systems. Like the rest of the island, they're 100% automated with no human oversight.

"The defense systems are designed to communicate outbound to the robots and drones. In other words, the orders only go one way. So if the machines lose contact with the central system, they'll function automatically. They'll continue to carry out their last set of orders.

"If I can get into one of their central computers, I should be able to upload a set of instructions that shuts the defensive machines down. If we can take out the communications system right after those instructions are sent, they'll have no way of recovering."

Tiberius and Ben liked Josef's idea. There was just one problem.

"I don't know how to get you within close proximity of their main computers," Ben said. He looked down at the plans and pointed to the center of the factory. "The central command is located half way up and deep inside the mountain. We'll need to get past their defenses in order to shut them down."

"Is there any way to remotely upload the data into their network?" Tiberius asked. He did not like the idea of relying on Josef to physically mess around with computers, while the entire operation was waiting outside the walls of the mountain.

"I'm afraid not," Josef answered. "The drones and robots only send limited information back to their central command. They upload pictures, video, and simple diagnostics. There's no way to upload code through their communications system."

"Well, we'll just have to find a way to get you inside," Ben said. "I don't know how we'll do it, but those defenses need to be neutralized before we can make an attempt to free Santa."

Tiberius looked over the plans for a little while longer. Baekdu Island was more like a fortress than a factory. He now thought travelling there may be the easiest aspect of the mission — and that alone would require quite a bit of luck.

Tiberius noticed the usually confident Ben David shared his concern. At first, Tiberius sensed the gloom he had previously experienced, rising within him like an unstoppable tide. He started to feel himself drowning in the misery that was washing in on the shores of his consciousness. Although this time, he was aware of its approach.

He looked at Josef. Josef also wore that familiar, worried look on his face. Tiberius focused his thoughts on the tide beginning to swamp his mind. He did not want to fall into the funk he had climbed out of earlier in the day. He took a deep breath, stood up and did his best imitation of Ben.

"Listen guys," Tiberius began. The tide of depression was already receding. "One way or another, I *will* get you to that island. We *will* get inside the fortress. When the time is right, Josef, you *will* upload your code into their system and neutralize whatever defenses are in place. And then we *will* rescue Santa.

"Keep working on it. We may need a miracle to pull this off. But if there's one resource we have in abundance around this place, at this time of year, it is miracles. Do the best you can, and fate will take us the rest of the way."

Tiberius caught up with Tomo and Gus as they headed back to dinner. Tomo was cheerful, but looked a bit tired. As usual, Gus was introspective.

"How'd the climb go today?" Tiberius inquired of Tomo.

"Great. We went straight up an ice wall and as soon as we got to the top, a flock of birds flew by," Tomo replied cheerfully.

"How about you, Gus? Any results?" Tiberius said turning to the quiet boy.

"I was able to listen to the birds. They described drones flying above the island and mentioned that the island had undergone some type of dark change recently, forcing them to vacate their nests." Gus turned gloomy and added, "But I don't think they understood anything I was trying to tell them in return. I tried to concentrate like I did with the spider, but the birds did not react. I was pretty tired from the climb with Tomo."

"You mean the drag," Tomo laughed. "I had to drag Gus up the wall. He's getting better, but this climb was too challenging for his level of experience."

"I feel empty," Gus lamented. "I would like to go to church and spend some time in prayer."

This caught Tiberius off guard. He had forgotten Gus was a very religious boy. Gus had been away from home for almost two weeks and Tiberius could not recall seeing him pray anywhere, at any time.

"Gus, let's talk to Ziggy and see if there's a place you can go to get some peace and quiet," Tiberius suggested. "Would that work for you?"

"Yes," Gus responded, looking a bit happier. "I'd really like that."

Gus was an introvert. He drew his strength from being alone. He liked being around the other kids, but the constant social interactions drained his energy. Tiberius hoped some time alone might help lift Gus's spirit.

As they headed in for dinner, Tiberius found Ziggy outside their quarters and told him of Gus's dilemma. Ziggy promised to take Gus to a special place the next day.

Tiberius felt hopeful about Gus. Each team member had an activity from which they drew their strength. For Tiberius, it was planning and talking. For Ben, it was commanding. Tomo's spirit always lifted when she engaged in physical exercise. Josef recharged when sitting in front of a computer and working on problems. Mithra could spend all night photographing snowflakes. Gus was the only one who did not seem to be participating in an activity which would help refresh his mental state. Tiberius hoped they had finally found the element that was missing from Gus's stay at the North Pole.

22

Early the next morning, Ziggy found Gus working out with the rest of the team and pulled him aside. They walked out of the village together, down a path that was lightly covered in snow and into a thick grove of trees.

This was the forest in the bubble Lucia had originally discovered. At first they walked through a dark green canopy of pine trees. Then they came to a cluster of quaking aspen. These white trees with yellow leaves gave a golden glow to the path they were walking on and Gus began to relax as he passed under their soothing cloak.

Further along, the aspen gave way to taller trees. These furs and pines were covered in snow that reflected the radiance of the morning sun. Gus looked around and saw small birds playing in the trees. He sensed more animals too, but could not see them. As they got further into the forest, the sounds of animals grew louder in Gus's consciousness.

The path led them to a wooden building. The building was a simple rectangle with a triangle roof resting on top. At the top of the roof was a spire with a golden bell in it. Gus noticed a small set of stairs that led to the entrance of the building. They climbed the stairs and stood in front of an arched doorway.

Ziggy opened the door and they entered the small structure. It was quiet, despite the presence of a few elves tending to the various plants at the other side of the building. The plants were mostly holly and ivy wrapped around a thick wooden table. Gus thought it resembled an altar. On top of the altar was a plain fir tree. It was perfectly symmetrical.

The green at the end of the room was contrasted by the brown of the natural logs that made up the walls. The morning sun cast a golden light upon the rows of half logs that provided seating, which Gus considered pews.

Ziggy gestured to the front row and Gus walked over and sat down. Without a word, Ziggy slipped away from Gus and left the building. Gus was immediately comfortable in this little sanctuary. There was no fire burning, but the temperature was quite mild.

Gus settled down into a meditative state. His thoughts rode on a spiritual wind that had no direction at all. At first his mind raced around the cognitive abyss, but soon the pace slowed and he gave up any control. He drifted through time and space, in and out of the familiar and unfamiliar.

He became a ghostly traveler across the expanse of the world. He dipped in and out of oceans, across barren deserts, and even through the densest cities. He soared above the highest mountains and dove deep into darkened canyons. A journey that seemed to take a millennia flew by in just a few minutes.

His journey continued as he entered into utter blackness. His mind seemed to be a complete void. He was no longer floating; he was nothing, in a universe of darkness. His senses faded away. There was only him. All of the external forces were gone. Gus was alone.

He became conscious of a series of sensations. His first sense came from underneath. He felt a cold, hard surface and began to walk on it. He was not sure where he was heading, but his eight legs had firm control of his movement. He tried to detect gravity, but that sense was not there. He just moved along in the complete darkness.

A pinprick of light appeared. He could see now. He walked toward the light and it became brighter as he approached. The pinprick soon grew to a crack. As he got nearer, the fragrance of earth filled the tiny hairs on his legs. He did not know how, but those hairs were providing a sense of smell he had never experienced before.

He approached the crack, but wanted to stop. He realized he was not in control. His eight legs continued to carry him through the little crack. The light on the other side was blinding.

He continued on. He noticed the scent of sweet pine overwhelming the other smells. His sight began to adjust to the bright world and he found himself in a sea of green. He felt himself give a little push and then there was a pull from behind. He was on a branch of a tree. Constantly feeling the pull on his back, he knew he had embodied a spider and was actively spinning a web.

After a long time moving about the tree, he dropped down and walked along the floor. He was not alone. There were others walking with him. They climbed up the wooden bench and Gus felt himself come to rest on a boy's shoulder.

When he looked up, his vision flashed and he found himself looking down at an Arctic spider. He felt as though he was staring at himself. Back in his own head, he glanced forward at the tree in the center of the altar. It came as no surprise to see it had been decorated in a beautiful web.

His attention was drawn back to the spider on his shoulder. He watched it crawl down his arm and move onto a log. It joined hundreds of other spiders. Gus felt them. He felt them all. There was no conversation, but he could feel their instincts, their senses; he could feel their souls — the soul that Nature's God put into all creatures.

As Gus drifted back into the present, he noticed the elves had opened the windows and doors. The conversation in Gus's head grew more complex as creatures big and small wandered into the tiny sanctuary. Birds, mice, bugs, and all sorts of animals entered the building and came to rest. There was now a chorus of thousands inside Gus's head, but it did not overwhelm him. He was not focused on any one voice, rather his thoughts were vibrating with the mass of voices.

Gus smiled. Every living creature in the room smiled with him. The vibration of joy floated out of the room and spread across the entire village. Gus had always listened to the animals, but now he felt like he really heard them as well. He felt their message. His brief moment as a spider helped him to understand his ability better.

He stood up and left the sanctuary. He ran down the path, toward the village. It was only then he realized it was getting dark. He had spent the entire day in that little sanctuary. There is no place he would have rather been.

23

Over the next couple of days, nothing interrupted the Naughty Team's routine. Each morning and evening, they all got together to discuss progress. In between, they focused on their individual tasks. As usual, Tiberius oversaw all the various activities.

Tomo taught each kid the basics of climbing. When she was on her own, she sought out the most difficult climbs and practiced new techniques.

Gus spent as much time as he could in the sanctuary. He loved the peace and quiet. He especially enjoyed the company of several animals that joined him for his daily meditation. Tiberius wanted to check it out, but decided it was best to let Gus have a place of his own, a place where he would never be bothered by anyone who was not invited.

Gus continued to improve his communication with the animals. It was important to hear them speak, but some animals lived in such a different manner that only Gus's meditation could help him understand the true meaning of their thoughts. He took a couple of trips through the lives of different animals. His favorite experience was hitching a ride on a whale's thoughts. He especially enjoyed the sensation of knowing his surroundings by using sonar.

Josef continued to strengthen his body. He remained quite large, but became a very powerful boy. He could run with the other kids, climb better than most, and his strength was second only to Nebo's incredible might. In the afternoons, Josef worked on a method to take out the central command of the Baekdu Island defenses.

Mithra experimented with the snowmen searching for a way to improve her ability to rebuild them. Her sensor had advanced to not only find cosmic dust, but also to attract it from a greater distance. There were a few times when she accidentally sucked the core right out of a snowman, but they never seemed to mind as she always reversed the process quickly. Her vapor diffusion chamber was also improved. She could rebuild the core snowflake in under a minute.

Tiberius was very interested in Mithra's work with the snowmen. After the first boat was complete with masts and sails, he began to train the snowmen to work the sails. He would take them out in groups of 10 according to their universe name. One day he would train the planets, the next day, the constellations, and so on. The best sailor from each group would be assigned as captain for one of the boats.

Hermey kept his promise to his son, Rudi, and maintained a watchful eye over Tiberius. He tried his best to stay close to him, while not interfering.

Ben continued to plan endlessly. He tried to consider every possibility and consequence, and how the team would overcome it. Ben took a moment to do a brief evaluation of their offensive capabilities. He believed in the competence of the core team to carry out their specific tasks. He was confident in the sturdiness of the ships and had faith in the increasing number of toy soldiers. His only concern was in regard to the flying drones. The elves would only be able to finish a thousand remote-controlled planes within the timeframe, and there was a possibility they would face an attack by tens of thousands of drones.

Nebo worked with the snowmen to push the ships out of the frames and into the water. He hoisted the masts and held them secure while the snowmen attached the rigging to support the large wooden poles. These massive vessels could not have been completed without Nebo's incredible strength.

The team possessed a great range of knowledge and skills, but it was Tiberius who had successfully molded them into a cohesive group. Only Gus remained a bit on the outside of everyone else. Despite his improved mood, Gus rarely spoke when the team was together.

Tomo was the only kid that Gus grew close to. He would occasionally join her on a climb, which pretty much consisted of her pulling him up some icy slope. At one point, he actually invited Tomo to go to the sanctuary with him. She enjoyed the visit very much, but did not experience the same spiritual lift Gus did. For Tomo, outdoor activity was her own form of meditation.

The two were returning from a climb one afternoon when they passed by reindeer that appeared to be playing. Tomo and Gus watched them fly in formation. They would then break apart and swing their heads side to side. They made quick turns and then kicked out their hind legs.

"What are they doing?" Tomo asked Gus.

"They're practicing to help us attack Baekdu Island," Gus responded. "They've been doing this for the past couple of days. The reindeer are insisting on helping us out.

"I've tried to explain to them that they need to have armed riders on their backs who can fire some sort of device during combat. Otherwise, I have serious doubts they'll be able to last long against a sky full of drones. Ziggy knows how to ride, but he has already refused to have anything to do with the actual attack.

"As for the rest of us, none of us are experienced enough to ride a reindeer into battle. It is one thing to do so on a leisurely trip, but during a fight while the reindeer are bouncing around the sky, is something else altogether. Even the best riders in the world would need months of training to ride the reindeer."

"Have you ever heard of the Epic of Jangar?" Tomo asked.

"No," Gus said flatly.

"When I was nine years old, I travelled to Mongolia with a small group of climbers to ascend Mount Khuiten. We had to travel across the Mongolian steppe to get to the mountain range. This is a large expanse of dry land with nomadic people living on it. We stayed with a tribe that claimed they were the descendants of Jangar.

"As a nine-year-old climber, I was accustomed to surprising people since my abilities were way beyond my age. This particular Mongolian tribe was not impressed. They had children as young as four riding horses on their own. By seven or eight, all kids were skilled at riding and shooting arrows. They would join older kids for horseback hunting.

"We stayed with them for a few days while a late spring snowstorm prevented us from moving on. They told us the story of Jangar, their ancestor. It's a story about a Mongolian child who was to rule a kingdom called Bomba. His parents were killed in battle when he was a baby. The story tells of him growing up among animals and tribesmen before becoming a fearful warrior at a very young age. He was always with his red horse, Aranjagaan.

"The Epic of Jangar is as much about the horse as it is about Jangar. Aranjagaan carried Jangar to battle and waged war with him. If Jangar was dismounted, the horse fought alongside Jangar, independently. If Jangar was hurt, the horse carried him to safety. This story helped me understand the tribe's high respect for their horses.

"The Mongols revere their horses. They believe their own human souls come from a wind horse that flies through the skies. Mongol riders do not break and train their horses like the rest of the world. They ride the horses and let the horses determine their own path. It's common for a young rider to mount a wild horse and ride it until they become one. They don't try to control the animal.

"When the snow stopped and my group continued its trek, a few young riders accompanied us to the edge of the mountain. There, we met another tribe, called the Dukha. They're reindeer herders. Similar to the Mongol horse riders, the Dukha are taught to ride reindeer from a young age. They're close to their reindeer and they're dependent on each other to survive.

"When I told Kiso this story, she was convinced Santa's reindeer came from the Dukha people. At the time, I laughed at her, but now I wonder if it's true."

Gus looked at the reindeer that were now surrounding them. They had stopped their practice when they heard Tomo mention Jangar. For a moment, all was quiet.

"The reindeer come from Russia," Gus said. "They say they come from a place called Tuva."

"That is right across the border from where I met the Dukha," Tomo said with enthusiasm. "Kiso was right. The Dukha are the ones who raised these reindeer."

The reindeer began to stomp their hooves with excitement. It had been a long, long time since they had been back to their birthplace. No one had mentioned it for decades. Gus could understand their emotion.

"The reindeer want to go back," Gus whispered to Tomo. "They want to find young Mongols to ride and fight with them in the skies above Baekdu Island. They seem pretty adamant about it."

"Tell them we'll check with Mrs. Claus and Ziggy," Tomo whispered back. "We're leaving in two days and it may be too late to adjust any plans."

24

By the time the team met on the morning of December eighteenth, everything seemed to be in place. The fifth ship was ready to come out of the frame and the snowmen planned to have it assembled by the end of the day. The kids had packed their gear on the first ship. Saturn would be the captain of their boat and the other planets would be the crew.

"Tomorrow we leave for Baekdu Island," Tiberius announced to the team. "We will load twenty thousand toy soldiers into four of the vessels. The one thousand planes will be loaded onto the *Planet*, our flagship. Josef and Ben will be in charge of programming the planes and adjusting their routes once they are engaged.

"When we reach Baekdu Island, we'll beach the four ships carrying the toy soldiers at different points along the shore," Tiberius continued pointing to places on the map in front of them. "The planes will be launched while the *Planet* is still at sea. They will give cover to the soldiers.

"After their outer defenses are wiped out; Josef, Nebo, and Ben will enter the factory and attempt to gain access to their computer network from the inside. Tomo will climb up the mountain fortress and look for an opening into one of the high passageways. Gus will stay with me and relay any information he gathers from the animals in the area. Mithra will also stay with us to analyze the weather and to manage the snowmen.

"Back here at the North Pole, Santa's sack will be loaded with toys and the sleigh will be ready to start its annual trip around the world. Once we locate Santa and transfer him outside of the fortress in the mountain, we'll burn a letter to let Ziggy know it's safe to bring the reindeer and sleigh to Baekdu Island."

"I don't think that will work," Gus said, startling almost everyone in the room. "The reindeer want to be more involved in the operation. They want to be flying in the skies, helping to take down the drones."

"It's too dangerous," Ben replied, staring at Gus.

"It may be," Gus continued, "But I don't think anyone is going to be able to stop them. They seem adamant about being there for the battle."

Ben was getting annoyed. He did not want the reindeer to be a distraction or, worse yet, to get hurt during the battle. "They'll need riders up there to attack the drones. The elves won't join us, so who is going to ride the reindeer?"

"I know," Tomo whispered. She cleared her throat and said with more authority. "The reindeer are ready to go home to recruit their own riders."

Gus looked at Tomo and they shared an understanding. It was evident to everyone that the two of them had already discussed this.

"Go home to Tuva?" Mrs. Claus asked. "Tuva is no longer what it used to be. The reindeer have not been back to Tuva since it was taken over in the 1940's by the Soviet Union."

"No," Tomo adamantly responded. "The Dukha people are in Mongolia too. There are not many families left, but they still herd reindeer near the mountains."

Mrs. Claus saw the plaintive expression on Gus and Tomo. She knew the reindeer well and did not think it wise to try to stop them. The reindeer had never been the property of the

North Pole. They had always been there by their own free will.

"Let the reindeer go home," Mrs. Claus concluded. "Let them find their own riders from their homeland. If they believe they will be able to help us, then I believe it too. They can fly back to the North Pole after the rescue and Ziggy can make sure they're ready to pull the sleigh."

"I don't like this idea," Ben responded. His frustration was obvious to everyone. "If the reindeer don't make it back on time, how will Santa make his trip?"

"There are some things we can control and some things we cannot," Nebo added to the conversation. "We must allow for each soul to choose its own destiny."

"Stop with the ultimate destiny baloney," Ben commanded, as his anger boiled over.

Nebo stayed placid as usual, but Gus's anger rose with Ben's.

"Animals have souls too!" Gus screamed at Ben. "The reindeer should be as free as we are to choose their part in this operation."

"This is a military operation," Ben yelled back. "Not a crusade."

The room seemed to be teeming with fury now. Ben and Gus were staring coldly at one another. Tomo was right next to Gus, ready to defend her good friend. Mithra stared down at her hands, obviously uncomfortable with the confrontation before her.

"If this is not a crusade, I don't know what is," Tiberius said as he rose to his feet. "The reindeer can go home and find their riders. This was not part of my plans, but we should allow the reindeer to help us in the manner they desire. After all, one of our biggest concerns is neutralizing the drones around Baekdu Island."

"Ziggy, please work with Gus this afternoon to design some type of armor for the reindeer," Tiberius continued. "If they're going to fight in the skies against those drones, I want the best possible protection you can provide. This is a time for all of us to come together for one purpose – to save Christmas. We'll need to employ as many resources as possible."

Tiberius had managed to diffuse the tension in the room. The team broke away from the meeting and went about their final tasks before their departure the next morning. Tiberius visited the ships along with most of the other kids. He was surprised to see Mrs. Claus and Hermey packing their own stuff onboard the *Planet*.

"I thought you two would be staying here," Tiberius said with a look of confusion.

"I know a bit about the sea," Mrs. Claus said, not looking up from her task. "Anyway, it is my husband you are trying to rescue. You didn't expect me to just sit back and wait for things to unfold, did you?"

"I guess not," Tiberius replied. He turned to Hermey and asked, "What about you, Hermey? I would think this is the last thing in the world you would want to do."

"It is, Tiber," Hermey replied apprehensively. "But I made a promise to your father that I would keep a close eye on you and I'm not going to break that promise. I hope you don't mind."

"I'm happy to have you both join us," Tiberius concluded with a grin. "I'm sure your wisdom will prove to be an asset to the mission."

Mithra barely noticed the new additions to the crew as she packed up her cosmic dust collector and vapor diffusion chamber before making her final weather observations. The wind would continue blowing from the North, so the fleet would have the wind at their back for at least the first part of the voyage.

Tiberius left the *Planet* and joined Nebo and Tomo who were busy working on the *Constellation* in preparation for the trip. The elves were there too, carving out the last of the cabins for the toy soldiers. Nebo had put the masts in place. Tiberius joined Tomo who was assisting the snowmen to attach the rigging and furl the sails on the yards hanging from the masts.

Once the *Constellation* was carved out and ready to go, Ben marched the last group of five thousand toy soldiers into the ship's hold. He was still worried about the reindeer ruining the operation, but hoped the toy soldiers and planes would clear the area of any danger before the reindeer arrived.

Josef finished the code he had worked on and was eager for the chance to cripple the Eastern Industries network. He downloaded it onto a USB drive. He kept it in his pocket and checked on it every couple of minutes.

The remote-control planes burst from the center of the village with a resounding buzz during the late afternoon. Josef had programmed them to fly in various formations and he wanted to demonstrate their capabilities to his teammates. After a successful test run, the planes were loaded into the Planet's hold.

Everything was in place when the team met that night for their final dinner at the North Pole. The kids were nervous. Ziggy and Scout were sad to know their new friends would be leaving the next day. They had really grown to like the entire team.

Mrs. Claus, on the other hand, had a steely reserve on her face. The warm, soft demeanor the kids had become accustomed to, now had a cold, hard edge to it.

"My children," Mrs. Claus said, calling their attention. "Once we get to Baekdu Island, we'll be on our own. No one will be able to save us if we get into trouble. If you want to back out now, no one will think any less of you."

Mrs. Claus looked around the table. The kids looked nervous but no one even considered abandoning the mission.

"Thank you for all of your hard work and dedication over the past three weeks," Mrs. Claus continued. "No matter what happens between now and Christmas, I want you to know I am proud of the effort you have made to save Christmas. Whatever the result, the world will know it was you who put an end to the Naughty List."

"I'm proud of you as well," Tiberius chimed in. "We've all grown and become stronger together. I know that after we save Christmas, I'm going to make some changes in my life. I'm sure some of you will too.

"I'm the luckiest boy on Earth. Being able to put together such a strong team has been the greatest experience of my life. Thank you all for your help and support."

Tiberius looked around the room. It was a quiet moment. No one was sure what to do next. Everyone was anxious about the voyage and looming battle.

"Naughty Team," Ben said, breaking the uncomfortable silence. "Back in military school, we would all write letters to our loved ones before a big mission. It helps us to remember what's most important in life. It makes clear what we're fighting for."

"Mrs. Claus?" Ben asked turning toward the matronly figure. "Would that be OK?"

"I think that would be perfect," Mrs. Claus responded. "Ziggy will make sure those letters reach their destination before Christmas Eve. I think all of your families would be proud to finally know what you've really been doing these past three weeks."

Ziggy handed out some pens, paper, and envelopes to the group. The kids began writing their letters home. Mrs. Bentley was the only person outside of the North Pole who knew about the mission, since Mithra had been writing to her mother and keeping her up to date. She finished her short letter first, looked up and saw Nebo staring straight ahead, an empty sheet of paper in front of him.

"Don't you have someone to write to?" Mithra asked.

"No," Nebo responded with detachment. "I am an orphan and I have never had a family. All of you are my family now."

Mrs. Claus softened her forced hardness. She turned to Nebo and whispered, "If we are your family now, maybe a note to Santa Claus would be appropriate."

Nebo took up the pen and slowly began to write. Mrs. Claus put her hand on Nebo's shoulder and said, "You will always have a home here, Nebo."

PART THREE

25

A dark blue news van barreled along a rural Vermont road with great urgency. Although Freya had only been a reporter at Burlington's WXMS for a few months she had quickly separated herself from the field with her uncompromising style of journalism. She and her crew were heading to a nearby farm to cover a story about a couple who apparently had gone completely overboard with their Christmas decorations. The hook was that they were claiming their daughter was at the North Pole trying to rescue Santa from captivity by an evil toy company. It was too good to be true – an eccentric couple still holding on to the "magic" of Christmas despite the world's mass transition to Winterval. Freya hoped this would be a turning point in making a name for herself.

As they entered Jericho, it was just getting dark and a light snow was falling. The van's headlights illuminated dancing snowflakes as they formed a swirling tunnel in front of the vehicle. Freya was reminded of how much she liked to get out of Burlington and into the countryside.

In the distance a dome of light rose from the horizon and gradually intensified until the van reached its destination.

Freya was awestruck as she stepped out of the van and peered down a long, narrow path that led away from the farmhouse. Above the entrance to the path was a huge six-pronged snowflake ornament. On either side, hundreds of old-fashioned Christmas lights cast a warm glow onto various holiday scenes. A few hundred yards onward stood a giant evergreen tree illuminated with thousands of lights.

Freya strolled up to the front door and rang the bell. Mrs. Bentley stepped out from the house dressed for the cold, snowy night. Mr. Bentley waved from the doorway and retreated back inside.

"Welcome to our farm," Mrs. Bentley said with a broad smile. "You must be Freya."

"Nice to meet you in person," Freya replied. "I'd like to have the cameras capture this incredibly magical setting. Are you okay with that?"

"That would be great," Mrs. Bentley replied. "We haven't had many visitors. I thought the decorations would have attracted more people."

"You're a bit off the beaten path," Freya joked. The cameras were already rolling. "Let's take a stroll through this wonderful story you've created. I think our viewers would appreciate a quaint, Christmas throwback."

"This is a Bentley farm," Mrs. Bentley began as she and the crew wandered down the path. "So we start with this big snowflake. My husband's uncle was Snowflake Bentley, famous for being the first person to photograph snowflakes. My daughter has been carrying on his work for a few years now.

"On your left is the barn where many of her snowflake images have been captured," Mrs. Bentley said as she pointed. It was decorated with bulbs that gave off a warm-white light. Around the edges of the roof and over the door to the barn hung crystal snowflakes of different shapes and sizes.

On the side of the barn was a wood burning fireplace. Next to it, was a small model of a child who was waving a letter in front of the flames.

"See that little figure?" Mrs. Bentley asked Freya as she motioned to the fireplace. "That's a scene of a child burning her letter to Santa. It will be carried in the smoke to the North Pole."

"I see," Freya said staring at the fireplace. "And you think that smoke is more reliable than the postal service?"

"Yes it is. As a matter of fact, it's the best way to reach the North Pole," Mrs. Bentley answered. "Now on your right you'll see dozens of snowmen. Notice how their heads give off a glow?"

"Yes," Freya responded, pointing the cameraman to the field of glistening snowmen.

"These snowmen represent the ones who are currently at the North Pole," Mrs. Bentley continued. "The glow emanating from their heads depicts the core essence of the snowmen."

"And what is the essence, Mrs. Bentley?" Freya asked as she pushed a microphone up to Mrs. Bentley's mouth.

"The glow represents the cosmic dust that allows the snowmen to become animate. Most people are under the illusion a magical hat brings them to life, but I've found out it's actually cosmic dust."

"Oh," Freya said. She paused before adding, "So you're telling us you've found the true secret of Frosty the Snowman."

"No," Mrs. Bentley replied with a smile. "Frosty is just a story for kids. I'm talking about actual snowmen who walk and talk."

"So, wait a minute, you're claiming living snowmen really exist?" Freya asked in disbelief.

"Yes, I met one myself. His name is Jasper."

"Oh really. Uh, can we meet this Jasper?" Freya asked with a touch of sarcasm.

"No, he went back to the North Pole," Mrs. Bentley replied as she continued strolling down the path. "Up ahead you'll see a scene I created that's meant to resemble what's currently underway at the North Pole."

The small group observed a variety of amusing activities in the Bentley re-creation of the North Pole. There were scenes of ice ships being built, toy planes flying through the night sky, and toy soldiers being constructed by elves.

"Looks like they're pretty busy this year," Freya remarked. "I would think things would be much calmer now that Winterval has replaced Christmas."

"Oh, Christmas is just fine," Mrs. Bentley responded. "Actually this scene represents the children who have been recruited by the North Pole to *save* Christmas. They're working along with Mrs. Claus and the elves to free Santa from Eastern Industries. I met the head of elves myself. He escorted my daughter to the North Pole so she could help with the task of building more snowmen like Jasper."

"You mean the animated snowmen containing cosmic dust?" Freya said seriously, trying to hold back her laughter.

"Exactly," Mrs. Bentley replied earnestly.

Freya smirked and whispered to one of her cameramen, "You getting all this?"

He nodded and continued filming.

As they got to the next area, a mountain of snow rose from a flat field. In the side of the snow mountain was a wooden door and an animated figure banging on it.

"What's going on in this scene?" Freya inquired. She was having trouble maintaining her composure.

"This is where the incredibly strong boy, Nebo, is pounding on the door of the God of Chaos. He will break open the door and free Marduk on Christmas Eve. This story goes back over four thousand years and is one of the first recorded winter celebrations."

"What's it called?"

"Zagmuk."

"Priceless. How about the next scene? Looks like men wearing dresses."

"That's part of the history of Christmas," Mrs. Bentley said. She did not notice Freya being disingenuous. "It represents the Roman celebration of Saturnalia. Just beyond it is a recreation of the Yule festivities from northern Europe."

As they got to the end of the path, the giant Christmas tree loomed above them. It was decorated in old-fashioned, incandescent bulbs. Many beautiful ornaments hung from the branches. Underneath it was a scene portraying a family sitting together as they opened a few presents. A young girl was holding a wooden soldier. "Silent Night" played from a set of speakers located below the tree.

"This is the end," Mrs. Bentley proudly announced. "Our final scene shows what will take place all over the world on Christmas day. All the excess of Winterval will be discarded and children everywhere will be happy with a simple gift that reflects their appreciation for the rescue of Santa Claus and Christmas being saved."

Freya had gotten the exact footage she wanted. Mrs. Bentley had explained the entire Christmas world she had built in the past two weeks. On their way back to the house, Freya asked, "Why did you build all of this?"

"I want the world to know Christmas isn't dead. It has been with us for thousands of years in one form or another. In a short while, Winterval will be the holiday that is forgotten.

"Right now, there are a group of talented, dedicated children working with the elves to free Santa Claus from the Eastern Industries headquarters. As you know, my daughter is one of them and I've met a few of the others. Once they succeed, the people of the world will realize the false promise that has taken hold of their hearts. They will throw away the antics of Winterval and embrace Christmas more fervently than ever.

"On Christmas Eve, we're hoping people will seek a place that takes them back to the old times. I hope this place, right here in Jericho, Vermont, will give them somewhere to revel in the Christmas spirit once again."

"How much did this whole display cost?" Freya asked, waving her arms in front of the camera to show the full expanse of the various scenes.

"It took all our resources to build this," Mrs. Bentley said. "We even had to mortgage the farm to pay for the lights. I'm not sure how we'll pay the electric bill at the end of the month."

"I guess you'd say you're *all in* this year," Freya remarked with a sneer.

"Absolutely," Mrs. Bentley said flashing her own confident smile.

"Thank you, Mrs. Bentley," Freya said concluding the tour. She motioned for the cameras to turn off.

"Good luck with everything," Freya chuckled under her breath.

"Have yourself a Merry Christmas," Mrs. Bentley replied as she turned back toward the house.

The next night, the Bentleys sat in front of the TV eager to watch their segment on the Burlington Evening News. The newscast began with a scene of the van driving through the snow at dusk as a voice-over explained they were going to visit one of the last Christmas holdouts.

The footage of the farm itself included some sound bites from Mrs. Bentley while Freya's voiceover made a joke of the whole story. Freya poked fun at the snowmen, the scenes of other winter celebrations, and laughed about the concept of a select group of kids gathered to save Santa Claus from Eastern Industries.

Freya concluded with a voice-over explaining how the Bentleys had spent all of their money putting the Christmas display together. Her tone turned serious when she added, "I hope they don't lose their farm because they invested in this extravagant, but ultimately useless exhibit."

When the segment cut back to the hosts in the studio, they joked about how the Bentleys had lost their minds.

"We've seen some crazy things here in Vermont, but this one takes the cake. I can't imagine spending all that money on some misplaced fantasy. And now to the weather forecast."

Mr. Bentley turned to his wife and put his hand on her shoulder. "I'm sorry, honey," he said softly.

"Why?" Mrs. Bentley asked as she beamed. "They successfully captured all the different scenes in the footage and I think my message was very clear."

"Well..." Mr. Bentley tried to be gentle, "they were making a joke out of the whole story."

"That's okay. It won't be a joke for long," Mrs. Bentley replied as she turned off the television. "They'll see."

26

On the morning of December nineteenth, the Naughty Team made their final preparations and loaded the ships. The elves had filled the cabins of the flagship, *Planet*, with tons of supplies. There was abundant food, expedition clothing, toy weapons, games, and an unusually large quantity of gingerbread cookies.

Mrs. Claus and Hermey were boarding the *Planet* when Lucia called out to them. "I would like to join you and the children, if it's okay."

Mrs. Claus knew Lucia was an experienced traveler and could help guide them to Baekdu Island. Unlike the other elves, Lucia was fond of travelling and it had been over two centuries since her last big trip.

"Of course," Mrs. Claus replied enthusiastically.

Lucia hopped on the ship with just two bags. One contained her clothes and the other was filled with her mistletoe wax candles. Mrs. Claus felt reassured by Lucia's presence. Lucia knew the northern world better than any living creature. If an unexpected problem came their way, Mrs. Claus was confident Lucia would know how to solve it.

With everything on board now, it was time to set sail. Every elf in the North Pole village came to the edge of the water to wish them good luck. There was a festive atmosphere in the air as the elves rang bells and sang carols.

The five ships unfurled their large mainsails and threw off their dock lines. Everyone gasped as the sails revealed a pleasant surprise. During the night, the elves had decorated each sail with a big green tree. The tree design had three triangles overlapping and at the top was a large gold star.

The rigging strained under the load and the masts creaked, but the ships eventually lurched forward on their southerly course. All of the kids donned their foul weather gear and lifejackets before going on deck to wave to the elves. The snowmen were up in the rigging, ready to do their work. As the ships moved further away, the North Pole village shrunk in the distance, until finally, only the white horizon lay behind them.

It was a beautiful day for sailing on the Arctic Ocean. Puffy white clouds drifted across a cobalt blue sky overhead. The temperature was just below freezing, but there was no bite to the cold. The wind blew around twenty-five knots and the ships pushed through the sea at ten.

Tiberius ordered all sail out and the snowmen climbed further up the rigging to unfurl the topsails. The ships soon hit speeds over fifteen knots. The snowman captains of each vessel had little trouble steering the ships with their large rudders.

It was a great start to the voyage. The ships were moving through the water quickly and their speeds were similar. It was easy to keep the fleet together.

As the ships sailed farther from the shore, ten-foot waves rose behind them. Fortunately, the sea ice in the ocean was thin for this time of year so the ships plowed through the water with ease. Lucia and Mrs. Claus were shocked by how little ice was in their path. They had never seen so much open water this far north.

Tomo was in a playful mood and decided to climb the mainmast to get a better view of the ocean. Her ascent went smoothly, but once there she realized that the top of the mast swayed side to side, more than fifty feet, over the rolling ocean. The motion started to make her queasy. She quickly climbed back down and raved about the incredible view from the top.

When it came time to eat lunch, only Nebo, Tiberius, Lucia and Mrs. Claus could keep their food down. The rest of the kids and Hermey were too seasick to even consider eating. They stayed on deck trying their best not to throw up. Gus was the first to vomit and the others soon followed.

Lucia joined her seasick companions on deck and offered them some gingerbread men. No one was interested, except Josef. Even though he was as sick as everyone else, Josef could not pass up a cookie. He chomped down two gingerbread men in no time.

"Ugh… not the tastiest cookies but I do feel better," Josef observed. "What's in these?"

"Ginger of course," Lucia replied. "I had the elves make these with extra ginger. I have been using ginger for centuries to fight off seasickness. There is also some peppermint in there. The combination seems to work well."

The other kids were so miserable by this point that they all tried a gingerbread cookie. Everyone soon felt better except Gus and Mithra.

"Look up," Lucia suggested. "The two of you have been staring down. You should look at the horizon for a while. It will help your balance become centered again and you will feel better."

It took some time, but everyone had recovered by the late afternoon. The weather conditions were consistent all day, so they were able to put one hundred and fifty nautical miles under their keels in the first ten hours of sailing. The crew was in a good mood.

As the darkness of night set in, the team went below to gather for dinner. They shared a quiet meal with little conversation. Soon after, they went back on deck to get some fresh air.

Behind the ships and to starboard, a fire seemed to rise from the horizon. Flames of green and orange shot up into the sky. The glow was so bright it cast a greenish hue over the ships.

"They must've attacked the North Pole," Ben said sadly. "I was worried they'd wait for us to leave and then hit the defenseless village."

"No, no," Mithra said laughing. "That light is the Aurora Borealis, also known as the Northern Lights. It's the reaction of the earth's magnetic field with the solar winds coming from the sun. Charged particles from the solar wind react with gaseous particles in our atmosphere to give us this wonderful light show. I see them, once in a while, in Vermont."

"It's beautiful," Tiberius observed. He couldn't take his eyes away from the spectacular phenomenon. "I've never seen such a brilliant show."

The ships were still pushing through the water rapidly when the kids retired for the night. The snowmen continued to enjoy the Northern Lights, but remained focused on their task of running the ships. They wondered if any more cosmic dust might emerge through the aurora.

Early the next morning, Tiberius pulled on his lifejacket and waterproof gear before heading up to deck. Mrs. Claus was already on the stern of the vessel, assessing the conditions. A red glow was growing brighter overhead.

"Red sky at morning," Mrs. Claus lamented.

"Sailors take warning," Tiberius finished her sentence.

They were referring to an ancient rhyme repeated by mariners. *Red sky at night, sailors' delight. Red sky at morning, sailors take warning.* They both knew bad weather was probable for their second day at sea.

"How did you know that saying?" Tiberius asked Mrs. Claus. He was surprised by her knowledge of the sea. Until they left for the trip, Mrs. Claus seemed to be playing the role of mother to the elves rather than an ancient mariner of the Arctic.

"Santa Claus is also known as Saint Nicholas," Mrs. Claus explained. "Everyone knows that Saint Nicholas is the patron saint of children, but not many remember that he is also the patron saint of sailors. Although we have not sailed in over two centuries, I still recall the old wisdom of the sailors."

Tiberius was impressed. He thought he was the only sailor in the group, but was relieved to know that Mrs. Claus also had experience on the ocean and that Lucia was an accomplished explorer.

The rest of the kids slowly joined Tiberius and Mrs. Claus on deck. Mithra looked at the red sky and her face grew concerned.

"Looks like we're in for nasty weather," Mithra commented. She did not know the saying, but understood weather conditions well enough to see the clouds were moving in from the west. In this region of the world, it meant a storm was moving in.

"Let's shorten sails before it's too late," Mrs. Claus suggested.

Tiberius ordered the snowmen to take in the topsails. They would continue on with just the mainsails until the storm passed.

Preparations went smoothly. Sails were reduced, loose items were stowed securely and the hatches were battened down.

The day never brightened from the pale red glow of the morning. Instead, the red faded into gray and the seas began to lash out at the mighty vessels. By noon, the first waves were beginning to wash over the decks. Tiberius ordered everyone to go below and ride out the storm in the safety of the cabins. Mrs. Claus and he would be the only people left on deck. Even the snowmen had to don foul weather gear as they did not want to risk getting frozen to the deck by the ocean water. They took short turns on deck to steer the vessel and climbed back up the rigging to chisel off the frozen ocean spray.

The sea grew angry. Furious waves of thirty feet slapped the fleet on their starboard sterns. The ships pitched and rolled. Tiberius looked behind to see mountains of dark water surging over the decks as foam capped the waves.

The ships continued to persevere through the tempest. At times they were surfing along at over twenty-five knots, while down in the trough, the wind was lighter and the boats would nearly splash to a stop.

It had been a long day for the kids. The pitching and rolling, combined with their fear, sent a nausea throughout the crew that even the gingerbread cookies could not relieve. Only Nebo seemed to be unfazed, whittling little wooden figures as he had since the beginning of the trip. Tiberius and Mrs. Claus shouted commands to the snowmen, but the snowmen had difficulty hearing them over the howling wind.

As the gray sky darkened to black, a tremendous puff of wind hit the boats like an avalanche. The heavy gust snapped the masts on the *Constellation* and the *Planet*. The mainsails on the other three boats were ripped to shreds. But even without sails, the boats continued to drift swiftly to the south.

The storm grew worse as the night wore on. The ships listed side to side wavering in their course. Without a sail to push them, the ships were at the mercy of the tumultuous sea. No one could suggest a solution to overcome this sudden disaster.

The storm was relentless as the brave little crew battled on. Nebo and Josef were inspired by the efforts and popped up on deck to help. Nebo grabbed one of the rigging lines and pulled the mainmast up against the howling wind. As it approached vertical, the rigging line snapped and the mast came crashing back down to the deck.

The only solace Tiberius found was that the pykrete hulls were taking a beating and showed no sign of weakness. Mithra had made the vessels as seaworthy as any ship afloat.

Gus peered from out of the main cabin. He saw the broken masts of the ship he was on and the shredded sails on the others. The ships were starting to drift apart in the gathering darkness. He ducked back down below and, in desperation, started communicating with one of the spiders which had climbed onboard before they had left.

"Our rigging isn't strong enough for this storm," Gus said as though he was answering a question from the spider. "Yes, please, it's worth a try," he continued. "Be careful!"

All at once, Tiberius noticed spiders spilling out of various cracks in the hatches on deck. At first, only a few emerged from the main cabin, but soon thousands were crawling all over the deck. The spiders seemed to be everywhere.

"Is this some sort of curse?" Tiberius wondered out loud.

"Look over there," Mrs. Claus said pointing to the rigging line that Nebo had held in his hands.

To everyone's astonishment, the spiders were spinning webs all over the line. The snapped part of the line was spun back together with spider silk in no time. The spiders were congregated on different parts of the rigging, twisting their fiber into long, thick strands.

Nebo took hold of the same rigging line that had snapped only minutes earlier. He valiantly pulled the mast back up. This time, the rigging line held and the mast was vertical again.

The spiders moved to the snapped section of the mast and encircled it so quickly that they looked like a blur. Within seconds, a foot-thick web was wrapped around the broken mast section. Tiberius grabbed the free end of Nebo's line and lashed it to a deck fitting. Nebo let go; the mast stood tall and withstood the screaming wind that was trying to knock it down.

The rest of the team threw on their gear and came on deck to witness this dazzling miracle. The spiders had repaired one mast and were working on the rigging for the other masts. Nebo was already pulling up the mizzenmast by the time everyone arrived on deck.

Gus turned to look at the *Galaxy*. A few minutes ago, its sails had been in tatters. Now the mainsail was back to its original shape. The only difference he noticed was the Christmas tree on the sail now seemed to be covered in tinsel. He took comfort in knowing the spiders were working on all five ships.

Out of the raging sea, the rigs of the fleet were once again defiantly standing against the storm. The ships moved back within sight of each other and continued on their course to Baekdu Island. The angry sea tried time and time again to smash the intrepid sailors, but the ships refused to yield to the merciless onslaught.

The spiders continued to spin webs on all parts of the rigging. By the time they finished, every mast and yard was covered in webs and the cotton on every line had been strengthened by the spider silk woven into it. The rigs still strained under their heavy load, but they seemed more flexible. The masts and sails pulled in harmony with the weather.

The ships handled the rest of the night well, despite the worsening conditions. Tiberius and Mrs. Claus grew more confident in the strength of the new rigging and ordered more sail to help make up for the time lost during the breakdowns. The ships began to roar like lions as they surfed along the mountainous waves. Spray shot out fifty feet from the sides of each bow. The sea whipped wildly in the ships' wake, looking more like boiling water than an icy ocean.

The only light left by midnight came from the sea itself. The water was illuminated by the tiny creatures living near the surface. The bioluminescence of these creatures was stirred up by the churning of the water behind the boats and left a glowing, green trail that stretched for miles behind them.

As the skies cleared just before daybreak, the trail was bright enough to be seen from an orbiting satellite and was picked up by NORAD. It was the first sign of the fleet seen by anyone outside of the North Pole.

The NORAD staff working that night was perplexed by the images. They inquired with Scout at the North Pole to see if she knew of any activity in the region. But the North Pole network was still down. There was no reply.

27

On the morning of the twenty-first, the sun's first rays rose from the ocean and revealed a clear, blue sky. The waves and wind from the storm were still robust, but the day dawned gloriously. As the crew came up from below deck, they were amazed at the transformation the ships had undergone during the night.

Each ship now had all its rigging and sails coated in spider silk. As the morning's first light hit the silk, it cast a rainbow of reflections. The masts looked like they were wrapped in thin bands of glass. The sails shined in the new light and their Christmas tree emblems were still visible under the magical coating.

The children's spirits had sunk low during the night. But the gloom and desperation that had threatened to drag them to the bottom of the sea gave way to a hope that sprang forth from the dawn's early light. Everything seemed different now. The waves and wind that once had appeared so threatening now blew with the promise of a swift journey across oceans.

They were leaving behind the cold and ice of the Arctic Ocean and entering the Bering Sea, the northernmost waters of the Pacific. Tiberius felt the shift in the oceans. They were ahead of schedule and it seemed like nothing could stop them now.

The gray lady of the sea had tested them the night before. Like an ancient hazing ritual, she had challenged the fleet and demanded a miracle to let them pass. Having received her bounty, she now blessed the fleet and ushered them toward their ultimate destination.

The team sat down and ate a hearty breakfast. It was like they were back in the bubble around the North Pole. The conversation was light and cheerful. Smiles and laughter had returned. The optimism, which had been nearly extinguished in the night, burst out once again. Nothing would dampen their spirits on this day.

As they passed the narrowest point of the Bering Strait, Tiberius was careful to keep the fleet out of sight from land. He thought it important to keep their mission a secret as long as possible. He was concerned Eastern Industries would discover what they were doing. He soon turned the fleet from its southerly course to a more southwesterly heading.

By late afternoon, the wind began to lighten a bit and all sail was put out to squeeze every ounce of thrust from the wind. The spiders were quick to scale back up the rigs and weave their mighty silk on the previously furled sails.

Tiberius was proud of the spiders, but felt a little uneasy at the sight of so many arachnids scurrying about all at once. He turned to Gus and asked, "How many of these little creatures did you bring?"

"I think they all came," Gus said shrugging his shoulders. "The night before we left, only one spider asked if he could join us on the voyage, but I guess they all decided to join."

"Well, I'm glad they did," Tiberius said as he patted Gus on the shoulder. "They saved our mission last night. Heck, they probably saved our lives."

"We owe them," Ben added with pleasure. "I never imagined a bunch of small spiders would be capable of saving such large ships."

Gus's heart filled with pride. It was only a few days ago that Ben had wanted to smash any spider he saw. Now Ben was giving them their due.

"I guess I don't have to worry about you crushing any of them," Gus joked.

"I don't think I'll ever recklessly kill any animal again for as long as I live," Ben answered with a broad smile. "You've shown me that the little creatures have the same souls as the big ones. It's a lesson I will never forget."

Ben turned his attention to the other ships. He asked Tiberius, "Are we sure everything is OK with the other boats? I'm worried the toy soldiers may have suffered some damage during the storm."

"The other ships are fine," Gus replied. "The spiders made sure of it."

But Ben wanted positive proof the soldiers were in good shape. He asked Tiberius, "Is it safe to assemble the soldiers on deck for a roll call? I would like to make sure they can still move efficiently. If not, we may still have time to fix them."

Tiberius looked around and considered the weather. The topsides of the ships were dry now so he saw no harm in ensuring the toy soldiers were functional.

Ben called Josef and together they programmed the toy soldiers to march on deck. Josef added a routine for the soldiers to play their marching music. The kids looked on as the soldiers began to muster on the decks of the other ships.

Soon they were filled with the three-foot-high warriors. On each boat, the sounds of drums and fifes could be heard. It was an impressive display of unison. The drumbeat they played over and over had the cadence of "The Little Drummer Boy."

As the crew relished the moment, they were suddenly interrupted by an urgent call from the mainmast of the *Planet*. "Ship on the horizon!" Mars, the snowman, shouted.

Up ahead was an Alaskan fishing vessel. It had its gear out and was moving slowly toward them. Alarm spread throughout the ships. There was no way for them to maneuver out of sight so Tiberius made an instant decision and ordered them to hold their course.

As the small armada approached the fishing vessel, its crew could not believe their eyes. In forty years of plying the Bering Sea, the captain of the vessel had never seen such a sight. The fishermen were worried some ghost from the North was coming to claim their souls.

One crewman on the fishing boat dropped what he was doing and instinctively reached for his mobile phone. He was intent on recording a video of the fleet cruising by as proof of what he was witnessing. He only got about thirty seconds of footage before they passed, but he managed to capture the strange spectacle. He focused in on a group of young kids standing on deck waving to the fishermen. He then panned over and recorded the extraordinary sight and sound of twenty thousand toy soldiers drumming their song in perfect harmony. Finally, he panned up to what appeared to be actual snowmen hanging from the rigging. To his astonishment, they were also waving.

The bass drums went "thump, thump". The snare drums rattled. The fifes played the melody. An incredible sound matched the unbelievable sight.

The crewman ran up to the captain of the fishing vessel. "Did you see that?"

"I don't know what I saw, but no one would believe me if I told them," the stunned captain replied.

"You don't have to tell them," the crewman said proudly. "Look at this."

The captain looked down at the little phone but still could not believe what had just transpired. He immediately took the video and uploaded it to his social media account through the boat's satellite connection. He added the hashtag, "#NorthPoleFleet" to his post.

Throughout modern history there have been a handful of images that have defined great moments. The first was an image of the carnage after the battle of Gettysburg that helped to bring the American Civil War battlefield into the popular mind. The picture of the "Migrant Mother" was instrumental in giving a face to the Great Depression. An unidentified Chinese man standing in the path of combat tanks in Tiananmen Square cast a light on a previously secretive Chinese crackdown.

As it turned out, the short clip of the North Pole Fleet would be the first video to achieve such a worldwide reaction. Right after it was posted, experts weighed in on the details. An old sea captain was able to plot the flotilla's course to Baekdu Island. An image expert blew up a frame with Lucia in it and highlighted the elf standing next to Mrs. Claus. A person in Vermont was able to connect the video to the news footage from the Bentley farm. Within a few hours the video had gone viral.

The madness of Winterval came to an abrupt halt as the fleet's mission became clear. People awoke from their daze and were suddenly filled with a new optimism for the season. As soon as they viewed the video, they instantly felt the magic of Christmas returning to their lives. The magic that had been stripped from the season by Eastern Industries, was planted like a seed in the minds of the world. It took root once again and was nourished by the hopes and dreams of the masses.

Business came to a stop. Employees in office buildings frequently popped their heads up from nine-foot-square cubicles and asked each other if they had seen *it*. For the rest of that day, the pronoun *it* was reserved for the North Pole Fleet video. Belief was rekindled in people's souls. A void that had formed over the past couple of weeks now yearned to be filled with the true spirit of the season. Christmas was reborn in the hearts of young and old.

Unlike the careful planning of its predecessor, the Christmas spirit had no marketing campaign. It did not have an army of Grandfather Frost's to woo the people. The spirit spread from heart to heart out of love. It was a sign that the nostalgia of Christmases past would not be discarded so easily. The pragmatic season of Winterval was finally yielding to the miracle of Christmas.

In cities big and small, people turned out into the streets. They held hands and began to sing their favorite carols. The few hearty Santas, who rang their bells for the needy, instantly found their pots overflowing with money. No one kept track or boasted about their newfound generosity, they gave from their heart and asked for nothing in return. Charitable giving became an anonymous practice as it once had been.

Toy collection centers not only overflowed with toys again, but they overflowed with volunteers as well. People left their businesses, closed their shops, and tried to fix what had been broken during their infatuation with Winterval. Christmas was not dead, it was alive again and had burst out from the ashes of Winterval.

After watching the video over and over, many kids abandoned their electronic toys and ventured outside. Wherever there was snow, young and old alike, came together to roll it up into balls. Parents joined their tots to recreate the waving snowmen in the rigging. Winter was no longer a burden on the people; it now represented a time to play.

Across northern Vermont, people again watched the sarcastic Christmas segment that Freya had aired a few days before on the local news. The images that had previously been presented as being absurd now seemed as if they had been a prophecy. By the time darkness fell over Jericho,

Vermont, a stream of headlights clogged the road to the Bentley farm. The local police and state troopers moved in to make sure everyone got a chance to take a stroll through the amazing Bentley Christmas display.

A fresh voiceover was recorded over the original Bentley news video and was aired across the world. This time there were no jokes or snide comments. In place of the original commentary, a positive perspective of Christmas was put forth. The new coverage talked about the wonderful spectacle that had been setup by the parents of a little girl on one of the polar vessels. It portrayed Mithra and the others as new-age Argonauts determined to save Santa Claus and Christmas itself. The world was captivated by the footage and desperately cried out for more information.

Even the commanders of NORAD joined in the euphoria that was gripping the entire planet. They posted an image of the phosphorescence they had captured from the night before. It showed the five glowing tracks of the ships emerging from a giant storm. They confirmed the passage of five ships south through the Bering Strait. The NORAD website was updated to post a real-time tracking of the crusading fleet so the world could follow the progress of the brave crew.

Overnight, the Eastern Industry stores had become a barren wasteland. Shoppers and employees abandoned the temples of greed and went back home to be with their families. Simple acts that had seemed like a chore only yesterday became delightful once again. People were decorating and baking, not out of obligation, but rather because they were listening to their hearts. The treats they now ate were not covered in plastic, but made with love and each bite warmed the heart.

The joy of Christmas had been reborn. The season once again typified quaint scenes depicted on postcards as dormant memories of Christmases past were revived. It was no longer a commercial race to outdo others. It was a tradition carried on out of love, not by force of habit. It was human affection taken to its highest tide. It was a reminder to the world that at Christmas, people often are closest to what nature's God sent them here to be.

28

Later that day, in a lonely office in New York, Rudi Kringle sat at his desk and stared out the window.

"It's all over," he thought. "Winterval is over, the stores are empty and my life is ruined."

He turned to his computer screen and looked at the video that had destroyed everything he had worked for. Watching it for the third time, he paused at the image of the kids. He zoomed in and could clearly make out Tiberius and Hermey.

The phone rang.

"What do *you* want?" Rudi answered, knowing it was his wife on the other end.

"I'm sorry dear." Her voice was kind for the first time in years. "I'm sorry everything you've worked so hard for, is gone."

"Are you calling to rub it in?" Rudi could not believe the sudden change in his wife's attitude toward him. "I really don't want to have another argument with you. This isn't the time."

"I'm calling because I love you, Rudi," she replied softly. "I'm worried about you."

Rudi was caught off guard by her warmth and kindness. Their love had faded as his career had taken over all of his time and attention. Now that he thought he had lost everything, her voice reminded him of the way things used to be. The way things could have been.

Within a moment, his life flashed before his eyes: the experience of finding out Hermey had been pretending to be Santa Claus; the ecstasy of falling in love with the woman of his dreams; the joy they shared when Tiberius was born. It all flooded into his mind. For a moment, he felt better.

Then his thoughts brought him to more recent memories. He recalled the many times young Tiberius asked if he would play with him and he always replied, "Maybe later." He remembered his wife asking about future plans and replying that he just did not have the time to think about it. He relived how those precious moments came and went. He missed them all. He had given up everything to make his career a success and now it lay in ruins.

"No Virginia," he replied to that far away voice. "I'm sorry."

"It's OK dear," Virginia replied. "You'll build your business back up."

Rudi began to cry. Years of misguided dedication unraveled in his mind. He had thrown it all away; his marriage, his child, even his love of toy making. He had given it all up in the chase for riches. No matter how much money he earned, it had never been enough. He had always strived for more.

"I don't give a flying reindeer about the business," Rudi sobbed. "I've lost you, I've lost Tiberius; and for what?"

"You'll never lose me," Virginia's sweet voice replied. "You'll always be the toy making boy I fell in love with so many years ago."

Rudi could not reply. He was choked up with regret. He had devastated so many lives. He had almost caused the downfall of the holiday his father cherished most. Suddenly, all of it meant something to him again. He felt like a blindfold was lifted from his mind's eye and he could now clearly see what mattered in life.

"Do you remember when Tiber was a baby and we lived in that small apartment in the Bronx?" Virginia asked.

"Please, don't remind me," Rudi wailed. He swallowed hard and added, "The memories are too painful now."

"So you do remember," she concluded. "And I'm sure you remember that first Christmas. You spent every night whittling little wooden toy soldiers for Tiber. They were the most beautiful toys I had ever seen. You must have made a hundred of them."

"One hundred and forty-four," Rudi robotically corrected her.

"You never noticed, but Tiberius played with those toys for many hours as he got older. He loved the little soldiers and always said to people, 'My daddy made these.' His favorite fantasy game was taking those soldiers and rescuing you from work. Seems like he is doing just that; right now," she added quickly.

"What can I do?" Rudi pleaded with his wife. "I wish I could go back in time and fix this whole mess."

"You can't go back in time," Virginia said with increasing authority. "But you can do *something*."

"What? What can I do?" Rudi repeated helplessly.

"You will make toy soldiers," Virginia ordered. "You'll make sure every child on earth has a toy soldier to cherish this year."

"Impossible," Rudi replied. He had lost the despair in his voice. His mind began to race with her words echoing in his thoughts. Since the video had gone viral, kids all across the world now wanted a toy soldier just like the ones they had seen on the ship. Rudi knew he could make them; they were just like the ones he had made for Tiberius as a baby.

"It just takes hard work and genius, Rudi. And I know you have both in abundance."

"Please come here, Virginia. I'll need help."

"I'm already on my way. I should be at your office in a few minutes."

Rudi hung up the phone. He called his marketing manager and told her to get the marketing team ready for a meeting in one hour, "To help give kids what they really want."

Virginia burst into Rudi's office and was surprised by his messy appearance. The usually dapper fellow now resembled a mad genius. He looked like he did when they were young. His eyes burned with a fire that had long ago been extinguished. They shared a brief but emotional embrace.

Rudi had his old carving tools laid out on his desk. He had some paints lined up at the edge. In the middle was a block of wood.

"Record this," he said.

Virginia held up her phone and began to record. The master toy maker made quick work on the block of wood and within a few minutes, a simple wooden soldier was formed. He talked to the camera, explaining the process while he carved the different sections. He then used red, white, black and gold paint to give color to the wood.

Ten minutes after he had begun, he held up a perfect, yet simple, toy soldier.

"What's the video for?" Virginia asked.

"I can only make a few hundred of these by myself before Christmas," Rudi replied excitedly. "If I get help, we can make millions."

"Who is going to help?" Virginia asked. "There aren't many people that carve by hand anymore."

"Yes there are," Rudi excitedly countered her. "They're just retired.

"When Hermey and I used to make toys for the children's hospital, we would go to the local retirement home and have the old woodworkers help out. They loved being able to use their well-honed skills once again.

"If I can get this video out to all the retired craftsmen in the world, I think we can make enough for every child to receive a toy soldier."

Rudi picked up the phone and called his marketing manager again. He explained his plan and sent her the instructional video. He asked that she spread the video to every woodshop in the country. He advised her to use every last advertising spot left on the airwaves to broadcast the following message.

"Santa needs your help. Kids around the world want one thing for Christmas — toy soldiers! Please go to the following website to view an instructional video on how to create the toys. On Christmas Eve, leave the soldiers outside your buildings in a red sack. Santa will take it from there."

Satisfied that his message was going out, Rudi picked up the phone and dialed.

"Mr. Kim?" he asked into the receiver. "This is Rudi Kringle."

"Yes, I know it's a mess," Rudi replied to the voice on the other end.

Rudi listened while Mr. Kim screamed into his ear. "I thought my father was crazy all these years, but you're the one who is insane. Kidnapping Santa Claus? I can't believe anyone would do that. I quit."

Rudi held the phone to his ear for another moment and hung up. His face sunk when he turned to Virginia. "Mr. Kim knows Tiber and Hermey are on their way to him. He said they will fail and Christmas will go down with Winterval."

"Oh my!" Virginia exclaimed.

"Don't worry," Rudi replied. "Mr. Kim is determined, but I know him well. He wouldn't hurt anyone. It would be bad for business."

Rudi took Virginia by the hand and hurried out of the office. They ran through the streets of New York and went back to their penthouse apartment.

"Pack some warm clothes," Rudi said to Virginia. "We're going north."

He scribbled a quick note and turned on his gas fireplace. He threw the note in and the two of them flew out of the apartment. He hurried down the street and hailed a cab.

"Airport please."

"Where are we going?" Virginia asked with the anticipation of a little girl on Christmas morning. She loved having her old Rudi back. "The North Pole?"

"Not that far," Rudi replied. "We're going to Jericho, Vermont."

29

Two days after the fleet had departed, Scout was pacing the E.I.N. headquarters. The computer networks were still down, so she was blind to many of the activities of the outside world. The only information she was receiving was from the forest elves and the occasional letter coming through the smoke collector.

An elf in the smoke collection area suddenly burst up from her seat and ran over to Scout while waving a new letter.

"This letter mentions our fleet out in the ocean," the elf screamed to the room.

Scout looked at the letter. It told about seeing a video of a fleet of frozen ships heading south in the northern Pacific Ocean. The letter just wanted to wish them good luck.

Scout was relieved to know the Naughty Team was still making progress. It was the first communication she had received about them since they had left.

"At least we know the fleet is still intact," Scout replied to the elf.

She sent an elf out to get Ziggy. She knew he would want to know about this new development.

By the time Ziggy arrived in the E.I.N., the elves in purple tunics were overwhelmed by the amount of letters coming in. They could not keep up with the huge increase in volume.

Ziggy rushed back out and put out a call for more elves to come in and help sort the letters.

"Thanks for the extra help," Scout said with a big smile. "Can you believe it? The fleet is a worldwide sensation. The rate of letters coming in keeps increasing. Read these."

Ziggy perused a couple of letters in his hand. His face softened as he turned over one after another. Soon a tear welled up in his eye and streaked down his face. More followed.

The letters Ziggy read had a new tone to them. They talked about Christmas miracles and hope. The letters contained apologies for giving up Christmas for Winterval. They talked about the good old days and expressed a desire to bring back the simple roots of the holiday. Most importantly, the letters contained the wonder of the season.

"I can't believe it," Ziggy muttered. "They have already saved Christmas!" he proclaimed. "They are barely half way to their destination, but they have already saved Christmas."

"Isn't that wonderful?" Scout wondered out loud.

"It is, it really is!" Ziggy shouted with exuberance.

An increasing volume of letters came in referencing the video. Requests for toy soldiers began to appear. Kids wanted the same toy soldiers they had seen on the deck of the ships.

"It seems like the whole world wants a wooden toy soldier like the ones on the ships. Do you think we can make enough of them for all the children?" Scout asked.

"We can make enough, but we just can't do it by Christmas," Ziggy replied. "We don't have enough time. We would need months to make enough for every child in the world."

An elf in a purple tunic ran up to Scout and Ziggy. She pushed a letter into Scout's hand and said, "You won't believe this one."

Dear Santa Claus,

Knowing that my father and son are heading to save you has made me realize how wrong I have been for many years. I have quit Eastern Industries and want to help save Christmas.

My plan is to get woodworkers across the world to craft toy soldiers, resembling the ones on the ship, and place them in red sacks. I hope this will help you give each child a piece of the miracle they are praying for.

Merry Christmas,

Rudi Kringle

Attached to the letter was a diagram of the soldiers Rudi planned to make. It detailed the aspects of the soldier's uniform, size, and shape.

"Rudi Kringle!" Ziggy yelled out loud. "Rudi Kringle is going to help us save Christmas!"

All the elves knew of Rudi Kringle. They knew about his naughty behavior over the years. They also knew he was an excellent toy maker, second only to Santa. After a brief pause, a cheer went out across the entire room.

"If Rudi knows that thousands of toy soldiers are on their way to rescue Santa Claus, then everyone else at Eastern Industries will know as well," Scout said with increasing concern. "We need to make sure everyone is safe. I doubt Mr. Kim will give up his machinations to end Christmas without a fight."

It took Ziggy a moment to process her words. He had been so overwhelmed with the letter from Rudi that he did not consider the increased danger the fleet would now face.

"Oh no," Ziggy said as his smile dropped away. "What can we do?"

"The reindeer," Scout said.

She thought about how the reindeer were going back to their homeland to find warrior riders. Up until this point, everyone had figured it would just be a nice distraction from the real effort coming from the ships. Then Scout considered the possibility that the reindeer could be a strong asset — one of the last surprises they could throw at Eastern Industries.

"Ziggy, we must make sure the reindeer can join the team in battle. We need to make armor for them and provide them with arrows the Mongol riders can use," Scout suggested.

"I already have armor," Ziggy responded with pride. "Tiberius suggested making it before he left and we've already outfitted eight of the reindeer with golden armor. All that's left is Rudolph's armor, but I need copper to finish it."

"Why copper?" Scout asked.

"Aranjagaan was the red horse that Jangar rode in the story Tomo told me. I thought we could make Rudolph's armor red to match Aranjagaan," Ziggy replied. "I just need to mix copper with the gold to make it into rose gold."

Scout considered Ziggy's request. There was no natural source of pure copper in the North Pole. She hesitated a moment before responding. "I'll get you some copper. We will tear apart the E.I.N. computer systems and take as much copper from the wires as we can. Please start making more arrows and I'll have that copper to you first thing tomorrow."

Across the village, bells began to ring. Any elf who was not already working in the smoke collection room rushed into the village square. Ziggy directed them all to participate by either making arrows or helping with the smoke collector.

Early the next day, thousands of arrows were piled up at the edge of the workshops. The arrows were made in typical elf fashion with a blunt point to make sure no one got hurt. The elves could not make a real weapon, but Ziggy thought the arrows would be useful nonetheless.

Ziggy found an old toy sack that Santa had not used in years. He cut it up into nine pieces and made quivers to carry the arrows. None of the elves were surprised the quivers could each hold an unlimited number of arrows, after all, they had seen a year's worth of toys stuffed into its original form as Santa's sack. The mountainous pile of arrows was now neatly packed away in nine red quivers.

Ziggy had another group work on mixing gold with the copper Scout had gathered, to create a brilliant rose gold armor for Rudolph. It took them the rest of the day to finish it.

As the sunlight was being extinguished by the horizon, the nine golden reindeer trotted toward the center of the village. The armor gleamed in the last rays of light. Ziggy attached a quiver of arrows to each reindeer. A large crowd of elves gathered around to give the reindeer a proper sendoff.

"Be safe," Ziggy gently ordered, putting his hand on Rudolph's muzzle.

Rudolph gave a quick nod before jumping skyward. The other reindeer followed and the herd was out of sight in a few seconds.

Turning his attention back to the crowd, Ziggy, sensing their concern, made an announcement. "Elves, we have one last task for this Christmas. We need to make as many toy soldiers as possible."

The elves cheered at this request. Their love for making toys washed away their worry.

"Let's keep it simple," Ziggy continued. "That is what the kids are asking for this year and we'll do our best to make sure it happens. We'll use Rudi's design and make as many as we can in the next forty-eight hours."

No one was sure how many toys they could actually make for the big ride, but they were determined to work straight through to Christmas Eve. The carols began again. Candles were lit in every workshop. The elves began to work and they would not stop until midnight on Christmas Eve.

30

Santa's reindeer were soon flying over the mountains between Russia and Mongolia. They looked down and observed small numbers of other reindeer and their herders. These mountains had once been teeming with reindeer, but now only a few thousand remained.

They crossed over the border a few times, looking for a specific Dukha family. Just before night fell, they found what they were looking for. It was a family of twenty herders who tended over a hundred reindeer. Santa's reindeer landed nearby and approached the family's tent.

At first, the native reindeer were spooked by their golden cousins. They let out a cry and the family of herders ran out from their tents to investigate. There was a brief moment of tension between the two parties.

Hearing the commotion, the family elder slowly emerged from his tent. He steadied himself with a cane as he walked toward the new arrivals. Donner and Blitzen moved forward from the others and stood before the old man, bowing their heads in respect.

The old man put his hand over Blitzen's muzzle and held it there for a few seconds. He repeated the same procedure with Donner.

"Donner, Blitzen," the old man said in his native tongue. "So good to see you again. I never thought you would come back."

He removed the champron from the heads of the two reindeer. The golden armor was handed to one of the younger members of the family. Additional family members gathered around the other reindeer and removed various pieces of armor.

"So the stories are true," one of the younger members said. "These are the reindeer that fly Santa Claus around the world."

The old man invited the entire family and the nine reindeer into his spacious tent where they were given food and water. He then motioned for the family to sit in a circle around a fire in the center of the tent.

"Over two hundred years ago, Santa Claus rode into our village on a sleigh pulled by donkeys during Shin Jil," the old man began, referencing the end of year celebration common in Mongolia. "He brought presents for the children and stayed the night with us.

"During the night, a great storm settled over the area and left behind a vast covering of fresh snow. The donkeys were not big enough, nor strong enough, to pull Santa's sleigh through the deep snow. But he was determined to continue on his trip and our ancestors felt obliged to help the kind man.

"They hitched eight of our best reindeer to his sleigh. At first, the reindeer struggled to pull their heavy load. Then Santa gave a whistle. This was not a whistle you or I could ever make. This was a whistle that rattled the snow off trees and echoed throughout the mountains.

"Immediately, the sleigh moved across the snow as if it was the down of a thistle. A moment later, they bounded out of sight and were gone.

"No one saw the reindeer for a whole month. When they reappeared they were strong and healthy, unusual for that time of year. Everyone was happy to have them back and the reindeer seemed to share the feeling.

"After that, spring turned to summer, and summer to fall; by the time winter was starting to set in, the reindeer left again. Our ancestors knew where they went each winter and were happy to let them go since they did not need the reindeer during the cold season.

"This continued for a century. The reindeer had outlived all the herders that were present during the original meeting. When I was just a little boy, Santa's reindeer made their last trip back to us. Poachers had begun to hunt for the special herd and it was no longer safe for them here.

"My grandfather told the reindeer to go back to the North Pole and never return. They heeded his advice and have not been seen around here, until now."

The family had heard this story many times before, but the words carried new meaning with the fabled reindeer in their presence. The old man watched as the younger members of the family played with the shiny pieces of armor.

"It seems the reindeer will be safe from the hunters if they wear that," he observed. Turning to the reindeer he asked, "What has brought you back to us?"

Donner bit into a quiver and picked out an arrow. Then he used his mouth to fling a young boy onto his back. He pranced around the tent, being careful not to knock the boy off. His meaning was clear.

"Ah, of course. You seek warriors to sit upon your armor. Tomorrow, you will need to head south. The riders you seek are out on the plains," the old man concluded.

Early the next morning, as a treat, the reindeer took each child for a ride through the sky. Children as young as four were able to ride as they bounded over treetops and back. After everyone had a turn, the older family members reattached the golden armor for their journey.

The reindeer took off toward the south. They were looking for the descendants of Jangar that Tomo had described. They flew over the Mongolian steppe peering down at the different tribes.

A large herd of gazelles was running along the horizon, leaving behind a cloud of dust. The reindeer flew low over the dust and spotted a group of Mongol riders chasing them. A child with a bow as big as himself pulled back on an arrow and aimed for a lone gazelle that had fallen behind.

Comet swooped down in the young rider's path and the arrow ricocheted harmlessly off his gleaming armor. The riders stopped and marveled at the golden creature.

"It is a wind horse," one of them said to the others. "It's here to claim a soul."

"It has antlers," another remarked. "Look, there are more."

All nine reindeer were now standing in front of the riders. Rudolph moved to the middle of the reindeer, his reddish armor catching the attention of the oldest rider. The rider dismounted and walked up to Rudolph.

Rudolph did not move. His red nose began to glow, matching the rose gold he wore. His fiery, red brilliance dazzled all the riders.

"It is Aranjagaan, the red horse! He has come back to carry us into battle," the oldest rider declared. "I, Batu Jangar, shall ride Aranjagaan once again to glory."

Fourteen-year-old Batu, jumped on Rudolph's back, bow in hand. He was surprised Rudolph remained motionless. Dasher poked Rudolph as a reminder that the young Mongol needed to ride with him first so their path could be determined. With that, Rudolph galloped into the sky, with Batu hanging on tightly.

At first, Rudolph worried about throwing his young rider. But as he looped and turned through the air, he realized the boy was able to ride him well. Rudolph gave some bucking motions and the acrobatic rider moved in perfect rhythm with him. Batu was so adept at riding that he merely felt like a shadow on Rudolph's back.

Batu's twin sister, Annushka, jumped on Donner's back and they took off immediately. She rode Donner as well as Batu rode Rudolph. The rest of the children, eager to mount their own wind horse, grabbed their bows and hopped on the remaining reindeer.

The nine reindeer had finally been paired with their riders. They were so excited that they flew higher and higher. They joyously danced in and out of puffy, white clouds, barely feeling the weight of the riders on their backs.

They flew over mountains that kissed the clouds and swooped down narrow canyons as they dodged between trees. The kids began to whoop in delight.

The riders were so nimble that it took some time for the reindeer to pick up on their subtle signals. A slight caress with their hand or a gentle squeeze with their legs were the only signals the riders used. Instead of controlling the reindeer, the kids' movements were more like suggestions. They had the sense they could be obeyed or disregarded, as the reindeer chose.

Annushka was the first to notice the red quiver located just behind her saddle. She pulled out an arrow and admired its perfect form. She took notice of the blunt tip and placed it in her bow. She pulled it back and launched the harmless projectile right into her brother's back.

Batu was shocked by the thump, but reacted quickly. He let go of Rudolph and fired an arrow back at Annushka. She moved to the side of Donner and the arrow pinged off the armor harmlessly. After watching this playful display, the other seven riders began to drawback on their bows and soon arrows were flying everywhere.

The kids cheered and hollered as the friendly competition intensified. The reindeer moved swiftly as they each helped their own rider to pursue the others. Besides the yelps of joy, not a word was spoken. The reindeer and riders bonded quickly in the games they played. By the time darkness set in, each reindeer and rider had developed a connection that joined their souls together. They had become one.

31

Rudi managed to carve eight toy soldiers during the one-hour flight to Burlington, Vermont. Virginia sat next to him and admired his experienced hands at work. She had always enjoyed watching him do what he loved most. Upon landing, the Kringles headed straight for the Bentley farm in Jericho. The traffic was heavy the whole way, but they made it there by dusk. As soon as they parked, a news crew immediately recognized Rudi.

"Mr. Kringle," a reporter called out. Soon every reporter on the farm was rushing over and barraging him with questions.

"Did your company really kidnap Santa? Can you tell us where he is?"

"Was Winterval your idea? How does it feel to see it end this way?"

Rudi and Virginia were being assailed from every direction. As they turned to get back into their car, Mrs. Bentley came through the throng of reporters and hurried the Kringles into her house. Mr. Bentley sat quietly in front of the television as the three entered.

Rudi urgently turned to Mr. Bentley and asked, "Have you seen me on TV today? There was supposed to be an advertisement about creating wooden soldiers."

Mr. Bentley slowly raised his head and glared at Rudi.

"I saw your advertisements; you scoundrel," Mr. Bentley said, insulting his guest. "How dare you say everything on the video was fake and Santa isn't real?"

"What?" Virginia asked incredulously.

"No, I didn't, I promise. Mr. Kim must have replaced the video I tried to circulate," Rudi said, keeping his composure. "My son and father are on those ships with your daughter."

Mrs. Bentley was surprised to hear this. "Which one is your boy? I assume the older fellow is your father."

"Tiberius," Rudi answered. His hands were shaking when he reached into his bag and pulled out eight toy soldiers. "I made these for Santa to give out on Christmas Eve."

The Bentley's looked at the little toys. They were perfect.

"You have quite the talent for that," Mrs. Bentley observed. "Why have you come to our farm?"

"Well, your farm is the center of attention right now. I had hoped to capitalize on that to reach out to woodworkers around the world and teach them how to make the soldiers," Rudi answered.

"So now you're a teacher," Mr. Bentley said sarcastically. "You better get out of here before I call the police."

"Please," Rudi pleaded. "I was wrong about Winterval. I know that now. It's not too late to help Santa give the world's children what they want for Christmas."

Mr. Bentley rose from his seat. Rudi backed away in fear, his body trembling all over.

"Sit down!" Mrs. Bentley commanded her husband. "I want to hear what the man has to say."

Rudi explained it all to her. He started with his father dressing as Santa. He talked about his love for making toys. He explained how that passion had been corrupted and how he had given up everything that was important in his life for Eastern Industries. He finished by explaining his ambitious plan to help Santa deliver the one toy that everyone wanted this year. The one toy that he hoped would forever represent the triumph of Christmas over materialism.

"Well, Rudi," Mrs. Bentley replied. "I think you *have* come to the right place."

She guided the Kringles to the front door and they stepped outside. In an instant, they were lit up by dozens of cameras. Everyone on the farm wanted to know what was going on.

"Friends," Mrs. Bentley began. "This is Rudi Kringle. His son and father are on the ship with my daughter. He wants to help Santa too."

Rudi said nothing. Despite his trembling hands, he sat down on the front steps and laid out his paints and his carving tools. He began to work while Virginia narrated the instructions. She explained Rudi's plan to the reporters and encouraged them to spread the word as swiftly as possible.

Within ten minutes, another toy was complete. Everyone was amazed how quickly the perfect replica had been created. The story was an immediate hit and played all over the world.

Back inside, Mrs. Bentley made some coffee for her guests. As Mr. Bentley watched the whole scene on television, he warmed up to Rudi. The four sat in the dining room for a while and talked about their concerns for the little crusaders.

Before long, there was a knock on the door. Four women stood outside the house and each had a little box tucked under her arm. Mrs. Bentley stepped out to greet them.

"Pardon us," one of them said to Mrs. Bentley. "Would Rudi mind showing us his technique again? We've come to help him."

Mrs. Bentley offered her barn to Rudi and the women. Rudi setup his tools and showed the women how to carve the figures. It took them a try or two, but they picked it up quickly. Throughout the night, dozens of local craftspeople came to the Bentley barn to help Rudi with his creations.

By the time the sun rose the next morning, hundreds were assisting Rudi with his project. By afternoon, the Bentley farm resembled the North Pole with its beehive of toy making activity. Donations of raw wood arrived, tents went up on other areas of the farm, and reporters sent out frequent updates to every outlet in the world; Rudi's plan was coming to fruition.

In Austria, the Ruprechts had seen their son on the fisherman's video. They were so proud that Josef looked fit and strong. Mr. Ruprecht was still convinced that Josef was at some type of exercise camp. He told his story to anyone that would listen. People were certainly listening now.

"You're all mistaken," Mr. Ruprecht tried to explain. "Those sailing vessels are just part of the fitness camp. They're not going to rescue anyone. They're just providing routines that help get the kids into shape."

When asked about the snowmen and silken sails, Mr. Ruprecht responded, "I'm telling you, that is all part of the grand plan. They pull out all the stops to make the kids think they're on a mission to help Santa. I guess that's how they motivate the camp children. Come to think of it, it's brilliant. It certainly is the only thing that has worked for my son."

Despite his denials, people flocked to Oberndorf, Austria. Many held a vigil in front of the little chapel where "Silent Night" was first written. They sang the beautiful song over and over.

Mrs. Ruprecht joined the impromptu pilgrims. She loved that Winterval was being swept away in a flood of Christmas spirit. She was also worried. Unlike her husband, she believed that Josef *was* on an expedition to save Christmas.

In central Pennsylvania, Mrs. Rauch realized what Gus was really up to when a coworker showed her Gus's image in the North Pole Fleet video. She immediately called Sam.

"Where's my son?" Mrs. Rauch began firing off. "You told me he was helping you on your farm all this time. Now I see him on some boat in... in... the middle of nowhere?"

"I'm on my way to your house now," Sam calmly replied. "I can explain it all when I get there."

"You better have Gus with you!" Mrs. Rauch ordered, slamming the phone down as she left work.

When she finally arrived home, Sam was standing near the barn. She stomped over to him, tears streaming down her face and fists clenched. Sam motioned for her to go into the barn.

She opened the door to discover over a dozen forest elves and dropped straight to the ground. The elves ran out of the barn and performed a comedic rescue of the poor lady. They moved her arms, listened for her heart, checked her breathing, and tried to get her back on her feet all at once. Sam explained that she had only fainted from the excitement and asked if they would help move her into the house. It took every elf, but they accomplished the task and laid her down on the couch.

When she awoke, the elves were scurrying about her house. They were cleaning, decorating, and making food. She sat up and rubbed her eyes in disbelief. The house never looked so good. Sam sat down on the couch and held her hand.

"What's going on?" she asked, still in a dreamlike trance.

Sam handed her the note Gus had written the night before the fleet set sail from the North Pole. She read it many times, glancing up every now and then at the dozen elves staring at her. They offered her some cookies and she accepted.

The letter explained everything. It revealed why he had left Sam's farm. It talked about communicating with animals at the North Pole. It ended with an explanation of why he had decided to help save Christmas.

*I came to the North Pole to save **my** Christmas. I wanted the world to put Christ back in Christmas.*

I have since learned Christmas is older and broader than I ever could have imagined. Since the beginning of civilization, this great holiday has given humans a chance to throw off the robes that separate each other and to be reminded that we are all the same underneath.

Christmas is a celebration for the whole world and Santa is the ambassador of this miraculous realm. Christmas is a reminder that we are all God's creatures. We are all equal spirits living on this little speck of dust flying through the Universe.

Mrs. Rauch did not fully understand what was happening, but she treasured this letter from Gus. She knew it was his writing and held it close to her heart. It had been a long, hard Winterval season for the exhausted mother. She was happy to rest and let the elves and Sam take care of her.

In Japan, Kiso Gozen read her letter from Tomo and squealed with delight. She never really believed Ziggy's note that told of Tomo recovering in some mountain refuge. Throughout Kiso's life, she had always known Tomo to be active. Unfortunately, Kiso was confined to bed again with another illness as she read the long, compelling letter.

It described Tomo's arrival at the North Pole. Tomo painted a magical picture with her words. Kiso loved the depiction of the towering fortress, the elves and their carols, and especially the portrayal of the daily life at the North Pole. It was all as Kiso had imagined.

Kiso called for both of her parents. Even though it was the middle of the day, her father was home. Mr. Gozen had missed work for the first time in his life when the fisherman's video spread over the internet. Despite his constant denials, everyone in Japan recognized Tomo on the ship. His presence had caused such a commotion at work that he was forced to take a leave.

Kiso's parents entered her room. She showed them the letter. Mrs. Gozen smiled as she read it, but Mr. Gozen's face dropped. He recognized the writing as Tomo's.

"We must keep this quiet, Kiso," her father ordered sternly. "This could bring shame to our family."

Kiso thought for a while as her parents peered at her with sympathetic eyes. She and her parents were together and Tomo was going to save Santa Claus. What could be better?

"Tell me a joke," Kiso asked weakly, blowing her nose for added emphasis.

She felt better than she had in weeks, but wanted her parents to stay with her. She begged her father to make her laugh and her mom to tell stories of Santa. She wanted to play games with them. She just wanted to be with them.

Her father obliged and began to tell his jokes. She had heard some of them before, but laughed all the same. Mrs. Gozen laughed as well. Kiso allowed herself to perk up and her parents assumed she had improved due to their actions. They spent the rest of the day in her room, simply enjoying each other's company.

"We cannot confirm nor deny the whereabouts of any of our students due to the sensitive nature of our institution," read the official statement from Ben David's military school.

But everyone in Israel knew the young soldier was with the North Pole Fleet. He could not be missed. He stood out among the kids. He personified the general the military school hoped he would someday become.

Nicola Abdou knew it as well. He was the recipient of Ben's letter, sent on the eve of the fleet's departure. Ben had asked that Nicola try his best to recruit more Santas in Israel and continue to spread the joy of Christmas. He wanted a Santa in every hospital, every refugee camp, and every orphanage.

Nicola had always been alone in this part of the world. There were very few Santas. Now that the world had changed in the wake of the fisherman's video, he suddenly found himself in the spotlight. By the time Rudi's message on toy soldiers was broadcast around the world, Nicola had hundreds of Santas ready to help spread the miracle of Christmas.

Nicola took charge of the recent recruits and sent his newly trained army of Santa Clauses out across the Middle East. They worked in Israel, Palestine, and North Africa. They collected toy soldiers from retirement workshops and came up with a plan to distribute them to every boy and girl they could reach.

Even Ben's military academy joined in the festive mood. Classes were cancelled as the school's commandant called for the students to make little toy soldiers for Nicola's campaign.

A reporter from a hardline newspaper in Israel tried to give Nicola a tough time, asking, "If *you* are Santa Claus, then who are the kids going to rescue?"

Nicola responded with his usual explanation. "When I put on this hat, I become a part of Santa Claus. You become Santa the first time you look into a child's eyes and they light up with the wonder of believing in miracles. It reminds us all to have faith: faith in families, faith in love, faith that we can have good will and peace on earth. The children are going to rescue the faith that the world so readily abandoned."

32

On the twenty-third of December, the fleet was less than two hundred nautical miles from Baekdu Island. According to Tiberius's navigation and Mithra's weather forecast, they would arrive at the island around daybreak on Christmas Eve.

Gus was on the front of the *Planet* when a pod of dolphins began to surf in the bow wake of the ship. Before long, they frolicked in the big waves in front of all the ships. Gus called out to the others to look at the playful mammals.

The kids' spirits were lifted as they watched the intelligent creatures perform a water ballet. Gus drifted off into thought then suddenly snapped back to reality.

"What is it?" Tomo asked with alarm.

"The dolphins want us to turn back," Gus responded solemnly. "They say it's very dangerous ahead."

"There will be no turning back," Ben responded.

Tiberius, thought for a moment and agreed with Ben. "We can't turn back now, whatever the problem."

Gus said no more since the dolphins could not explain exactly what the threat was. They just knew that evil activities were taking place up ahead. Like most other animals, they had been avoiding the sea around Baekdu Island.

The team was unsettled by the dolphin's prognostication of danger but nonetheless stayed the course. They left the bow of the *Planet* to prepare for the next day's rescue mission.

Tiberius and Mithra headed down below to check the condition of the hull. Although the frozen vessels had been sailing in warmer water since leaving the Arctic Ocean, the hulls were in great shape. Tiberius and Mithra saw no evidence of any problems.

Ben and Josef powered up the toy soldiers and assembled them on deck. This time they marched and practiced military maneuvers, rather than play their musical instruments. Ben was satisfied they would be ready to go ashore the next day.

Tomo tested her climbing gear by scaling the masts and rappelling back down. At the top of the mainmast, she scanned the horizon and saw nothing but the big blue expanse of the Pacific Ocean.

Nebo quietly gathered the fifty wooden figures he had been busily carving since he had left the North Pole. The others began to huddle around as he placed his little creations in a tight circle around the mainmast of the *Planet*.

Despite the rolling of the ship, the figures did not fall over.

"That one looks like Jesus," Gus observed. "Is this some type of nativity scene?"

"I think that one is Moses," Ben offered as he pointed to a figure with a long beard.

Tomo gestured toward a figure sitting cross legged. She asked, "Is that the Buddha?"

"They are what you want them to be," Nebo responded to no one's satisfaction. "These fifty carvings represent many gods gathered to consolidate their power to Marduk."

"Interpret them as you will," Nebo continued. "In my religion, the gods get together and give their power to Marduk to defeat the God of Chaos. What you see is your interpretation. These carvings have been made every winter for over four thousand years."

"That one looks like Ronald Reagan," Tiberius said calling attention to another figure.

The kids all laughed. Even Gus broke a smile.

"Your mind will interpret these based on your experience," Nebo added. "Whatever forms you interpret them as being, understand no one else sees them exactly the same way. You should respect the forms others see as well. No one is wrong in their interpretation of the carvings. After all, they are just little pieces of wood, whittled from my imagination."

Nebo asked for a moment of silence and everyone complied. He spoke words no one understood. Even Mrs. Claus could not decipher the meaning.

Nebo then rose and said, "As long as these figures come together once a year to defeat chaos, the world will go on. If they remain apart, our world will be returned to the state of chaos preceding our creation."

As Nebo picked up his carved figures, an albatross began to circle overhead. Gus looked up at the bird and picked up on its thoughts.

Everyone turned to Gus as he stared at the distressed wanderer.

"What is it?" Tomo asked, concerned.

"She is telling us to turn around. There is nothing but danger and ruin up ahead," Gus answered. "She was born on Baekdu Island, but no creature goes there anymore. It was once full of nesting birds, but they have all been forced to leave. The island is a blackened wasteland now."

As the day wore on, more birds circled the fleet. Some of the birds were tired and landed on the *Planet* for a rest. Gus, Tomo, and Lucia did their best to make them comfortable. Many flew away after a brief time, but a few still remained. Gus felt terrible for the avian refugees.

Each bird talked about being expelled from its home on Baekdu Island. Gus tried to reassure the birds they would be back there by Christmas. He did not know if he could keep that promise, but he was more determined than ever to make it come true.

Just before nightfall, the snowmen spotted five drones heading their way from the southwest. The drones took no action, but hovered above the ships as they raced through the sea.

"Should we launch the planes?" Tiberius asked Ben.

"No," Ben replied. "Let them fire the first shot. We don't want to be the aggressors."

Ben whispered in Tiberius's ear, "I'm concerned they sent five. How could they have known we have exactly five ships? They must know we're coming."

Dark clouds began to blow in as night fell. The full moon rose from the horizon behind the ships, but the clouds soon covered it up again. The night turned to total blackness.

Some of the kids became frightened. They could no longer see each other on deck. The darkness left them blind. They groped around trying to find their way back to the main cabin.

"Do not fear the darkness, my children," Mrs. Claus called out. "Black is the true color of Christmas."

She opened the hatch to the main cabin and a bright red light spilled out from below. Lucia had lit a candle in the cabin that made it almost as bright as day.

"The red candle is perfect," Tiberius said as he turned to Lucia. Tiberius was the only child who understood a red light would not compromise their night vision if they returned to deck.

As they gathered in the cabin, Gus turned to Mrs. Claus and asked, "Why did you say black is the color of Christmas? I thought it was red and green."

"Don't forget silver and gold," Tiberius added.

"No, no," Mrs. Claus responded. "Black is the color of Christmas because it is the absence of light that makes our holiday stand out. The glow of a fire, the twinkle of a string of Christmas lights, the bright stars at night; they are extra special at Christmas because they defy the total blackness which would otherwise cover the world. Black is the background that makes Christmas shine the brightest."

"You need to get some sleep now," Mrs. Claus instructed the children.

The kids turned into their sleeping berths and nodded off. After only a few minutes, Gus woke up screaming, "Left! Left! Turn Left!"

Everyone else woke up to his pleas. They were fully conscious when a loud boom came from the starboard side of the bow, shaking the entire ship.

"What was that?" Tiberius called out.

"It was a mine," Gus stated, regaining his composure.

"How do you know?" Lucia asked.

"The dolphins were warning me," Gus continued. "I thought I might be dreaming until I heard the sound."

"Mithra, check the hull for cracks," Tiberius commanded sleepily. "Gus, get your lifejacket and come on deck. Let's see what's out there."

Lucia joined Gus and Tiberius in the darkness. She lit a white candle that glowed like a flare, illuminating the entire ship. Even Mercury, at the perch of the mast, was visible. Up ahead, they could see a pod of dolphins.

"Follow them," Gus called out, as the dolphins swam to the port side of the bow.

Saturn was at the helm of the *Planet* and turned the mighty vessel to port. The dolphins then turned back to starboard and the ship followed, avoiding another encounter with the unseen danger lurking below the surface.

Recognizing the dolphins' purpose, Lucia lit four more candles and threw them with perfect aim to the other vessels. Saturn called out to the other captains to follow the dolphins in front of the ships. Each vessel now had a bright candle on its bow allowing each captain to follow the dolphins' course precisely.

Mithra returned to the deck and told Tiberius, "There are some cracks in the pykrete, but no water is coming in."

"What does that mean?" Ben asked nervously.

"It means we're fine," Mithra replied. "But we don't want to take another hit like that."

"Gus, can we follow the dolphins for the rest of the night?" Tiberius queried the animal expert.

"Yes," Gus replied. "The dolphins use sonar to locate objects, so they can find the mines even in total darkness."

"What if they swim off?" Ben asked.

"They won't," Gus responded.

The kids went back below. No one took off their lifejackets this time. They laid down, but sleeping proved elusive. The best they could hope for was to get a few hours of rest.

33

The team gathered around a table in the main cabin before first light on Christmas Eve. In the middle of the table was a pale brown object about the size of a bowling ball.

"What's that?" Josef asked pointing to the ball.

"This is a traditional Christmas pudding," Mrs. Claus announced to the group. "It's a special mix of ingredients that was specifically made for today. Each portion will give you enough energy to last the entire day.

"There's an old custom with Christmas pudding. Inside the pudding is a gold coin. Whomever gets the gold coin in their portion will accompany Santa on his ride tonight. Usually it's just the elves sharing the pudding, but they wanted one of you to get it."

Mrs. Claus sliced the steaming ball into eight pieces. At first, the kids just stared at the unidentifiable lump in front of them. After Josef took a bite and smiled, the others dug in. Despite its odd texture and spicy smell, it was quite delicious.

Everyone ate carefully, with most hoping they would get the coin. Toward the end of the meal, Tomo reached into her mouth and pulled out one gold coin. She immediately placed it on the table and slid it over to Nebo.

"Is that OK?" Tomo timidly asked Mrs. Claus.

"That's perfect," Mrs. Claus said with a smile. "I think it's the best way to start this day."

The kids returned to their cabins and put on specially tailored uniforms made for their mission. The boots and pants were black. They wore a tight shirt with traces of gold fiber running through a dark burgundy material. Over that was a black jacket with dark burgundy threads which gave the slightest hint of red. Their gloves and woolen hats matched the jacket.

As the team climbed to the deck in their matching uniforms, they barely recognized Mrs. Claus. Instead of the bright red cloak they were accustomed to seeing her in, she wore a dark one which matched their jackets. Her iron gray hair was pulled back and was barely visible under the hood that covered her head. She held a simple wooden staff in her hand which was slightly taller than she was. At the top of the staff was a small twig with two green leaves on it.

She pointed her staff toward the front of the vessel and the kids looked ahead. The increasing light of dawn revealed a towering black mountain in front of them. A heavy, dark smoke poured out of the peak. Everyone immediately recognized it as Baekdu Island.

The birds that had visited the day before were nowhere to be seen. Only the dolphins remained, still guiding the ships around the mines. As the ships got closer, the kids could make out charred tree stumps jutting out from the base of the mountain. The eerie reflection of the icy, dark sides resembled black onyx.

As the snowmen continued to steer the ships toward the imposing island, the kids began to tremble. The immensity of the island was more than anyone had imagined. It appeared as though it was a monument to the nightmares that lurk in the shadows of consciousness. With every mile of approach, more twisted features of the island revealed themselves.

A look through binoculars exposed piles of discarded metal strewn about the rocky shoreline. The weathered bones of a whale carcass were washed up at the edge of the water. Every element of the island was black, covered in a sooty blanket of ice.

"Well, I guess if hell froze over, this is what it would look like," Ben observed, trying to hide his fear.

Mrs. Claus looked at the children with pity. She now regretted the whole Naughty List idea.

"These kids are too young to be facing this challenge," Mrs. Claus thought to herself. "I should have come alone."

Feeling the fear growing in the group, Tiberius decided to give voice to it.

"I am afraid," Tiberius confided. "I am afraid of that island. From the depth of my soul, I fear that place.

"We *should* all fear it. It is a monolith of greed built to appease the worst desires in each of us. It's normal to be afraid of the darkest places.

"But remember, we are the light, my friends. We are the children that delight in miracles. We carry the wonder and hope of all creatures in our hearts. Let us shine our light on this dark place today. Let it be the Naughty Team that sends this darkness back to the shadows."

Ben pointed overhead as a dull hum suddenly filled the air. The mountain had released a squadron of drones.

"Launch the planes!" Ben took command as he yelled to Josef.

Instantly, one thousand toy planes took off in unison from the *Planet*. They flew in tight formation and began to execute the flight patterns Josef and Ben had worked on so diligently. They shot soft projectiles into the blades of the drones and a few of their aerial counterparts immediately crashed below.

The drones did not fire back. Instead, they dangled nets that caught some of the planes and together they fell into the sea. Josef rapidly reprogrammed the plane's flight patterns to gain altitude and swoop down on the drones. The sky was soon filled with hundreds of dogfights.

The toy planes pivoted and turned much faster than their opponents, using this advantage to shoot down the enemy. But the drones were able to rise and descend more quickly, catching many of the speedy planes in their dangling nets. Despite the toy planes' superior maneuvering, the outnumbered squadron was taking heavy losses.

All around the ships, drones and planes plummeted from the sky. After only fifteen minutes of fighting, there were just a few dozen planes left flying above the fleet. Fortunately, their gallant efforts had prevailed — there were even less drones remaining and they were still dropping from the fight.

"Looks like the planes are doing what we need them to," Ben cheered. "Too bad there won't be many left when we land on shore."

Having endured their first obstacle, the ships were now only two nautical miles from the island. Tiberius gave out the order to reduce sail. What had been the wharf for the delivery ships was now in ruins. The fleet would have to beach themselves to get ashore.

With one mile to go, the dolphins swam away from the fleet. The kids turned to Gus and he explained there were no mines left in their path. In his special way, Gus thanked the dolphins.

The snowmen moved gangways to the bow of each ship. Ben had the soldiers muster on deck and they began to play their marching music. The drums and fifes gave out a spectacular sound. The grand display made the kids extremely confident that their army could win any battle.

The *Planet* dropped to the back of the fleet. The *Constellation* was the first ship to hit the rocky shore. It landed with a thud, but took little damage. The toy soldiers marched down the gangways to become the first to step foot on the sinister island.

The *Galaxy*, the *Star*, and the *Comet* beached and offloaded their soldiers next. The landing went unchallenged and the soldiers formed ranks for the two-mile march to the base of the mountain. The objective was just beyond that, a large iron gate protecting the entrance to the factory.

Twenty thousand toy soldiers now advanced along the shores of the island. Their golden bayonets were angled forward, ready for attack. The soldiers' painted white pants and red jackets created a burst of color flooding over the blackened landscape. The bayonets glimmered in the light of the sun. Tiberius's analogy of an army of light invading the darkness was made real in this moment.

The wooden soldiers were just toys. They weren't capable of feeling emotions like the kids on the *Planet* were experiencing. The imposing landscape was irrelevant to them. They marched on without hesitation, without fear.

The *Planet* finally hit the shore and Mrs. Claus leaped off onto the icy black rocks. It was very slippery, but the metal spikes in her boots gave her a sure footing. The kids were impressed with her nimbleness.

Ben, Josef, Nebo, and Tomo followed. Ben was using the controller to guide the soldiers' movements. Josef kept his hand in his pocket, tightly gripping the USB drive he hoped would turn off the Eastern Industries defense network. Tomo had her climbing gear and was prepared to scale the mountain. Nebo followed the group quietly.

In the distance, a dark nemesis began to rise. Robots climbed out from behind the black rocks, directly into the path of the marching soldiers. These robots did not resemble toys. They were twice as tall as the soldiers and moved about on four legs. Above their legs, two arms waved about menacingly. The robots held a strong, silver sword in one arm and at the end of the other arm was a black pincer that resembled a crab's claw held aloft, opening and snapping shut.

The toy soldiers marched on without hesitation. As they neared the first line of the enemy, thousands more crab-like robots rose from the desolate landscape. The menacing mass of metal began to close into ranks as they prepared for the soldiers' arrival. The combined movements of the robots created a terrible sound of creaking metal and pounding footsteps.

The approaching soldiers lowered their bayonets and prepared to engage the enemy. They kept their steady pace right up to the point of contact. As the first toy soldiers readied for attack, their enemy stood over their heads and raised their silver swords. The golden bayonets rose up to deflect them, but the pincers swung around and snapped the bayonets with ease. The swords thrashed the helpless soldiers and the first line was lost.

Ben saw the futile effort and feverishly adjusted the formations of the soldiers. He grouped them tighter together as four soldiers took up the same space as one robot. He also adjusted the attack pattern to chop at the legs of the mechanical beasts.

His adjustments worked immediately. While one soldier had his bayonet stuck in a pincer, the soldier next to him was able to block or deflect the silver sword. A third soldier would then take a swing and chop off one of the robot's legs. They would repeat this until the robot was destroyed.

Up and down the line, the soldiers executed this strategy. The robots adjusted their own attack strategy and began to flail with both sword and pincer. The losses on both sides were heavy. The toy soldiers splintered apart from the destructive blows while the robots were dismembered by the soldiers' accurate swipes.

On the left side of the line, the robots had stopped the toy soldiers and were starting to push them back. Ben sent up reinforcements to bolster the weakened flank. No sooner were the reinforcements on their way when thousands of new robots rose from beyond the next hill and crashed into the middle of the line. The weight of numbers now pushed the middle of the line in and it looked like the robots would break the attack in half.

The fight was too large for Ben to properly control all aspects. As he shifted his focus to the imperiled middle of his line, toy soldiers came in from the right to attack the robots from behind. The soldiers now moved without explicit commands. They caught the robots by surprise and were able to quickly disable hundreds to reestablish the middle of the line.

The toy soldiers pressed forward again. The robots made them earn every foot of advance. Neither side seemed to tire. Throughout the duration of the battle, both sides attacked without pause. The soldiers slowly regained their momentum, pushing forward with greater speed.

After two hours of hard fighting, the din of battle began to quiet down. The toy soldiers had fought ahead for half a mile. Behind them lay thousands of destroyed robots and shattered toy soldiers.

Seven thousand toy soldiers had survived the fight and were now in formation at the base of the mountain. The main gate was just a few hundred yards further. Mrs. Claus and the four kids followed closely behind the soldiers, hopping over the carnage from the battle.

As they got close to the front line, Tomo quietly left the others and proceeded to the side of the mountain. The few remaining robots did not notice her. Within minutes, she was well above the battlefield and looked back at the ships washed up on the shore. Their webbing sparkled in the late morning sun.

Ben ordered the army up the mountain toward the main gate. He kept a few hundred soldiers back to protect their flank. Mrs. Claus joined the advancing soldiers and left Nebo, Josef and Ben with the rear guard. As she got ahead of the soldiers, a group of robots emerged from a crevice and headed directly for her. Toy soldiers, at Ben's command, tried to intercept the enemy, but the robots reached her first.

A flurry of swords and pincers swirled toward her, but Mrs. Claus did not retreat to the safety of the toy soldiers' formation. Instead, she lifted her staff high and brought it down hard on the robots, smashing away at the threatening machines. By the time the small detachment of soldiers arrived, she had finished off the pack of robots.

"Wow," Ben said to Josef. "She sure can fight. Who would've thought?"

"I wonder what else she can do. She probably has a few more surprises," Josef said admiringly.

A few thousand soldiers were busy cleaning up the rest of the robots as Mrs. Claus reached the gate of the factory. She looked around, but saw no way to open it. Before long, Ben, Nebo, and Josef had joined her.

Nebo took a long moment to inspect the entranceway. "This must be the door to Marduk," he said to no one in particular. He took a few steps forward, drew a deep breath and began to pound on it. The door bent in from the weight of his fists, but did not fall.

Suddenly, a darkness fell all around them. They looked up and saw so many drones flying out of the mountain that day seemed to turn to night. Like a big black cloud, the drones spread out above the victorious army and began to swoop down.

"Take cover!" Ben yelled.

The four ran from the gate and looked for a place to shield themselves. Nebo saw a little spot between two rocks and lifted a boulder over them to make a shelter as the drones approached.

Burning oil sacks could now be seen hanging from the bellies of the drones. As they flew over the wooden soldiers, they dropped their incendiaries. Ben and Josef tried to send out instructions ordering the soldiers to hide, but it appeared to be too late. Flames spread across the combat zone, catching most of the soldiers by surprise. They were helpless against this new terror.

As the fire melted the ice covering the landscape, a black river of waste flowed downhill toward the ships.

From the *Planet*, Tiberius looked in horror as the toy army was being incinerated. He watched fire rain down and burn everything on the ground. He scanned the battlefield and could not find Mrs. Claus nor the kids that were with her. Before long, the drones reset their focus and moved toward the helpless ships.

The few toy planes which had survived the first aerial battle were launched to meet the advancing squadron, but were severely outnumbered. The drones quickly overwhelmed the little aircraft and continued their approach toward the ships.

The snowmen saw the advancing threat and quickly climbed the rigging in an attempt to defend their post. They ripped the sails to pieces and used them to swat away at the drones. Many drones were destroyed by this courageous resistance, but as they crashed to the deck, their fiery payload damaged the ships all the same. The heat of the flames carried by the drones intensified as more drones clustered over the ships. The snowmen began to melt, but fought on for as long as they could. Eventually the volume of drones outweighed the effort of the snowmen and they ended up as puddles on the decks of the ships.

Mithra jumped from ship to ship, bravely dodging the fireballs, to collect the cosmic cores of the melted snowmen. Once her task was complete, she hid below deck on the *Planet* with Gus, Lucia, Hermey and Tiberius. The only good news was she had managed to retrieve every last core from the snowmen who had fought so valiantly.

Thump, thump, thump. The small crew listened as the fireballs continued to fall like hail on their frozen vessel. A wet pulpy drizzle began to rain down in the cabins as the fire took its toll on the pykrete. They were safe for now, but no one knew how long the pykrete could hold out during the assault.

"Tomo!" Gus exclaimed.

He jumped onto the smoldering deck and looked through binoculars at the mountain. Tomo was perched on a steep section of the mountain, just under a rock outcropping. The drones could not strike her from above, but he could see them flying near her position looking for an opportunity to attack.

"Please help her," Gus thought, directing his mental plea to the spiders.

Out of the bowels of the vessels, the spiders emerged without delay. They shot out webs and created a path which hovered above the flames. They charged from the ships, swarmed up the shore and weaved their way around the charred battlefield. Gus watched as the dark patch of spiders began a rapid ascent of the mountain toward Tomo.

He refocused the binoculars on Tomo right as a drone smacked into her arm. He flinched as she lost her grip and fell.

Tomo thought it was all over. She watched the rock outcropping above her fade away as she plummeted about fifty feet. To her great relief, she suddenly hit a soft surface and bounced upward. Fortunately, she did not rise very far. She realized she was stuck to an elastic substance. She had been caught in a spider's web.

Tomo was suspended in a giant cocoon surrounded by a cluster of spiders. They had spun their silk to make a protective web where she had landed. At the edge of the cocoon, there were flashes of fire, but nothing seemed to penetrate it. Like the others below her, she was temporarily safe, but she was uncertain if she'd be able to make any progress from this point forward.

The fire continued to pour down on the vessels. They had already lost two feet of the ten-foot-thick deck. The cabins were starting to fill with wood pulp and water. Mithra worked with Tiberius and Lucia to chisel out a channel for the pulpy water to drain. Based on the rate of melt, Mithra calculated they had until nightfall before the deck was completely melted away.

The assault by the Naughty Team had been neutralized. Three separate groups, huddling from danger in different locations, were all that remained of the stalled mission. Although everyone felt very alone in the moment, no one felt defeated.

The fires that raged across the island continued to melt away its black coating of ice, and the rocks and tundra that had been buried, were once again visible. Despite the calamity of the past six hours, the island already seemed to be coming out of the dark shadow of Eastern Industries. Above the fiery cleansing, a few birds began to circle and take notice of the change to their former breeding grounds.

From his shelter, Nebo glared at the gate, waiting for another chance to pound his way through to free his sacred Marduk. Ben was still getting readings back from a few toy soldiers who had survived the fire bombs. Joseph clutched his precious USB stick, hoping he would find a terminal to activate his code.

In the cocoon, Tomo was sure she could reach the unprotected passageways at the top of the mountain. She felt Gus's presence there with her.

In the bowels of the melting *Planet*, Gus was relieved to hear from the spiders that Tomo was safe — at least for the time being. Mithra earnestly believed the team may yet have a chance to save the day. The barometer was dropping. A huge storm was brewing and its first snowflakes were descending upon the island. Mithra thought to herself, "The snowmen will rise again."

34

Mr. Bentley was up late on the night of the twenty-third. He had not slept much since his farm had been converted into a toy soldier factory. He settled down into his chair and, as usual, turned on the television. Satellite images of Baekdu Island were on every channel. The headlines blared, "The Battle for Christmas is Lost."

He stared at the television as a few grainy images of the conflict flashed on the screen. Even though the images were taken from space, he could clearly see the aerial dogfight and the ships landing on shore. He could make out the toy soldiers marching to the mountain and a dark army emerging to challenge them. Finally, he watched with concern as the cloud of drones dropped fire on the island and ships.

No one knew what had happened in the hours since the storm had settled over the island and created a whiteout. Satellite images were the only source of real-time information as no nation was willing to risk war by violating the island's sovereignty. Mr. Bentley listened to reporters hopelessly talking about how something needed to be done to help the kids.

Mr. Bentley went into the kitchen to share the news with his wife.

"That's great," Mrs. Bentley replied. "That means they made it to the island and are about to rescue Santa Claus."

"They're at the island alright," Mr. Bentley replied in shock. "I don't understand what's so great about our daughter being attacked by drones."

"They're just drones," Mrs. Bentley said, trying to cheer up her husband. "You said a storm is covering up the island. That means the fire they are dropping won't hurt the ships. It will also allow Mithra to keep making snowmen, no matter what else happens to them."

Mr. Bentley did not agree. He turned and walked back to the television in the living room while shaking his head. Whenever life gave his wife lemons, she always found a way to make lemonade. He just hoped that would be true for Mithra as well.

Mrs. Bentley walked outside her house to check on the Kringles. As soon as she did, a crowd of reporters ambushed her. They fired off many questions about the satellite images that had the world wondering what was unfolding at Baekdu Island.

"I don't know anything more than you do," she replied to the questions. "I'm confident we will all know the details by Christmas."

She brushed by the horde of reporters and entered the barn. Rudi was sitting at a bench, whittling away at another toy soldier.

"How many have you made?" Mrs. Bentley asked.

"A few hundred," Rudi replied with a tired smile. "But with all the help that has arrived, we have over ten thousand here."

Across the world, millions of toy soldiers had been created. People loved making the toys, especially the older folks in retirement homes. Woodworkers that had been idle for years, suddenly found themselves involved in a project they hoped would bring smiles to the faces of children all over the world. They loved the opportunity to engage in their old craft. They felt they were doing their part in helping to save Christmas, like the kids in the North Pole Fleet.

As the morning wore on, more and more people arrived at the Bentley farm. They were sad, and worried, after viewing the video of the battle and wanted to do something, but did not know what. So they congregated on the farm and did what came instinctively — they began to sing Christmas carols.

The image of complete strangers singing together in the bucolic setting of the Bentley farm, touched a nostalgic nerve across the world. People got caught up in the beauty and simplicity of it and began to gather and create spontaneous choirs. No one really knew what to make of the battle for Baekdu Island, but joining together and singing the carols made them feel better. Raising their voices to the heavens gave people a feeling they were part of something bigger than themselves. They felt connected to others, and experienced an expanding happiness within, because of the newly formed bond.

Around the globe, bells began to ring from hillside to village. People climbed towers that had been deserted for years and the old bells tolled once again. Cars were abandoned at the side of the road as the occupants dashed to take part in the festivities.

In cities, bands of carolers streamed through the streets. People left their apartments and readily joined the impromptu parades. After a short time, the parades turned into a march of thousands. The sound of drums and trumpets could be heard along with the chiming bells. The chorus of voices soared above the din as every person opened their heart and swayed to the rhythm of the melodic carols.

Many animals took notice of the unusual activity and participated in their own way. Dogs barked and followed behind the revelers. Birds flew above the crowds while squeaking and squawking. Spiders cast silvery webs on many Christmas trees and decorations.

Anyone who was out on Christmas Eve felt as though the whole earth was vibrating with one wish. The carolers, the drummers, the trumpeters, the woodcarvers and the many Santa Clauses all seemed to long for the same thing. They wanted Christmas to be saved. They wanted the Naughty Team to reach into that mountain of darkness and pull out the one miracle that made Christmas so special. They wanted Santa back.

35

In a valley in northern Mongolia; Batu, Annushka and the seven other reindeer riders were sitting around a fire preparing for battle. They fixated on the flames and visualized their ride through the sky. They did not know what type of enemy they would face, but they pictured themselves maneuvering on their mounts and attacking from every direction.

The reindeer knew the battle should have started by now and they were anxious to leave. They snorted and pushed at the young Mongols, but they would not be persuaded to depart. The reindeer took off and landed again, but the riders did not budge. They sat passively, focused on the fire.

The valley was absolutely silent. The riders stood up in unison and opened their hands to the skies. With palms facing up, they petitioned the skies for aid. In the distance, a bell started to chime. The ringing grew louder as the riders began to move their hands in small circles. Far away voices sang songs of the old heroes and the horses that had carried their riders into battle for many generations.

As the valley filled with music, the riders turned to Batu. He looked intently into each rider's eyes before yelling, "Morindoo!"

The kids immediately grabbed their bows and jumped onto the backs of the reindeer. Annushka hollered, "Yavyaa!"

In an instant, the reindeer and their riders had charged into the sky. They flew low over the mountains and heard bells echoing from each valley they passed through. They swooped over cities in southern Russia and noticed the sounds of caroling. In a short time, they were out over the Pacific Ocean.

As the reindeer neared Baekdu Island, eagles, albatrosses, and many other birds of prey swarmed behind the sky warriors. The reindeer huffed and snorted as they prepared to meet the enemy. Their heads bobbed up and down, looking like they were ready for a mighty fight. Their riders rode with ease and focus despite the undulations of the reindeer.

They flew up over the dense clouds of the storm that had settled over Baekdu Island. The sinking sun, low in the west, cast a golden glow which was mirrored in the clouds.

The reindeer angled down, pierced the clouds and entered a foggy, gray void. The young Mongols pulled arrows from their quivers and drew back hard on their bows. The reindeer continued on their rapid descent. The gray darkened to charcoal as the sky cavalry sunk deep into the heart of the storm.

They burst through the bottom of the cloud into a blizzard. Below them was Baekdu Island, half covered in snow and half on fire. The flames reflected in the snow, making the whole sky seem as if it was ablaze.

As the reindeer emerged from the heavens, the black drones could be seen everywhere. Tens of thousands of them swarmed over the flames, still dropping their fire onto the helpless survivors. Their payloads could be seen hitting the ground, creating a brief flash before joining the sea of fire that was still raging. The Mongol riders guided the reindeer into their attack formation.

Batu cried out, "Clear eyes, full hearts, can't lose!"

Arrows began to rain down on the bringers of fire, but the blunt tipped arrows had little impact. They simply bounced off the center of the drones. Annushka adjusted her aim quickly and launched a shot at one of the rotors on a drone. As it began to plummet, the other riders adopted her strategy. Within seconds, countless black drones had met their demise. But the top of the mountain spewed forth more drones, crowding the sky with the automated monsters. The riders did not flinch. Arrows flew in all directions and each one seemed to find its target. But despite the devastation the reindeer riders inflicted on the enemy, the number of drones continued to increase.

The reindeer flew higher, taking their riders above the drones, but the drones were quick to catch up. However, as they approached the edge of the storm clouds, out of nowhere, a massive flock of birds gushed out and joined the fray. At first, the young Mongols did not know what the birds were doing. It became clear when a Steller's sea eagle grabbed a drone with its talons and smashed the center with its powerful beak. The eagle dropped the damaged drone and it fell from the fight.

Thousands of birds joined the reindeer riders in the fight above Baekdu Island. The drones fought back, but their numbers began to shrink. Instead of fire, drones now poured down from the firmament. The mountain had released everything it contained as the battle above Baekdu Island raged.

36

Despite the commotion in the snowy sky, the Naughty Team was buttoned down safely in their makeshift shelters on Baekdu Island. On the *Planet*, only Gus had noticed the aerial battle when it began. He was the first to emerge from below deck. The reindeer had announced they were about to engage the enemy. When the birds joined the fight, Gus detected their chatter about taking back their island.

The fire had stopped raining down and the deck was only half melted when Gus called for the others to come up and watch the fight. Tiberius, Mithra, and Lucia climbed up to see the wonder for themselves. Hermey was still in shock over the battle and could not muster the courage to leave the safety of the cabin.

Above the island, golden reindeer flew in all directions. From each one, an explosion of arrows seemed to shoot out in every direction. Drones fell on all sides. Everyone cheered the heroic deeds they were witnessing overhead.

Mithra only took a quick look before retrieving the precious cosmic dust cores. She placed the first one in the vapor diffusion chamber and within a minute, she had produced a snowflake core ready for building. Rolling the core into a small snowball, she enthusiastically proclaimed to the others that it was time to rebuild the snowmen!

Tiberius ran below and tugged at Hermey.

"Grandpa, we need your help," Tiberius pleaded to the suddenly old-looking man. "Please Grandpa, we need to rebuild the snowmen and move along the shore with them."

"I can't, Tiber," Hermey muttered. "I'm too scared to move."

Tiberius pulled on Hermey and got him to his feet. He continued to press the issue. "I know you're scared, Grandpa. I am too."

Hermey looked at his courageous grandson and saw his fierce countenance and the determination in his eyes. He squeezed Tiberius's hand and allowed the boy to guide him up to the deck. Hermey took in the wonder of the continuing battle. The reindeer sparkled in the orange glow that peeked out from the trailing edge of the storm. He saw the brave Mongol riders performing acrobatic motions while precisely shooting their arrows into the mass of drones. He noticed the birds swooping down and doing their part. He felt empowered by the bravery surrounding him.

The fight dropped from the clouds and ended up right over the heads of the trapped army. The tide had turned in the skies. The hunters were now the hunted. The young Mongols continued to fire arrows into the blades of the drones, rarely missing a shot.

The last of the snowstorm put out most of the flames on the island. As the battle in the sky wound down, the setting sun gleamed from the horizon. A warm glow illuminated the snow covered island. Many of the birds that had fought with the reindeer riders were able to see their old perches for the first time in months. They slipped away from the fracas, en masse, and returned to their welcoming mountainside abodes.

The reindeer riders broke out of their formation and chased the retreating drones. The little black targets tried to flee from their golden pursuers, but the effort proved futile.

What had been a highly pitched battle was now just a turkey shoot. After a few more minutes, it was all over.

In celebration, the reindeer proudly carried their Mongol riders alongside the ships to wave to the cheering kids onboard the *Planet*. They then flew toward Mrs. Claus and saluted as she emerged from her shelter. They climbed higher and circled the island a few times, making sure there were no more drones to take on.

Satisfied the enemy had been eliminated, the reindeer set a course to return to their ancestral home in Mongolia. They needed to return their riders safely before heading straight to the North Pole. They anticipated a long night ahead.

"Let's go. We haven't a moment to spare," Mithra urged. She handed out the newly formed snowballs to the others and they headed down the gangway and onto the charred shore. Within a hundred yards, they found a patch of fresh snow and began to roll the snowballs into six-foot-high snowmen.

"Hello Universe!" Jasper shouted out as he came to life again with a big smile on his face. He looked around and asked, "Is it over? Who won?"

Tiberius pointed up and Jasper realized the skies were clear of danger. Within minutes, Hermey finished Saturn, Gus rolled up Mercury and the snowmen immediately engaged in lively chatter. Tiberius instructed them to go back to the ship to get more snowballs from Mithra who had reformed the remaining core snowflakes. In a short time, all fifty snowmen had been reanimated and were ready to rejoin the mission.

The snowmen scooped up their creators from the Naughty Team and started off toward the others. They trudged through freshly fallen snow for the first mile, but the snow soon gave way to bare rock and smoldering soldiers. Everything around them was in ruins. Smoke hovered over the barren field of destruction. It was eerily quiet.

"I hope we have enough force left to get into the factory," Tiberius said to the snowmen.

As he looked up toward the gate on the side of the mountain, he noticed the imposing figure of Mrs. Claus standing above the shelter she had been hiding under. Her dark cloak matched the grim battlefield around her. Nebo, Ben, and Josef were soon standing next to her. They immediately noticed the piles of destroyed drones that were a new addition to the carnage around them.

Tiberius ran up to Mrs. Claus and gave her a big hug. He repeated the gesture with the others.

"I'm so glad to see you guys," Tiberius happily greeted them. "Are there *any* soldiers left?"

Ben looked down at his controller and hit the button calling the toy soldiers to muster. Everyone waited in anticipation to see if there were any brave toys left to answer the call.

They knew it was unlikely any wooden creation could have survived the inferno. But to everyone's great surprise, black hats began to rise all around them. It was a sight to behold. The toy soldiers stood up tall and soon an army of red jackets was visible. They were charred and chipped, but they indeed rose again. They were a defiant hope against the destruction that had been assumed to be their graveyard. Hundreds were now upright and marching to form a line in front of the gate.

The team's spirits lifted with the resurrection of the toy soldiers. Ben flashed a broad smile and said, "I can't believe anything survived that fire. I'd fight a thousand battles with these tough soldiers by my side."

Nebo stomped toward the entrance. His usually placid expression had turned fierce. He walked straight to the gate and lifted his arm to strike it. But to everyone's surprise, just before his strong fist found its target, the gate opened.

"Get out of the way!" Mrs. Claus shouted as she ran up to the gate herself.

The soldiers broke out of their orderly march and charged to the gate without being commanded to do so. Ben looked down at his controller and was shocked.

"I did not do that," he said. "The soldiers are acting on their own."

Out of the gate, various types of robots emerged that were of different shapes and sizes. They were painted in bright yellow and white. They had a torso, two legs and two arms that had assorted devices attached. Some arms resembled tools and claws. It was apparent to the team that these robots had been designed to work inside the factory.

"They must be getting desperate," Ben concluded. "These robots look like they're toy builders, not defense machines."

Regardless of their design, they were menacing. As soon as they marched out of the gate, Mrs. Claus engaged them in combat. The soldiers were by her side with their golden bayonets lowered for battle.

"Tomo!" Josef shouted, looking up.

Robots had emerged from a gate above her. They were the same type as the original battle robots the soldiers had encountered on the ground and were advancing quickly to her position. Josef ran to the base of the mountain and began to climb toward Tomo. Tiberius ordered the Constellation and Galaxy snowmen to join Josef; Gus followed.

The rest of the snowmen rushed into the battle in front of the main gate. They picked up rocks and hurled them at the robots that were swarming out. The team was now engaged again on two fronts.

Hermey and Lucia stayed back with Mithra as Tiberius also charged into the melee. The new ground action was smaller, but no less fierce than the previous engagement. Mrs. Claus swung her heavy staff into robot after robot and knocked them over. The toy soldiers hacked away at the dangerous arms with their bayonets. Tiberius and Ben guided a few dozen soldiers to surround the horde of robots and attack them from their flank. Nebo stood back from the fight and observed the action.

Up on the mountain, Orion was the first snowman to reach Tomo. He arrived at the cocoon just as the robots descended to the perch it was hanging from. Orion tried to throw them off the perch, but the robots overpowered him, tossing him off. More snowmen reached the robots and halted their progress as the two sides pounded away at each other.

On the ground, Mithra hurried over to the pile of snow that had previously been Orion. She sucked out the core from the pile and created another core snowflake. Hermey and Lucia rolled Orion back into shape and he quickly scrambled up the mountainside once again. This process was repeated many times as the snowmen were hurled by the robots. They were not winning the fight, but they were buying precious time for Gus and Josef to get Tomo out of the cocoon before it became her tomb.

Gus heard the spiders talking about the danger outside the cocoon. Countless voices bounced around his mind as the spiders debated what to do. Their debate ended when a robot's sword knifed through the top of the cocoon. Immediately, the spiders spilled out of the opening and began to wrap the robot in a web that immobilized it.

The hole opened further and Tomo spilled out, disoriented. She fell about five feet before the strong hand of Josef grasped hers and held on. She looked up and smiled.

"Took you long enough to get here," she joked with him. "I thought I was going to spend Christmas all alone."

Josef swung Tomo up to his ledge where she was able to obtain her own grip. She looked down and was surprised to see Gus.

"You climbed up here too?" she blurted. "I guess you two were holding back when we trained at the North Pole."

"No," Gus replied through heavy breaths. "We just climb better when we have a really good reason to do it; like saving you."

Above them, the snowmen were still battling robots. Both were being flung off the mountain, but the snowmen were returning to the skirmish within minutes of falling, thanks to Mithra and her builders down below.

"If we can get by these robots, I think we have a good chance of gaining entry inside," Josef said, pointing up to the gate. "Once I locate a terminal, I should be able to shut the whole place down."

Tomo assessed the situation and plotted a clear path up to the gate. It was about one hundred yards to their left but there was no way for them to climb over to it. She pointed and asked, "Gus, can the spiders help us get to that spot right there?"

"I'll ask," Gus responded.

He connected into the spiders' thoughts and made the request. Within seconds, they had scurried halfway toward the destination. Next, they effortlessly climbed up a ninety-degree slope that would have been impossible for any human to scale, even Tomo. From there, the spiders quickly spun a thick, silk rope, attached it to the rock face and guided it toward Tomo.

Tomo gripped the rope, swung across the gap and secured a good hold on the other side. Gus and Josef followed suit and the three now had clear access to the upper gate. Tomo led their ascent and threw down safety lines to help the two boys follow her.

Far below, the robots were being worn down by the superior fighting of the toy soldiers so they adjusted their tactics and headed straight for Mrs. Claus. She was soon overwhelmed by the large concentration of robots. As she was fighting them off one of them snuck up from behind and raised its massive arm to smash her. Before the arm lowered,

Nebo's hand grabbed it and the robot wheeled around to face him. The robot smashed down on Nebo with its other arm, but Nebo maintained his grasp. He stood steadfast while holding the robot's arm. Tiberius and Ben yelled from their flanking position to slam the robot, but Nebo would not.

In a flash, Mrs. Claus pivoted toward Nebo and buried her staff directly into the robot's head. The robot fell to the ground. Tiberius and Ben arrived at the scene from their flanking position.

"Why didn't you just smash it, Nebo?" Tiberius screamed, still filled with the rage of battle.

"I cannot fight," Nebo replied. "I am a peaceful being. I cannot harm anything."

"They're trying to harm us," Ben chided the strong boy. "It's not even a living creature. I thought you were going to battle to get Marduk or something like that. I haven't seen you do anything but pound on a door."

"That is all I came here to do," Nebo replied calmly. He did not seem to be affected by the scorn the boys were heaping on him.

"Leave him alone," Mrs. Claus said sternly. "We each have a part to play in this battle and Nebo must follow his own path."

"His path is to be a coward," Ben said harshly.

"There is too much violence in this world," Mrs. Claus lectured. "It's easy to meet force with force. The more difficult choice is to stick to one's values. Nebo is living the life he has chosen and he doesn't allow outside pressures to change him into something different. The world would be a better place if more people followed their hearts rather than react to what is going on around them."

"Remember," Mrs. Claus added with a smile. "I'm very close to a strong, peaceful man myself."

Ben suddenly saw the gentle boy for who he was. Mrs. Claus's words had made an impact on him so he turned to

Nebo and apologized. "I'm sorry. I was wrong to call you a coward."

The robot army was now split in half and the toy soldiers were having an easy time finishing them off. The soldiers had suffered only light losses. Those that had survived lined up in front of the gate, ready to march in. Lucia ran up to Mrs. Claus and the boys and gave them each a candle.

"You'll need these in there," she said peering into the darkness beyond the gate.

As the battle on the ground wound down, the snowmen on the mountain managed to gain the upper hand. They noticed the three climbers had made it to the entrance of the upper gate. In a powerful surge of effort, the snowmen tossed the remaining robots from the ledge and began to climb up to the kids. At the bottom of the mountain, Lucia handed Jasper three candles as he began his ascent to join them.

The snow had stopped falling on Baekdu Island. The sun had set and cast a soft, purple glow on the snow-covered terrain. Simultaneously, at each gate, Mrs. Claus and Tomo lit a candle, took a deep breath and entered the Eastern Industries factory.

37

The toy soldiers had hurried ahead of Mrs. Claus into the dark tunnel at the base of the mountain. She and the boys followed closely behind with candles illuminating the way. Nebo placed a large boulder in the entrance to prevent the gate from closing. The snowmen stayed outside the entrance, wary of any more surprises.

The group cautiously stepped further into the dark tunnel. There were no doors on either side. After two hundred yards, they came to a large, open room. Conveyor belts crisscrossed the space at various levels. The kids glanced up at the ceiling which was over two hundred feet above their heads. They knew they were in the heart of the factory.

All the toy producing machines were strangely idle and partially assembled toys were strewn about the floor. There was an uneasy feeling to the whole place. From the outer walls of the great room, the sounds of machines could be heard. Abruptly, the conveyor belts that surrounded the would-be rescuers sprang to life. Despite the commotion, the only light in the room besides the candles came from the flashing indicators on the various machines.

The production lines rolled, but there were no factory robots left so the toys just fell to the floor. Mrs. Claus ordered the toy soldiers to surround her and the kids. They obeyed once again, lowering their golden bayonets and anticipating a fight. But there was no movement; nothing approached the vigilant soldiers. For an intolerable amount of time, the machines just churned on and on.

Mrs. Claus motioned with her staff to move to the far side of the room toward a large door. The toy soldiers continued to envelop the group, as they made their way. Without warning, a dozen soldiers at the front of the group disappeared from sight. Ben looked ahead and saw a trap door that had opened in the factory floor. Another door behind the group opened and more soldiers fell through.

"Get away from the ends of the conveyer belts," Ben yelled.

They tried to run, but it was too late. The door beneath Ben's feet opened and he began to slide into the darkness. Tiberius slid next to him. Mrs. Claus thrust her staff toward the boys and they were able to take hold of it.

Mrs. Claus started to lose her footing. She had nothing to hold onto. Nebo laid flat at the edge of the opening and reached out to Mrs. Claus. His mighty hand found hers, and in one motion he adeptly lifted all three out of the chute and onto a slow moving conveyer belt.

"Thanks, big guy," Ben said with a warm smile. He was relieved he hadn't discovered where the chutes went.

"Let's find a safer spot to chat," Nebo suggested, flashing his own smile.

Doors burst open beneath the ends of every conveyor belt now. Nebo jumped from one belt to another, reaching under and flinging the toy soldiers up to safety. By the time he was done, only a few dozen remained. The rest had been lost down the chutes.

The machines kept grinding on. As the group continued along the conveyer belts, they had to sidestep the partially built toys moving along the line. Unfortunately, this included a few toy soldiers that had been picked up by the automated builders and destroyed.

"We must move up," Nebo said pointing to the ceiling. Above the group was a walkway adjacent to an office that overlooked the factory floor. At that moment, it seemed like the safest place to take refuge.

Everyone began to run up the conveyer belts, dodging the machines that were designed to cut, polish, and paint. They jumped from one belt to another, as they made their way to the walkway.

Tiberius stopped on a stationary edge of one of the belts and looked back. He could not see Mrs. Claus and was worried they had left her behind. "Mrs. Claus! Where are you?"

"Up here," Mrs. Claus said as she appeared on top of one of the big machines. "Stop dawdling and get your butt up here."

Mrs. Claus peeked into the office as a figure dressed in a dark suit retreated out a back door. Ben, Nebo, and finally Tiberius, caught up to her.

"I think I just saw Mr. Kim," Mrs. Claus said. "He was in the office but just left through that door in the back."

As the group turned to investigate, metallic blue robots silently appeared on the walkway. These robots were a type that Mrs. Claus and the kids had not yet come across. They were six feet tall, had arms and legs, and moved like humans. The robots had armor protecting their core and were much faster than the ones outside of the factory.

The robots glared at the kids and Mrs. Claus through their glowing red visors as they blocked the only way into the office. The toy soldiers were too far below to help and besides, the three-foot-high warriors were unable to climb the conveyor belts. The blue robots leaped from the office walkway onto the conveyor belts, heading straight for the team.

As the first robot reached their position, Mrs. Claus swung her staff, scoring a direct hit. The robot took no damage and was only slowed for a moment. Ben looked behind and saw a better place to defend from. They retreated across two conveyor belts and huddled on top of an assembly machine in the corner of the great room. Nebo smashed the last conveyor belt they had used so the robots could not follow their route.

They were safe for the moment, but the robots were already swinging around to the sides to approach from another direction. Their swift movement struck fear into the hearts of the kids. Mrs. Claus resolutely stared down the assailants and braced for another round.

A robot on their left ripped off a large piece of metal from one of the assembly machines and heaved it toward them. Mrs. Claus swung with her staff and just barely managed to change the direction enough to make it miss hitting its target.

The robots surrounded the team and began to approach from two sides. A pair of robots leaped onto the bottom of the assembly machine the team was on and began to climb up. Mrs. Claus hit one repeatedly with her staff, but only slowed the progress of the evil tormentor. They were trapped. There was nowhere left to go.

38

Further up the mountain, Tomo, Josef, and Gus had made some headway upon entering the large upper gate. Just beyond the doorway, the path ended and they observed thousands of empty bays that had previously held drones.

The hangar was immense. Row after row of drone bays filled the dark room. They were tightly grouped with just enough space for the drones to fly through. In the center of the hangar, was one large open area, at the back of which was a full-size, black helicopter.

Tomo pulled out some climbing line and they rappelled about a hundred feet down to the floor of the hangar. They fanned out across the bays and searched for an entrance into the heart of the factory.

"Over here," Gus called out.

He was standing below the helicopter. Above him, a light burst out of a door as it opened. A shadow moved against the opposite wall.

"I think someone's getting into that helicopter," Gus said pointing to the light. "Look at the gate."

Josef looked over at the entrance at the far side of the room, well above their heads. The spiders were starting to spin a web across the open gate.

"What are those spiders doing?" Josef asked Gus.

Gus focused his thoughts back to the spiders and said, "They're making sure no more drones can leave."

Above them, the helicopter's rotors began to whirl. A strong breeze hit the kids below. Tomo immediately jumped onto a row of empty bays and began to climb. Gus and Josef followed, but were too slow to keep up.

The wind felt like a hurricane as the rotor spun faster and faster. The helicopter lifted off its platform and flew toward the gate.

"Take cover," Gus yelled to the spiders. His thoughts echoed the command.

The helicopter sliced right through the weakest part of the web and left the hangar. The snowmen ducked as it whirled right above their heads. The helicopter turned to the southwest and quickly flew away from the island.

By the time Josef and Gus reached the helicopter launch pad, Tomo called out to them from inside an adjoining room, "Hurry, this is the defense control room."

The room had monitors all along a large wall. In the center of the room was a seat for just one person. The kids looked at the images on some of the monitors, but many of them showed nothing but darkness. One monitor displayed the shredded spider web the helicopter had just flown through. A few showed the candlelit factory floor.

"Oh no!" Tomo exclaimed, pointing to a monitor that showed the robots advancing toward Mrs. Claus and the kids. "We have to do something."

Josef jumped into the command chair in front of the main control terminal. He inserted his thumb drive and began typing furiously.

"We're lucky that person left in such a hurry," Josef said. "He left this terminal unlocked."

"You have to save them," Tomo pleaded.

"Working on it," Josef said while focused on the screen in front of him.

He navigated through the main control screens and found the factory controls. He shut off the conveyer belts on the automated machines, but the robots continued to close in.

"I just uploaded the virus I made for the defense systems," Josef said, gesturing to his thumb drive in the machine. "I hope it works quickly. There's no other way to shut down the defenses."

The three kids anxiously stared at the monitor. The robots had reached the team and Mrs. Claus was swinging her staff to keep them just out of reach. More were heading in.

Gus heard a door open and looked to the back of the room.

"Security breach," five metallic blue robots said in unison as they entered.

They advanced toward Josef's command chair. He ripped his drive out of the main computer and ran to the edge of the hangar opening.

"What now?" he asked Tomo.

"I don't know," Tomo responded. "Can the spiders help us?"

"There's no time," Gus answered as a robot grabbed his arm and restrained him.

Tomo and Josef were also caught by the robots who began to march them out of the control room.

"Where are you taking us?" Tomo demanded, trying to wriggle free.

"Do not resist," the robot responded. "We are going up the elevator to the detention center on the..."

All at once, the robots froze in place. The lights in the room flickered for a moment and then went black. Josef wrestled out of the motionless robot's grip and pushed it over.

"It worked!" Josef exclaimed. "The defense systems are shutting down!"

In the toy factory, just as the robots were about to pounce on Mrs. Claus and the boys, they froze. Tiberius and Ben pushed the disabled robots off the conveyer belts and they smashed onto the factory floor.

"Hurray!" Tiberius yelled, giving Ben a high five.

"He must have done it," Ben said, referring to Josef.

Nebo led the team up to the factory office. They looked around using Lucia's candles to illuminate the area. Nothing seemed to be working. They went through a backdoor and found themselves standing in front of an elevator. It too was disabled.

"I guess we'll be walking," Tiberius said pointing to the stairs.

The group ran up dozens of flights of stairs before coming to a sign that read, "Defense Control Room." They opened the door and found Tomo, Gus, and Josef combing through files in the room.

"I've never been happier to see anyone in my life," Tomo said to the new arrivals.

"Where's Santa?" Mrs. Claus asked, adding, "Have you seen Mr. Kim? He was down in the factory office a few minutes ago."

"We just saw someone leave in a helicopter, that must've been him," Gus replied.

"Nice work, Josef," Ben praised, resting his hand on the computer whiz.

"Thanks," Josef replied. "The system went down before I had a chance to locate Santa. We're going through the paper files now to see if there is a blueprint or something. The robots mentioned a detention center."

Suddenly, the lights flickered on and off. Some of the monitors lit up for a moment before going blank again.

"What's happening?" Tiberius asked.

"I think the systems are trying to come back online," Josef said. "They're more resilient than anything I've ever seen."

"How much time do we have?" Ben asked Josef.

"I don't know," Josef replied, adding, "Some equipment is already starting to reboot."

"We need to get Santa as soon as possible and seal off this mountain," Tiberius implored.

"Found them!" Josef exclaimed. "I found the floor plans. The detention area is near the top of the mountain."

"I thought so," Mrs. Claus replied. "Do you see a way out from there?"

"It looks like the exhaust vent runs next to the stairwell," Josef declared, still studying the plans. "There's an access door at the top of the stairway that leads to it."

"Any other openings in the mountain?" Tiberius asked.

"Yes," Josef answered, pointing to the plans. "Here and here."

The gates he indicated were low on the mountain. The first was about a thousand feet from the main gate and the other was down by the old docks.

"Tiberius, Ben, go back to the factory floor and retrieve as many functioning toy soldiers as you can," Mrs. Claus commanded. "Bring them outside to join forces with the snowmen to block the main gate with ice and rocks – whatever they can find.

"Tomo, Gus," Mrs. Claus continued. "Go out the hangar gate and seal that off. Leave enough room for Josef to get out..."

"Let's go Ben," Tiberius said urgently. "Once we seal the main gate, we'll split up and close off the other gates."

Tiberius and Ben ran back to the stairwell and jumped down. Mrs. Claus and Nebo entered the stairwell behind the two boys and went in the opposite direction. Tomo, Gus, and Josef were again alone in the defense control room.

The main terminal flashed back to life. Josef began to type commands into the various screens that were coming back online.

"Go now," Josef said to Tomo. "I can probably delay the systems for a few more minutes, but those robots will be back online shortly."

Josef pointed at the disabled robots. The monitors were buzzing back to life and camera images were available again. One monitor showed Ben and Tiberius running around the factory floor guiding toy soldiers into the tunnel that led to the main, lower gate.

Tomo and Gus moved out to the hangar and climbed across the drone bays, leaving a climbing line for Josef to use during his own departure. Gus sent the spiders into the control room and they began to spin webs around the frozen defense robots.

"That should buy him a few more minutes in there," Gus said proudly.

The robots in the defense control room started to wake. At first, their movements were twitchy and uncoordinated. Within a minute, they were fully functioning.

"Security breach," the muffled sound of the robots announced.

They began to push and pull at the webbing but could not move. In an instant, saws snapped out of their left arms and began to cut away the webs. The spiders rushed out of the room, followed by Josef.

Josef used the line Tomo had left behind to climb across the drone bays. He arrived at the upper gate which was now almost completely blocked by ice and rocks. There was just enough room for him to crawl through. Once outside, the snowmen filled up the remaining space. The gate was sealed.

Josef looked below. Tiberius and Ben had made it out and split up with each leading a small group of soldiers and snowmen around the bottom of the mountain. They had sealed the main gate and were moving to the next.

"Hurry," Josef yelled down. "The systems are back online."

At the top of the mountain, Mrs. Claus and Nebo reached the end of the staircase. Above them was the access door to the exhaust vent. They exited the stairwell into a large, round room. The area had six armored doors, each with a small window in the center. Two disabled robots were standing motionless in front of the first door.

"Santa?" Mrs. Claus cried out.

"In here," came a faint reply from behind the guarded door.

"Stand back," Nebo ordered as he lifted his fist high.

He brought it down onto the door with such force that the whole mountain shook. Although they were spread across the island, the entire Naughty Team knew at once that Nebo had found the door he had been looking for. A series of loud booms rang out from inside the mountain.

Nebo pounded on the door again and again until it finally fell over. Mrs. Claus ran past him into the small cell. At the far end, stood Santa. They fell into each other's arms. As they separated, Mrs. Claus looked him up and down checking for any signs of distress.

"You look better than I expected," a surprised Mrs. Claus observed.

"Well, it's the first time in centuries that I've rested during the season. I may be getting too old for this," Santa said with a smile. "Ho, ho, ho."

Before Mrs. Claus could reply, the robots in the hallway began to stir.

"Let's get going," Nebo calmly suggested.

Mrs. Claus returned to the round room and opened the door of an empty cell. Nebo helped her drag the wakening guards in, and they locked the door. Soon the robots were pounding against the door, but noise was the only result.

The trio entered the stairwell. Nebo lifted Mrs. Claus high enough to open the access door to the vent. She climbed up, followed by Santa and then Nebo. Behind them, the sound of robots climbing the stairs could be heard.

They moved through a short access tunnel that led to the main exhaust vent for the factory. As they travelled to the end of the tunnel, they could see the light at the top of the exhaust vent, but there was no way for them to climb the steep vertical sides and exit. The sound of the approaching robots grew louder.

Mrs. Claus looked into the staircase and saw them making their way into the access tunnel. She pushed them downward with her staff. "We can't turn back," she said to Nebo and Santa. "We have to find another way out."

39

Tomo, Gus and Josef scrambled up the mountain with Jasper and the snowmen following. Tomo quickly outpaced the others and reached the peak before anyone else had even made it half way.

She scurried over to the opening of the exhaust vent and looked below. About fifty feet beneath her was a small light shining out of the side of the sooty flue.

"Hello?" Tomo called. "Is anyone there?"

Nebo leaned into the vent and waved to Tomo. Realizing the position he was in, Tomo immediately fastened a climbing line to the largest boulder and threw it down. Nebo grabbed hold of it.

"We have a way out," Nebo said to Mrs. Claus. "Tomo threw us a line from above."

"Go!" Mrs. Claus ordered Nebo.

Nebo followed her command. When he reached the top, he looked below, but saw no trace of the Clauses. The commotion of the robots was escalating.

After a few more seconds, he saw the Clauses appear from the edge of the access tunnel. Santa drew his wife near and held her tight. "Why you clever fellow," she teased. "I've seen that look before — you're up to one of your old tricks."

"Ho, ho, ho. It is Christmas Eve, after all," he twinkled.

And laying his finger aside of his nose, and giving a nod, up the chimney they rose.

Just behind them, the robots emerged from the access tunnel and used their magnetic arms to climb the sides of the exhaust vent.

With Santa and Mrs. Claus safely out, Nebo pushed the large boulder with the line still around it, into the opening of the vent. The muffled pounding of the robots was all that could be heard now. Tomo stared at Santa, but could not speak. She was trying to figure out how he had shot up the chimney so fast.

Santa took in a deep breath. He looked around the mountain and the island and noticed the crashed drones, the smoldering battlefield, and the wrecked ships on the shore. "All of this destruction... because of me?" he sighed.

"Not because of you," Nebo said. "This happened because of evil. What has been destroyed will allow a new beginning for this island."

Mrs. Claus took Santa by his hand and said, "The world needs you now more than ever. Eastern Industries tried to destroy Christmas and create their own version of the holiday. Many have embraced the new holiday, but it has left them feeling empty inside. When the world sees you again this year, the Christmas spirit will be renewed and stronger than ever."

"You need to get back to the North Pole right away," Mrs. Claus concluded. "We don't have much time. Nebo will help you this year."

Santa did not bother to argue with Mrs. Claus. He trusted her completely and always followed her advice. He took in another deep breath and let out a whistle that rang from the mountaintop and echoed through the heavens. The sound carried far across the ocean, reaching the North Pole.

As they continued their ascent, Gus, Josef, and the snowmen looked toward the sky when they heard the whistle. They noticed the first star appearing in the west. It was so bright it cast a glimmering reflection on the ocean far below. They looked to the east and admired a clear moon rising above the storm that had retreated to the horizon. As they paused for a moment, they were thrilled to see the shadows of all nine reindeer and a sleigh fly across the face of the moon.

Within seconds, the sleigh landed on the summit of the mountain. Ziggy was in the driver's seat and jumped for joy when he saw Santa.

"Take Santa and Nebo back at once," Mrs. Claus said to Ziggy. "You can come back for us next."

"You won't believe what's going on!" Ziggy burst out. "Every child in the world wants a toy soldier from Santa."

"Then we have even less time than I thought," Mrs. Claus responded, confused by Ziggy's comment. "Please hurry and get Santa ready for his trip. You can give us more information when you return."

Santa removed his soot covered hat and gave it to Tomo. Recognizing the stunned girl, he said, "Please give this to your sister. I know how much she loves my visits."

Tomo, still too overwhelmed to speak, clutched the hat and waved as Santa and Nebo hopped into the sleigh. Santa gave another whistle and the sleigh bounded back to the northeast.

Gus and Josef reached the summit right after Santa had left. Tomo and Mrs. Claus were the only two waiting for them there.

"What happened?" Josef asked, catching his breath. "Where's Nebo?"

"Nebo went with Santa back to the North Pole," Mrs. Claus replied. "Ziggy and Scout are going to fill Santa in on the new route for this year. With the Naughty List gone, Santa is going to have many more toys to deliver and more stops than ever."

"Ziggy will come back with the sleigh any minute," Mrs. Claus continued. "It's time to get you all home for Christmas."

Jasper and the snowmen arrived on top of the mountain and piled rocks around the boulder Nebo had used to block the exhaust vent. Satisfied with the work, Jasper offered, "Hop on our backs, we plan to slide down the mountain."

Mrs. Claus and the tired kids were happy to oblige. They jumped on the snowmen and raced down the hill. What had taken over an hour of climbing, was now flying by in a two-minute descent. The snowmen came to a stop by Lucia, Mithra and Hermey.

From both sides of the mountain, Tiberius and Ben joined the group with the rest of the snowmen and a few hundred toy soldiers. The soldiers looked beat up, but stood proudly in their formation. Some began to rattle their drums.

"Now what?" Tiberius asked Mrs. Claus.

"Now we'll sit under this tree and wait," Mrs. Claus replied, thrusting her staff into the ground.

"There are no trees left," Gus replied, glancing at the staff. "This island is a wasteland now."

"Mrs. Claus, look. There are four leaves on the top of your staff!" Mithra said excitedly.

The kids all looked at the staff and noticed twigs sprouting. Soon there were eight leaves, then sixteen.

"This staff is made from the Glastonbury Holy Thorn," Mrs. Claus explained. "It was a gift to the North Pole from the people of Glastonbury, England.

"A few years ago, vandals cut down the famous tree. It had bloomed every Christmas for hundreds of years. The people of Glastonbury made a staff from the trunk and left it out for Santa to pick up on Christmas Eve. I have waited years to find the right spot to plant it. This is it."

The kids sat back and observed the tree as it continued to grow right in front of their eyes. Within minutes, a large trunk was firmly rooted with branches spreading out from the center. Thousands of leaves soon formed a canopy over their heads.

"I doubt any vandals will get to it now," Mrs. Claus said looking around the desolate island.

Roots quickly spread beneath the ground where the kids sat. Further away, a few tender shoots were visible in the moonlight as they sprung from the rocks.

"Look!" Ben shouted, pointing to the moon.

The reindeer and sleigh had returned and were descending straight toward the team. Ziggy was alone in the empty sleigh as he landed it softly a few yards away.

"We must hurry," Ziggy said by way of introduction. "Santa must ride by midnight. There are only a few hours left."

"Does the world even care about Santa anymore?" Gus asked.

"They care more than ever!" Ziggy replied, starting to get emotional. "A fisherman took a video of your fleet sailing through the Bering Sea. He posted it online and the whole world found out what you were doing here. They know about the toy soldiers and snowmen – everything! For the past couple of days, the Christmas spirit has spread clear across the whole world.

"We've received millions of letters, sent to us through smoke, requesting toy soldiers like those seen on the ships. The Bentley farm became a symbol of your struggle to get Santa back. Even Tiberius's father is there making toy soldiers for Santa to give to kids around the world."

Hermey smiled when he heard Rudi was making toys again. Tiberius was in a state of shock.

"But my Dad tried to kill Christmas," a stunned Tiberius countered.

"He may have tried, but he's now leading a worldwide effort to make sure every boy and girl on earth gets a wooden toy soldier that resembles the ones here," Ziggy explained. "Christmas was saved the moment the world found out about all of you. Now you have saved Santa. What a merry Christmas this will be for everyone."

Ziggy jumped out of the sleigh and gave each child a hearty hug. Tears streamed down his face. He turned to Mrs. Claus and said, "I only have enough room for you, Hermey, Lucia and the kids. We can return for the snowmen and soldiers later."

"Wait," Mithra interrupted. "I'll collect the cosmic cores of the snowmen. They'll fit into a few jars."

As Ziggy pondered her suggestion, Mithra did not wait for the answer. She picked up her dust collector and approached Jasper.

"Good idea," Jasper said as his soul departed and left behind a stationary snowman. The kids helped Mithra pack up the rest of the snowmen.

"What about the soldiers?" Ben asked, purposely leaving out the "toy" part of their description.

"They should stay on this island and guard it from future threats," Tiberius suggested.

Everyone liked the idea. Ben quickly entered some commands into the control box for the soldiers, but they marched away before he finished. The soldiers spread out across the edges of the island and stood tall with their golden bayonets resting on their shoulders. Once in position, they did not move.

As everyone crowded into the sleigh, Lucia walked away silently and sat under the tree that had grown from the staff. She relaxed into it.

"Aren't you coming with us?" Ziggy asked. "I can't leave you here alone."

Lucia looked from side to side before fixing her gaze on Mrs. Claus. In a tired voice she replied, "I'm going to rest here for a while. When the others are ready, they'll come out and join me in the new forest here."

Mrs. Claus looked back at the wise, old elf. She now understood there were still forest elves on the island. It would take some time, but eventually they would emerge from their hiding spots and join Lucia in the rapidly expanding forest.

Mrs. Claus was not saddened by leaving her companion behind. Instead, she was thankful for the long time the two had shared at the North Pole. She had always known Lucia would eventually veer off on a new adventure. This seemed like the perfect time to part ways.

Mrs. Claus bade the ancient traveler farewell. "Good luck with your new home. Thank you for everything you have done for us."

Ziggy gave a whistle and the reindeer pulled the sleigh up into the air. With the moon at their back, they headed toward the bright star in the western sky.

"First stop Japan!" Ziggy called out as the reindeer carried the exhausted kids into the moonlit night.

40

Everyone looked back as the island grew further away. The reflection of the moon on the snow-covered island made it look like a completely different place than what they had seen at the first light of this long day. Instead of a black fortress sticking out from the ocean, they left behind a shimmering, silver bastion with seabirds nesting on the mountain. There were quite a few trees around the one Lucia was resting under, and the first had begun to flower. All around the edges of the island, golden bayonets sparkled in the moonlight.

Gus stared back at the mountain, listening to the birds.

"What are they saying?" Tomo asked, knowing the look on Gus's face when he was hearing the animals' language.

"Thank you," Gus replied, lost in thought. "They are relieved to be home again."

The sleigh sped over a thousand miles of ocean in under a minute. Soon the tall peak of Mount Fuji could be seen in Japan's evening glow. The sleigh had caught up to the sunset here. Ziggy had the reindeer circle Mount Fuji once, before landing on its lower slope.

"We are about two miles from your house," Ziggy said turning to Tomo as the sleigh landed. "Can you make it home from here?"

"I have done so a hundred times," Tomo replied, referring to her many training runs up the mountainside. Realizing this was the end of her time with the group, she began to cry.

"I will always treasure my time with all of you," Tomo stammered. She was not used to being emotional, but there was no stopping her now.

"Tiberius, thank you for picking me. Being part of this team saved me as much as we saved Santa Claus," Tomo said as she gave Tiberius a big hug.

She turned to Mrs. Claus and made a request. "Please make sure Santa stops by our house tonight and waves to Kiso."

"I'll see what I can do," Mrs. Claus replied. The warmth had returned to her face as she added, "You should be proud of yourself, Tomo. You are a great teammate."

It was a simple compliment, but Tomo had never heard those words before. She melted into Mrs. Claus's arms for a long hug. She soon gave everyone a warm embrace.

As the sleigh was about to leave, Gus reached into his uniform pocket and pulled out an Arctic spider. He handed it to Tomo.

"Please, take her," Gus implored. "She was the first spider I connected with and I would like you to take her home. She wants to go with you. She's the only spider that did not make Baekdu Island her new home."

Tomo stretched out her hand and the Arctic spider climbed onto it. She walked up Tomo's arm and nestled into her chest pocket. Tomo just stood there, overwhelmed.

Ziggy gave a whistle and the sleigh took off to the west. Tomo watched as the sleigh flew out of sight.

It was getting dark quickly as she headed along the familiar path back to her village. She ran the two miles to the center of town. She did not go home. Instead, she joined her family in the long line outside of the local fried chicken restaurant.

She immediately noticed her father and mother were different. Kiso looked as well as she ever had. The family shared a heartfelt greeting as the others in line noticed the reunion. All the people outside the restaurant insisted that the Gozen family go to the front of the line, but Tomo refused.

"This is exactly where I want to be on Christmas Eve," she responded to the kind gesture.

Tomo's father began to tell jokes, continuing their perfect Christmas tradition. The wait in line did not seem long enough.

Once back home, Tomo told her story to her parents and Kiso. She started with the rescue from Everest. She talked about how she had almost traded her life for the chance to attain one more accomplishment. As she explained that her records were meaningless and having been part of a team was the greatest accomplishment in her life, her father felt a sudden remorse for pushing her so hard.

Kiso squealed with delight as Tomo recounted the first day at the North Pole. Tomo talked about her new friends, the training, and finally the trip to Baekdu Island. Kiso clasped her sister tight when Tomo spoke about being stuck on the side of the mountain. Kiso cheered when she heard about the spiders coming to the rescue. When Tomo described her silent meeting with Santa, she presented the sooty hat to her sister. Kiso donned the gift and felt the first inkling of the power of the hat resonate through her body.

As midnight approached, Tomo's father read "The Night Before Christmas" to the family, and the parents tucked the young girls into Tomo's bed. Kiso and Tomo waited for their parents to leave before getting up and watching out the window for Santa's sled. Tomo hoped Santa would wave to her sister. They would not be disappointed.

41

The sleigh chased the sun as it headed west. By the time they reached Mongolia, the sun was once again above the horizon. The reindeer swooped down over their ancestral homeland looking for their Mongol riders. Voices rose from the valleys and greeted the victorious team in the sky.

The reindeer flew close to a mountain and descended into a narrow valley. They noticed a golden glow in the distance and realized it was the armor they had left behind with the riders, as a reminder of their bravery. As they drew closer, they saw the Dukha herders had been reunited with the young Mongol riders. The Dukha tribe had invited the Mongol heroes to be their guests for Christmas. They were having a feast in honor of the great sky battle. Each rider had taken a turn describing the battle, mesmerizing the children with each telling of the aerial fight. They sang old songs and celebrated, waiting to see if Santa would ride through the sky once more. The reindeer made a quick flyover to the cheers of all and swiftly resumed their course to Israel.

A short time later, the sleigh descended toward the mountain where Ben had originally been picked up. As they got closer, Ben could see Nicola Abdou's old station wagon alone in the abandoned parking lot.

"Nicola!" Mrs. Claus cried out as she stepped from the sleigh. "So good to see you."

The two shared a hug before Mrs. Claus asked, "How did you know we would be here?"

Nicola grabbed Ben tightly and answered, "I knew you would succeed, so I figured you'd be bringing Ben home soon."

"We don't have much time left," Ziggy reminded Mrs. Claus as he gestured to get her back in the sleigh.

"Keep up the good work," Mrs. Claus said as she hopped back in next to Ziggy.

Ben saluted the kids in the sleigh and said, "It has been an honor to serve with you on this important mission."

He turned to Tiberius and added, "You are a born leader, Tiberius. I would follow you to the ends of the earth."

Tiberius and the kids saluted back. Mrs. Claus thanked Ben for all his help and the reindeer took off for their next destination.

It was a warm, late afternoon on Carmel Mountain. Ben removed his jacket and took a moment to let everything settle in.

"Your whole school knows what you've been up to," Nicola said, breaking the silence.

"Uh oh," Ben responded. "Am I in trouble?"

"Trouble?" Nicola laughed. "Far from it, the school cancelled all classes and the students are busy making wooden toy soldiers as we speak. They are calling you a hero."

As they drove down the mountain, Ben explained the whole story to Nicola. Ben was most proud of the toy soldiers and was excited so many kids wanted one. As they got close to the school, Ben was surprised to see all the news reporters out front.

"What's going on?" Ben asked.

"People can't get enough of the story since the fisherman's video was posted," Nicola explained. "They saw you on the boat and now the whole country wants to hear from you; if you're willing to speak."

Ben motioned for Nicola to stop the car. He stepped out and was immediately surrounded by a throng of reporters. They peppered him with questions. Ben held up his hand and they went silent.

"It was a tough battle," Ben began. "Santa has been rescued from Eastern Industries and tonight he will ride through the skies once again."

The reporters cheered. Ben waited a moment and continued. "I would like to thank the entire world for their support. Especially in this part of the world, a holiday that celebrates peace and good will is desperately needed.

"Nicola Abdou is the real hero in Israel. For over twenty years, Nicola has spread the magic of Christmas across this land. I hope more people will embrace this holiday as it transcends all religions and includes all who want to celebrate the beauty of a child's wonder. Let us pause once a year to remember the hopes and dreams of our youth and to shed the armor that years of tough living have given us. I hope each and every one of you has a Merry Christmas."

Ben pushed past the reporters and got back into Nicola's station wagon.

"I thought you were going to go into the school," a confused Nicola said.

"I'm not going back," Ben countered. "Please take me to the hospital where we first met. I want to return the favor you did for me many Christmases ago."

Nicola was excited to hear this and they sped away to the hospital. Ben went room to room for the rest of the day, telling his story to the sickest of kids. They were overjoyed to be talking to one of the saviors of Santa Claus.

Toward the end of the night, the kids that were not bedridden gathered in the hospital's cafeteria for one last telling of the miraculous rescue of Santa Claus. Nicola, dressed as Santa, handed out one toy soldier to each child. With that, he planted a seed he hoped would slowly spread over the entire Middle East. The values of Christmas had taken root and were just beginning to create change.

42

The sun was high as the sleigh began its descent into the woods near Oberndorf, Austria. The sounds of caroling could be heard in the distance. Ziggy touched the sleigh down near the Ruprecht home and the reindeer trotted along the empty path on top of a deep snow.

Ziggy reached into the bottom of the sleigh and hung two signs on either side. They read "North Pole Fitness Camp". They were the same signs Ziggy had used when he had picked Josef up under Tiberius's ruse.

Josef, Tiberius, Mrs. Claus and Ziggy chuckled together.

"What's so funny?" Mithra asked.

"My parents thought I was going to a fitness camp," Josef explained. "Ziggy picked me up in the sleigh and did not take flight until we were out of their sight. He used those signs to help with the deception."

"It was all Tiberius's idea," Ziggy said defensively.

They trotted along the lane toward Josef's home. As they approached, people from all over town looked on and clapped. It was a victory lap of sorts. The sleigh finally came to a stop in front of Josef's house.

Due to the commotion, Mr. and Mrs. Ruprecht were already out front.

"See," Mr. Ruprecht said, turning toward his wife. "This was just a fitness camp with a North Pole theme. Those reindeer can't fly."

The kids in the sleigh laughed when they heard the comment. Josef gave everyone in the sleigh a big hug and then effortlessly hopped over the side. The Ruprechts were amazed. They had never seen Josef move so nimbly.

"Wow," Mr. Ruprecht said, walking up to Ziggy. "You've done a fantastic job. Feel free to put me down as a reference."

Mrs. Ruprecht ran up to her son and kissed him all over his face. Josef was happy to be the object of her affection again.

"You look amazing," she observed. "I can't believe what great shape you're in."

Mr. Ruprecht reached into his wallet and pulled out all his money. He tried to inconspicuously hand it to Ziggy with a "Thank you."

Ziggy laughed at the gesture and replied earnestly, "Sorry sir, we don't take tips."

"Well, you run a first class operation, Ziggy," Mr. Ruprecht praised. "Absolutely first class. As a matter of fact, I think you fooled the whole world with that sailing trip you took with the kids."

The kids in the sleigh went from quiet giggling to the type of belly-busting laughter that hurts. No one had the heart to explain that Josef was not really at a fitness camp.

"Please pardon me, I have to go and drop the other kids off at their homes," Ziggy said, staying in character. "Josef, remember to keep exercising and eat right. Have a nice day."

"Thank you for everything," Josef said with a wink.

The reunited family went into their house. Mrs. Ruprecht began to fawn over her son. She pointed up the stairs and said, "We have all your computers running again. You can play some games while I make you a late lunch. You must be hungry."

Josef smiled at his mother's kindness. He turned to her and said, "I would rather take a walk to the chapel. I heard the caroling going on there and thought it would be nice to join in."

Mrs. Ruprecht was shocked. She called her husband over and they put on their coats. The family walked the mile to the chapel without stopping. Despite the long day's exertion, Josef showed no sign of tiring. As a matter of fact, it was his parents who had trouble keeping up with his pace.

Outside the chapel, people cheered when they saw Josef in his uniform. Despite his father's objections, everyone knew Josef was part of the team that had saved Santa Claus. By this time, the news from Japan and Israel had spread far enough that people knew the rescue team was arriving home.

The crowd broke into a heartfelt rendition of "Silent Night." Josef joined the chorus and everyone sang until it got dark. The Ruprechts went home that evening and ate a hearty Christmas Eve meal. When Mrs. Ruprecht brought out a tray of cookies for dessert, Josef only ate four before telling his parents what really happened at the North Pole.

Despite the details of the story and the way it matched what was on the news, Mr. Ruprecht would not believe that Santa had been kidnapped. To this day, he tells anyone who will listen that the North Pole Fitness Camp made up the whole kidnapping story as a ploy to get the kids into shape.

43

The dwindling group continued on its westward journey, crossing the Atlantic Ocean. The sun shone from behind the sleigh in the eastern sky, as they approached the United States of America. They eventually came to rest in a light snow, on the Rauch farm outside of Lancaster, Pennsylvania. Gus's mom rushed out of her house with a dozen forest elves around her as Sam trailed behind.

"Hi Mom!" Gus greeted his mother as he jumped out of the sleigh.

Mrs. Rauch ran up to her son and hugged him with all her love. Ziggy hopped out behind Gus and introduced himself. The forest elves had never met one of their cousins from the North Pole; after looking Ziggy over, they swarmed around the sleigh.

Mrs. Claus was next out of the sleigh and approached Mrs. Rauch.

"I see you've met the forest elves," Mrs. Claus said as the elves turned their attention to the reindeer. "I assume they were helpful."

"They were!" Mrs. Rauch replied. "They cleaned up the house, cooked meals for Sam and me, and did our laundry. This has been like a little vacation for me. I feel relaxed for the first time in years."

When Sam reached the sleigh, he waved to the reindeer and introduced himself to Mrs. Claus. She knew how he had assisted with Donner's past mishap and thanked him. "You saved Christmas back then and now your great-grandson has helped save it again. Without Gus, we would have never made it to Baekdu Island."

Mrs. Rauch showed Mrs. Claus the letter from Gus and added, "I was so glad Gus was able to be a part of a team. Ever since his father moved away, he rarely leaves the barn. It made me happy to hear he was up there working with other kids for a good cause. I'm very proud of him."

Gus smiled when he heard all of that. Usually, his mother was stressed and busy. Seeing her relaxed was a welcome change. Gus had always hated the fact that his mother had to work so hard and was very pleased she finally had gotten a break.

Gus turned back toward the sleigh and waved to everyone as Mrs. Claus climbed in. Mithra, Tiberius and Hermey waved back as the reindeer pulled the sleigh upwards toward the north.

After watching the sleigh fly out of sight, Sam, Mrs. Rauch and Gus headed straight for the barn, with the dozen elves following behind. The animals were very happy to see Gus again. He petted each one and turned toward the door.

"It's OK Gus," his mom said. "You can stay out here all day. I know how much you like to spend Christmas Eve with the animals."

"No, Mom," Gus replied. "I missed you. I want to spend more time with you and I think I know how to make that happen."

Mrs. Rauch hugged her son for a long time. Sam stood back and appreciated the new connection between mother and son. The three went inside the house and invited the elves to spend the rest of the holiday with them. The elves put together a wonderful Christmas Eve meal.

Later that evening, everyone went out to the barn together and gave the animals a special Christmas helping of extra food. Outside the barn, Gus put out wheat stalks and seed for the birds to enjoy on what he considered to be the most holy of nights.

After the elves had gone to sleep, Gus told his mom and Sam about the improvements in his ability to understand the language of animals. He was confident he could now use his gift year round, but this time he wanted to use it for good, rather than spreading rumors. With Sam's help, they planned to found an animal hospital where Gus could help the veterinarians better diagnose animals through his understanding of how they felt. They hoped their plan would revolutionize the way animals were treated.

44

As the sleigh left the Rauch farm, Ziggy turned to Mithra and asked, "Is there a place near your farm where we can land without the news reporters seeing us?"

"Why? I think it would be great to land on the farm right in front of the cameras," Mithra responded.

"We can't do that Mithra," Mrs. Claus joined in. "With all the attention, we can't afford to be held up by the commotion we will attract."

"Ok, then we can land on the west side of Mount Mansfield," Mithra suggested. She worriedly added, "But it's over ten miles from the farm. With all the snow, it would take us a long time to make it home."

"That'll work," Ziggy responded, reaching into his pocket.

He took out Tiberius's mobile phone. Tiberius had forgotten he had brought it to the North Pole a few weeks ago. He blushed a bit as he threw a quick glance at Hermey. Tiberius recalled his obsession with his phone when the two had made their original trip to the North Pole.

"Tiberius, your father and mother are at the Bentley farm," Ziggy continued, unaware of Tiberius's uncomfortable recollection. "You can call them and I'm sure they'll pick you all up as quickly as they can."

The sleigh was now flying above the clouds. Without warning, Ziggy made the slightest move on the reins and they plunged into darkness. Rudolph's red nose glowed brightly as he guided the sleigh through a blinding snow.

Ahead was a small woods road on the side of Mount Mansfield. Ziggy guided the sleigh to a gentle landing in the middle of a narrow path. They came to rest in an idyllic alpine landscape.

Tiberius powered on his phone and when the screen lit up, he felt an instinctive urge to check in on *Legend Quest*. It was a force of habit more than anything else, but Tiberius resisted and waited for the phone to receive its signal. He handed the phone over to Hermey.

"I don't want to use it," Tiberius said quietly. "Can you please make the call?"

Hermey put his hand on Tiberius's shoulder and replied. "It's OK, Tiber. I understand. I'll call your father."

Hermey pulled up Rudi's contact information and connected the call.

"Hello?"

"Hi Rudi, it's Hermey."

"Dad! Where are you? So glad to hear from you," the sincere voice replied.

"I'm with Tiber and Mithra Bentley. We're on the west side of Mount Mansfield, not far from you. I'll send you the location in a text message."

"I'll let Virginia and the Bentleys know. Please tell Tiber I can't wait to see him. We'll be there as soon as we can. I'm so sorry Dad. I love you. I..." The quivering voice trailed off.

"It's all right Rudi. Everything is going to be all right."

Hermey disconnected the call and sent their location. He handed the phone back to Tiberius.

"We're late, we need to get going," Ziggy said to Mrs. Claus.

"Just a moment," Mrs. Claus responded back sternly. It was clear they would leave only when she was ready.

"Mithra," Mrs. Claus said, pulling her in for a hug. "Thank you for all your brilliant ideas. Without you, we would have never made it to the island. Your great uncle would be so proud of you."

Mithra could not respond. She just hugged Mrs. Claus with all her might.

"You gave all those snowmen a new life," Mrs. Claus continued. "Keep following your passion. I'm sure the past few weeks are just the first of many more accomplishments for you."

With Mithra still clinging to her, Mrs. Claus turned to Hermey and said, "Thanks for bringing Tiberius to the North Pole. You've always been there for us. We owe you a huge debt of gratitude."

The slight, old man was crying now. He looked into the endlessly compassionate eyes of Mrs. Claus and stammered, "No one could be more thankful for this whole affair than me. I have my family back."

Mithra was soon replaced by Hermey in Mrs. Claus's grasp. Mithra jumped back into the sleigh and gave Ziggy an unexpected kiss on the cheek. The poor elf tried to maintain his composure, but was quickly overwhelmed in the moment. Tiberius jumped up to the sleigh and joined the embrace.

"I'll miss you all," Ziggy cried out. "Take care of yourselves."

Tiberius turned to climb down from the sleigh when Mrs. Claus lifted him out with a tight grasp.

"And you, young man," Mrs. Claus proudly said. "You will be known as the boy who put an end to the Naughty List."

She placed Tiberius back on the ground and held him by the shoulders. She looked him straight in the eye.

"Forget the past Tiberius, that's not who you are. You're not the boy with the naughty behavior. You're a young man that rescued Santa Claus and saved Christmas. You found

313

your true self. You'll continue to do great things for this crazy world we live in.

"You will forever be remembered as the boy who showed us that we are not defined by our mistakes. Parents will begin to understand that naughty actions do not define their children. All kids are good at heart. Instead of punishing naughty behavior, your example will be a model for forgiveness. If compassion and redemption replace anger and punishment, children will be happier and work harder to be nice. That is the lesson you have taught all of us at the North Pole and hopefully the whole world."

Tiberius beamed as he tried to respond to the generous praise. He hoped the look on his face conveyed his thankfulness and appreciation for everything Mrs. Claus and the North Pole had done for him. He wanted to mention each and every part of the past four weeks he was thankful for, but could not find the words. He could only reply with, "Merry Christmas."

Mrs. Claus let go of Tiberius and leapt into the sleigh. This time, *she* gave a whistle to the team. It echoed from the mountains and was heard all the way down at the Bentley farm.

As the reindeer hopped up into the sky, Mithra yelled, "Please take care of the snowmen."

"I will," Ziggy replied as the sleigh climbed into the clouds and out of sight.

The three tearful rescuers just wandered around for a moment. A heavy snow was falling and there was almost no sound in the woods. The occasional bird song was all that broke the silence.

Without saying a word, they headed down the path in the woods toward the main road. The deep snow under their feet made a squishing sound as the three marched on. Tiberius reached over without thinking and took Mithra's hand in his own. They glanced at each other, smiled and looked forward again. Hermey, following in Tiberius's footsteps through the snow, smiled too. It would be a long time until any of them lost their smiles.

As they reached the main road, the Bentley pickup truck was just pulling up. Mrs. Bentley was driving and Rudi was in the seat next to her. They stopped and jumped out of the truck; running to embrace their children.

"We did it, Mom!" Mithra exclaimed as she squeezed her mother.

"I know," Mrs. Bentley replied. "We've been following your progress since yesterday. I'm so happy to have you back for Christmas."

Rudi and Tiberius both tried to apologize to each other at the same time. Tiberius backed out of his father's arms, looked up at him and said, "We've all made mistakes, Dad. I love you and that's all that matters now."

Rudi pulled Tiberius to him and said, "Thank you, son. You saved me from myself."

After a few more moments, Rudi looked over at his emotional father.

"You were right, Papa," Rudi said through tears. "You were always right. I believe again, and it is the greatest feeling in the world."

Hermey had not heard Rudi call him "Papa" since the Santa suit incident long ago. He hugged him and gently said, "It's okay, my son. Everything is going to be all right."

They all got into the pickup truck and drove back to the farm. In a flurry of excitement, Mithra and Tiberius shared their experiences at the North Pole. Rudi explained how he had quit his job and started the toy soldier campaign. Hermey listened to the joyous conversations with great contentment.

The initial thaw the Kringles experienced soon turned into a torrent of emotions. Tiberius and Rudi laughed with each other. Rudi cried when Tiberius explained how the Naughty List had been eliminated. Tiberius got choked up when Rudi talked about his reunion with Virginia in his office and how she had been by his side ever since. Any awkwardness the reunion had created, vanished by the time the Bentley pickup pulled up to the farm.

When the kids got out of the truck, they were instantly swarmed by reporters. Mr. Bentley rushed out of the house and tried to shoo the reporters away, but Tiberius stopped him. Many questions were asked all at once.

"How did you save Santa?"

"How'd you get home so fast? I just saw you on the television in Austria."

"Santa's sleigh has just been picked up by NORAD, was he really kidnapped?"

"How did you pull off this elaborate hoax?"

One reporter accosted Rudi by asking, "Is this just another trick engineered by Eastern Industries?"

Tiberius waved his arms up and down to try and hush the crowd. Soon, reporters were telling each other to quiet down so Tiberius could speak.

"What I'm about to tell you is all true. Santa Claus was kidnapped by Eastern Industries before the Thanksgiving Day Parade," Tiberius began as the noisy questions subsided. "Since the elves at the North Pole are purely good and because of their beliefs, they were not capable of rescuing Santa on their own. So, I worked with them to recruit kids from the Naughty List. We trained for a few weeks and then sailed south to Baekdu Island on ships made from ice."

He pointed to Mithra and added, "She came up with the design of the mighty vessels."

As the cameras moved to Mithra, she shyly stared at her feet. Tiberius took the attention back as he continued.

"In a nutshell, we fought our way into the center of the island and freed Santa. I believe he has already begun his yearly ride to deliver a toy to every child for Christmas."

"Every child?" Freya asked as she pushed her way to the front. Everyone recognized her as the reporter who had originally broadcast the satirical story about the Bentley farm. "What about the kids on the Naughty List?"

"There is no longer a Naughty List," Tiberius said with pride. "Mrs. Claus burned it. She doesn't believe naughty behavior determines a child's worthiness to receive a present from Santa. Every kid who helped with the mission found the good in themselves and that's what Christmas should be about. Santa does not and will not judge kids, he will give *every* child a present. I want parents around the world to join Santa and focus on the good in children during this season of miracle and hope."

"No Naughty List?" Freya asked above the others. "What's Christmas without the Naughty List? You can't just change Christmas."

"We must change Christmas!" Tiberius commanded with authority. "If we don't, Christmas will become a dead force of habit that will eventually fade away. Its traditions are constantly evolving – that's what keeps it alive. This holiday has survived in one form or another since the beginning of humankind. Its continual transformation is what makes it stay so special in our hearts."

Some in the crowd applauded Tiberius, but others were not satisfied. Tiberius realized there was no way to make them all happy. He finished by saying, "I promise to tell the whole story to the world when the time is right. Please, go home now and spend the rest of the holiday with those whom you love. Let us, for just a moment, put strife and cynicism on hold in the name of good will and peace on earth. And when we return to our normal lives, we should carry the season with us – all year long."

The people on the farm heeded Tiberius's advice and began to depart for their homes. Freya tried to squeeze more questions in as Tiberius headed into the house with the

Bentleys and his family. She soon found herself standing alone in the cold.

Virginia and Mr. Bentley had prepared a banquet for the returning heroes. As the two families sat down to eat, Mrs. Bentley placed an electronic candle in the window. She noticed Freya standing outside.

"Please come in and join us," Mrs. Bentley said, opening the front door.

"I think I am the last person you want in there," Freya replied.

"This candle in the window is a welcome sign to anyone who needs a place to go," Mrs. Bentley continued. "Frankly, you look like you could use a warm meal and some company."

Freya joined the two families at the table and an all-day feast began. Tiberius sat between his parents and beamed with satisfaction over the new warmth they now enjoyed. Hermey quietly reveled in the amazing stories the kids shared with everyone.

Late in the evening, everyone settled down in front of the Bentley Christmas tree. Despite their effort to stay awake, Tiberius and Mithra fell asleep to the twinkling of the lights just before midnight. The next morning, like homes all over the world, the only evidence of Santa's visit were cookie crumbs, half drank milk, and a neatly wrapped toy soldier for each of them.

The food had been modest, the décor somewhat plain, but everyone present in the farmhouse would cherish the memory of that Christmas Eve for the rest of their lives. Like so many other Christmas memories, it was not the perfection of the preparations or the lavish gifts that made Christmas so special. It was the good times shared with others that brought pure joy to their hearts.

45

By the time the sleigh reached the North Pole, the first midnight had passed just west of the International Date Line. Santa was dressed in a fresh red suit and had been filled in on what transpired since his kidnapping. Nebo stood next to him, holding an enormous red sack, filled with toy soldiers.

"You're late," Santa scolded as Ziggy pulled the sleigh to a stop. Then his face brightened. "You've done great, Ziggy. I think this new route is going to work out just fine, despite the late start."

Mrs. Claus was overwhelmed with emotion seeing her husband back in his familiar red suit. She gave him a big hug and joked, "At least you're well rested for the longer trip this year."

"Ho, ho, ho!" bellowed the jolly fellow, his stomach shaking with each laugh.

Bells across the North Pole village began to ring. Everywhere, elves joined in a chorus of "Here Comes Santa Claus." As Nebo flung Santa's sack into the sleigh and climbed aboard, Mrs. Claus had a tear in her eye. She walked up to the placid boy and gave him a kiss on his forehead.

"I'm glad you found us Nebo," Mrs. Claus confided. "I hope you'll stay with us after the season."

"I think you already know the answer to that," Nebo said with a wink.

Santa jumped up into the sleigh and gave his special whistle. The reindeer effortlessly carried their heavy burden up into the sky. They flew across the Pacific Ocean with greater speed than ever before, dropping toy soldiers into every cherished place a child slept.

Along the way, the sleigh touched down at retirement homes and picked up millions of toy soldiers that had been created to fulfill the wish of all the world's children.

To Nebo, it was all a blur. He made out the faces of Tomo and her sister in a window in Japan and gave them a wave. He recognized the chapel in Josef's town. He saw Ben standing with a man dressed as Santa on top of a children's hospital. He could feel the happiness in the animals near Gus's house. Finally, he saw the candle in the window of a farmhouse in Jericho, Vermont. A trip around the world seemed to go by in an instant, but he had many lifetimes worth of memories.

Nebo could not explain it, but he remembered Santa riding a kangaroo in Australia, a white horse in the Netherlands, a donkey in Switzerland, a camel in Spain and Latin America, a helicopter in Brazil, and finally a dugout canoe in Hawaii. Memories overlapped as thousands of them seemed to flood his mind at the same time.

He recalled eating a mountain of cookies and drinking an ocean's worth of milk, along with many other delicious foods over the course of the night. He felt as though each stop had been his only one, but in reality he had experienced billions of adventures within a span of twenty-four hours. He did not understand how they had made this incredible voyage, but he would never forget it. He hoped it was the first one of many more to come.

When the sleigh finally came to rest at the North Pole, Nebo turned to Santa Claus and asked, "How did you do that?"

"Ho, ho, ho," Santa laughed. "I am not the producer of this Christmas pageant. I'm merely an actor, playing my part."

"If you're not the producer, then who is?" Nebo continued, departing from his usual contentedness.

"If you look into your heart, you will find the answer," the wise, old man explained. "I cannot tell you what love is, but I know that I feel it. To me, it is the most real thing in this world, yet sometimes it is shrouded in a veil that keeps us from understanding or explaining it.

"You are now a part of the miracle of Christmas Nebo," Santa continued. "As long as this miracle endures, it will remind people there is more to life than what can be seen or heard. Children have a beautiful ability to wonder and believe in something outside of themselves. They will always remind us there is a supernatural perfection beyond this world which often lies dormant in our minds.

"That is the true gift of Christmas."

THE END